Dedication

In Loving Memory of Mrs. Bertha Mae Nelson. A light that shined bright in this world. Quietly you lived your life in faith, quietly raising a family, and quietly serving God. Never in search of fame or glory, you departed this world in the same subtle way that you lived in it. Leaving a lasting impact upon all those who were blessed by the comfort of your presence, the wisdom of your instruction, and the gentleness of your speech. Now a light shining amongst the stars your quiet and loving devotion to your children will never be forgotten.

Surviving Life!

A Novel by Brian Nelson

Table of Contents

Introduction

The year 2020 was a year of turmoil, confusion, and anger for a lot of people. There was a global pandemic, political unrest, and division created during the election season leading to violence, and protests were rampant and sometimes out of control across the country. During the midst of all of this emerged a local battle that most were unaware of but was a microcosm of a larger problem.

In the novel "Choose Life" by Brian Nelson, Conrad James and Harry Jacobs were two men from decidedly different backgrounds when they first met over two years ago. Conrad an African American man from Chicago had been raised in the projects on the city's westside, while Harry was from a successful "football family" in southeast Texas. Neither could have imagined that their lives would take them on a collision course that would one day require choosing between life and death.

Both were shaped by loving single parents who wanted the best for their children. Conrad a single mother struggling to make ends meet, and Harry by his father a former professional football player and all-American at the University of Texas. On the surface, decidedly different people the morals, beliefs, and systems of right and wrong taught to them were not that different. However, life's sometimes bitter pills made them appear to be. Despite both being raised primarily in single-parent homes the parents of both men were people of integrity. Hardworking, honest people at their core.

It would seem that the two would be able to get along reasonably well under normal circumstances, however, the circumstances presented to them turned out to be anything but normal. They became instant competitors, even fierce adversaries as fate brought them together under adverse conditions. Two men both looking to live out a lifelong dream. But there was a problem. Their dreams would collide as it seemed only one could obtain it, at the expense of the other. Unknowingly, they had embarked on a collision course from different parts of the country. Both were raised men of faith, but the faith was about to be tested in unforeseen ways.

Faced with choices set before them they grapple with finding the wisdom, integrity, and judgment needed to navigate obstacles before them. Some challenges of their own making others by the randomness of life.

Surviving Life! is the sequel to "Choose Life" the groundbreaking novel that first introduced the two proud adversaries to one another in the year 2020. However, if you haven't read Choose Life, it's okay this book brings you up to date skillfully in a way that most sequels don't, you can enjoy one independently of the other.

Chronicling the twists and turns of ten people whose life choices will take them and the reader down roads that they or the reader would have thought unimaginable. Some of the obstacles were real others were being manufactured by forces behind the scenes. Some will live, some will die. Some will continue down the road to destruction while others will emerge victorious.

Life has a way of connecting the destinies of people in both unpredictable and unforeseen ways, and God has a purpose for them all. Will their faith sustain them? Will they be able to find that purpose? Are they willing to follow it to its conclusion? Or will human frailties like pride, greed, envy, and hatred blind them from seeing and fulfilling that purpose?

Chapter 1

Reliving Choices Better Left in the Past

It was a blistering hot morning in the city of Houston and Conrad James was out for his morning run in an affluent suburb of the city. An area out of reach to those who have yet to attain the "American dream," known as the "good part" of town to them, but to its wealthy resident's commonplace, routine, the natural order of things.

As Conrad jogged smoothly through the area, he took in the beautiful sights the community had to offer. The stately homes, perfectly manicured lawns, and palm trees, which lined the streets gave the area a tropical feel.

In a moment of reflection, Conrad thought to himself, this is a long way from the west side of Chicago and the Henry Horner projects that he grew up in. I know I'm still in America, but this seems almost like a foreign land he laughed to himself. Most Americans will never experience anything close to this level of opulence he thought matter-of-factly while playing music from one of his favorite artists and attempting to run to the rhythm of the music.

It was the music that provided him with the outlet to escape into his own imagination while out on his daily morning runs. Conrad liked to pride himself on having a broad range of musical tastes. Some days it was Marvin Gaye or Bob Marley, some days Tupac or Jay-Z, but today it's Alicia Keys. The combination of running blended with the musical infusion took his mind off the worries that life and the world can bring, and into an escapism of his own choosing both serene and nostalgic. A world he believed he could control. Conrad was in that zone.

Suddenly, and without warning came red and blue lights flashing from behind him and within seconds out of a police squad car jumped two uniformed officers, guns drawn, an elevated sense of urgency in their voices, and determination on their faces. Almost simultaneously as if choreographed came a second squad car and out jumped another pair of police officers also with guns drawn. Conrad abruptly froze in his tracks as if in shock from the sudden onslaught of police officers and guns pointed at him. The serenity he enjoyed was instantly changed into a whirlwind of high intensity, a sense of danger lingering in the air.

Commands came at him loud, fast, and from all directions. Put your hands up! Don't you move! On the ground! Stay right there! Let me see your hands! Freeze! Hard and fast, like a blur they came and with increasing intensity with each flickering moment. The commands kept coming. Hands up! On the ground! Don't you move! Show me your hands! Halt or I'll shoot!

Conrad wanted to obey the commands being screamed at him, but the commands contradicted themselves. When one yelled up the other shouted down, one shouted move, the other hollered don't move. It was as if time itself was frozen and the few seconds he was in the officer's crosshairs appeared to last an hour. Not knowing what to do Conrad reached for his earbuds to hear more clearly what was going on. That was a mistake.

Conrad felt a hard and sharp pain on the back of his head followed by a flash of light. Then came a punch from another direction and after that an intense pain from his kneecap. The result of being struck harshly across the knee by another officer's night stick which he welded with speed and precision. Within seconds Conrad was lying on the ground with an officer's knee pressed against the back of his neck as he struggled to relay to the officers that "I can't breathe."

The police radio had broadcast reports from several members of the affluent Houston suburb of a black man "running through the community" they described it. The residents there appeared greatly disturbed by the sight of the 6 ft. 4 in. black man jogging in their community. The police quickly responded to the perceived threat with a sense of urgency, appearing to be on heightened alert because of the hysteria of the residents. This transferred hysteria caused the policemen to create a confrontation out of what could have been a casual interaction with the perceived suspect.

Conrad James, like most people, never carried a wallet or identification with him when out for a morning jog. All he needed was his music and some fresh morning air to get the morning started, but now he was pinned to the ground. A knee to the back of his neck, guns pointed in his direction, and gasping for air. After a few seconds that seemed like minutes of being assaulted and peppered with questions, he was lifted up and placed into one of the squad cars. The officers wanted to know who he was and more importantly, “what are you doing in this area boy?” He didn’t look like he belonged they said to one another.

What’s your name boy? One of them coarsely yelled after a moment of calmness.

Conrad James! He answered quickly.

This brought an outburst of laughter from the two officers who had gotten into the vehicle with him. No! Your real name shouted one of the officers in a mocking tone. Conrad repeated himself. The squad car moved from left to right through traffic, speeding unnecessarily as the officers hurried to get back to the police station, enticed by the prospect of applying more pressure, and interrogating Conrad more intensely.

They continued to mock him for the name he provided them. Conrad James huh? One of them said. Are you sure it’s not Assad, Denzel, or Shabazz X? And they laughed hysterically at what they considered “black names.” Well by the time we get you to the station you had better come up with a better name and the reason for why you were running through that respectable neighborhood. They spoke threateningly reverting back to a serious tone.

Conrad James sat silently in the back of the squad car as it headed towards the local police station his mind took him back to an earlier time in his life. Back to the days of his youth in the projects on Chicago’s Lower West Side. In those days, the police appeared to have the authority to harass the residents of the area, the majority of whom were black. They would approach a group of us and ask in anger "What are you doing outside?" It seemed a strange question, but we grew accustomed to it. Conrad thought to himself.

Often, unprovoked they would grab someone and push them against the wall or force them to the ground while rummaging through their pockets and clothing. He'd seen a number of people arrested by the police over there, but never once seen or heard them read them their rights or anything like that crap you see on tv," Conrad told a friend once. In those days there were no cellphones or cameras around, and neither was there a respect for "civil rights." Ignoring the comments from the police, his mind faded off into the distance.

As he sat in the back of the police car Conrad posed a question to God, did I misunderstand God? "this can't be what you had in mind when you told me to move forward with this mission.

Back at the police station young police officer Erick Kemp, who transferred to the south Houston police district a month prior to be a part of the new anti-carjacking task force assembled at the station. Officer Kemp made a name for himself by being involved in the capture of a serial house burglar turned unlikely killer in the Houston area. Avery Wright killed Daphne Jackson, the wife of prominent news executive Andre Jackson of WKROC in Houston. Officer Kemp was on routine patrol when he heard the call over the radio and thought he recognized the name of Conrad James, the suspect who was being held for "running through the neighborhood" of a prominent Houston suburb. The name sounded familiar, but he couldn't quite remember from where. By the time the other officers brought Conrad into the station to question him Officer Kemp had already found out who he was and moved to quickly get the information to the arresting officers.

Do you know who that is? Officer Kemp asked, walking hastily towards the arresting officer. No. But I know he's a criminal who we caught with no business being in the type of neighborhood he was in. Declared Officer O'Reilly, a 20-year veteran of the police force known throughout the department for his racist beliefs and actions.

I looked him up and that's Conrad James. He's the CEO of some big engineering company, and he's in the area for some type of convention. It says on their program that he's the keynote speaker for some big event tonight. Oh really? Asked Officer O'Reilly feigning ignorance and half laughing as he talked. Officer O'Reilly already knew the truth about who Conrad was he was simply following the instructions of Rex the leader of his White Nationalist movement and the one orchestrating the actions from behind the scenes.

Rex learned that Conrad would be in the area and knew about his habit of going out for a morning run, in fact, Rex knew about most of Conrad's habits because he had him under surveillance for two years, so he directed officer O'Reilly as to when and where to accost him. "Don't do too much damage just shake him up a bit using a case of mistaken identity as an excuse," Rex told him. Officer O'Reilly would have liked to have a little more fun but thought better of it now that this “meddling young boy” was in my way. Well, you’d better release him then. O’Reilly said handing the handcuff keys to Officer Kemp.

Officer Kemp and other officers then attempted to apologize to Conrad and calm the situation. They were concerned about the possible bad press and legal ramifications the department could receive.

Conrad James now unhandcuffed stood before the police officers at the station. Have you now reached your morning quota for today or are you going back out hunting for more blacks later? Conrad asked them in disgust.

Watch who you’re talking to in that tone boy! Officer O’Reilly said flatly.

I know who I’m talking to. A redneck cop who gets his kicks out of looking down on and harassing the people in the community that he’s sworn to serve and protect. A corrupt and racist cop who has little else to feel good about in his life other than to go around harassing, hounding, and attempting to intimidate people. There’s nothing new or interesting about you. Do you think you’re the first redneck that I’ve run into? Do you think I’ve gotten this far and not been targeted by your kind, or felt the looks of jealousy and disbelief that a black man can accomplish what I have? I’ve overcome hundreds of people like you and kept my head high and that’s what I’ll be doing today.

But I have your name and just memorized your badge number which I’d be willing to bet that as long as you’ve been on the force you probably don’t have memorized. You can count on hearing from my legal team soon. Conrad said as he strode out of the police station. The other officers had looks of shock on their faces at the audacity of Conrad's speech to officer O'Reilly who they knew walked in dangerous circles.

Chapter 2

The Choice to Continue Down the Wrong Path

It was two years ago that Harry Jacobs and Conrad James became unlikely adversaries of one another. Two men who were remotely positioned from one another, growing up in vastly different worlds and circumstances, yet were inextricably connected by life's unpredictable twists and turns. A testament to how life's roads can lead down some strange paths at times. Almost immediately they collided on a multitude of issues, but the main issue to Harry was the fact that Conrad James, an African-American man from Chicago had been given "his position" and was named the CEO of Houston Exponential Engineering.

Harry was a dedicated and trusted employee of the company and was thought by many to be the natural successor to the soon-to-be-retired CEO. However, the Board of Directors told Harry that they needed someone different, a person of creativity and vision. This hurt Harry deeply when he was not able to obtain his lifelong dream, but it was only the beginning of the pain he would feel. When Conrad arrived to great fanfare and celebration Harry was pushed over the edge, and the sight of seeing a black man celebrated for receiving what was "rightfully his" infuriated him. "Damn affirmative action!" Harry cussed to himself at the sight.

This singular event was the tipping point for Harry who was in the process of mulling a significant choice in his life. Harry was being recruited by Rexnord

Rutherford known to his inner circle as Rex - A sinister and shadowy figure who was the leader of a white nationalist, Neo Nazis movement he was mobilizing in south Texas.

Rex set his sights on Harry as a potentially powerful ally to "the movement" he called his white nationalist followers. Rex, who possessed a degree in psychology was a master at manipulation, excelled at sizing up people, and specialized in exploiting the disappointments and hurt feelings of their past. Using these skills allowed him to rise quickly up the ranks of the white nationalism movement that he now leads in the region of south Texas. Highly educated, Rex chose to use his skills for sinister reasons instead of uplifting his community.

Harry arrived for a meeting with Rex at the local park on a typically hot summer morning. "1488." Rex greeted Harry. "1488." Harry replied. This had become one of their standard salutations towards one another when people outside of the "movement" were not around. 1488 was code speak for the Neo Nazis and white nationalist movement and is now used in online posts and other forms of media for these like-minded individuals to identify and support one another covertly, without the knowledge of the general public. The numbers have taken the form of an endorsement for white supremacy, and its racist beliefs and principles. They can be found hidden stealthily in artwork, graffiti, graphics, and tattoos. Others use a form of it in their email addresses or even online merchandise sales with the price of $14.88 requesting financial support from people of similar beliefs all over the world. Regardless of its use, the "movement" sees it as a way to adjust to both verbal and online communications and keep up with the changing technological times.

1488 is broken down into two parts. The first symbol which is 14 stands for the 14-word slogan "We must secure the existence of our people and a future for white children." The second symbol 88 refers to the eighth letter of the alphabet H and they are saluting "Heil Hitler". A salute to the Nazis' death tyrant.

Our friend is back on our radar at least temporarily Rex said to Harry. What friend is that? Asked Harry. Conrad James Rex said, hiding a sly smile that he kept in check. Rex knew that even the mention of this name would get a rise out of his associate, and he delighted in arousing Harry's anger. One of our people at the police department says that they have him in custody at the moment but will have to release him soon. The damn Black Panther! Replied Harry incredulously. One day soon I'm going to deal with him personally for what he's done to me and my family! But what is going on I know you didn't want to meet with me for the likes of him, so what's on your mind?

We're about to enter a new phase in our efforts to "take back America" and I wanted to make sure that we're on the same page with everything. Rex said. We saw the great job that you are doing as our "Director of Homeland Internal Defense," during the time when these Jews, niggers, and immigrants were protesting and attempting to change our way of life. The way you and your team were able to infiltrate their protests and create chaos through violence, looting, and destruction of property was brilliant. We've always been able to take the country's mind off the real issues that these groups of outside agitators complain about and having the media focus shifted to the violence will work every time. We've been doing that since the 1960s. We've evolved into "White Nationalists" there is too much of a negative stigma attached to the "White Supremacist" label with many of our brainwashed white brethren.

However, you also need to know that Conrad has started an organization that he hopes can change some of our gun laws and will hurt our people in the gun industry. His activities have caught the eye of some of our higher-ups, so we wanted to start feeling him out by having him arrested this morning, just to let him know that we're still around. Guns have become a major source of revenue for our movement, and they have also served a dual purpose for our mission of taking back America. This could also affect your work as Director of Homeland Defense and the chaos that you have been able to inflict in certain areas while showing the urgent need to protect gun manufacturers and distributors. Not only do guns play a major role in the inner-city violence that we want to see they also help to fill our prisons with those lowlifes. This has been a dual boom for our pockets and allows us to invest in the NRA and other pro-gun groups. We have to keep the politicians on our side of the debate, so nothing changes. Let them continue to offer their "thoughts and prayers" and do nothing. Rex said with a smile on his face.

But now we want to move into other areas and we're going to need more of our white brothers and sisters to be awakened to the dangers of all these illegal immigrants being allowed in our country. But first, we must know are you fully with us Harry?

Harry was still struggling with his personal life since the tragic death of his only son Harry Jr. He was being tormented with the choices that he made leading up to his son's death. Harry Jr. was badly in need of bone marrow and a blood transfusion and there were only two potential donors that came up in the hospital blood bank, both matches resided in the Sun Park, Tx area. The first was Jordan James, Conrad's son. Harry sr. rejected the notion of having an African American give bone marrow or a blood transfusion to his son.

Convinced by Rex and other members of his "white brethren" to not mix the pure white Aryan blood with Jordan's. "God would never provide that as a solution that would corrupt the pure white blood," they told Harry. The second potential donor, Rex never came forward wanting to keep secret that his blood and Jordan's were essentially the same. Fearing it would hurt his potential advancement within the white nationalism movement. Harry's choice to delay while waiting for a "suitable" donor to come forward resulted in the death of his son.

Harry's wife Judy also left him a short time later because of his participation in his newfound white nationalism which she correctly saw changed Harry from the man he was into an empty one. She also blamed him for the death of their son.

Harry at first blamed himself for the bad choices he made, but he attempted to move beyond self-blame by now blaming God for "allowing" his son to die. He was still being held captive by his past - the feelings of disappointment that he felt from his childhood and his relationship with his father. Believing he never lived up to the name of his father and grandfather always gnawed at Harry and he walked through life as if carrying a heavy burden on his back. A "spirit of rejection" gripped Harry tightly whenever he thought about his father.

Harry although financially a wealthy man and an engineer by trade, was greatly unhappy, he was feeling mentally and spiritually shallow, empty, and unfulfilled. A prisoner of his past now stuck in a repeating cycle of failure because of his unresolved feelings of rejection from his father and disappointment in his career. Harry first attempted to go through life without any resolution of his past issues, then he started to deny their existence. When this didn't work Harry simply told himself that he was ok and could live with them. Carrying the weight of this baggage, Harry was about to be faced with yet another potentially life-changing choice.

Harry leaned back in his seat as he contemplated the question that Rex posed to him. "Are you fully with us?" Despite all that he had gone through, all he endured over the past two years Harry felt like God was giving him another chance. That God was speaking to him through the words of his parents that echoed in his mind during times of reflection. He also remembered those words of repentance and redemption of the pastor at his mom's church from what he thought of as long-ago days from a distant past. Another lifetime it seemed. It's as if the words were still speaking to him, chasing him from behind, pursuing him. At times they even haunted him. Let go of the past and live they called to him, "Choose Life" his pastor would say, but would he listen?

Was God giving him another chance at life, an exit ramp off the road of destruction he was traveling down? A chance for a change of direction and destination from the road to perdition. Would he take it? Would he take heed to the voice of repentance? Or had the voice of hate, and revenge that he allowed to fester in his mind now stronger, more influential than the voice of God?

Harry had become accustomed to listening to this voice of destruction through daily practice as the last two years he listened to little else, and now it ruled him, pulled at him, mocked him. Making his heart callous to God's word. Harry had a choice to make. Was his hate and need for revenge stronger than his need for redemption and salvation? "It's too late for me!" Harry lied to himself. I've made my choices for the direction of my life even for my final eternal resting place. If I'm doomed, I'm doomed. What do you have in mind? Harry replied to Rex.

Chapter 3

Living With the Consequences of our Choices

Alex Alvarez was serving a double life sentence in the Texas state penitentiary. He was now in year twenty of paying for one bad choice that he wished he could have back. There was a time when he hoped for and dreamed of a miracle that would allow him another chance at life. But the passage of time has dimmed that hope, and now he has come to terms with his present reality. Alex had been a straight-A student in school and was about to graduate at the head of his class. He was always told that greatness was in his future. That he would one day make his parents and even the entire Fifth Ward of Houston proud. Alex dreamed of one day becoming a doctor and he would always excitedly tell others about his dreams.

Those dreams were dashed by one bad choice on a hot summer day in Houston. Alex had foolishly bought a gun from someone selling illegal guns on the street one day while walking home with his best friend Louis Hernandez who pleaded with Alex not to make the purchase. "No good is going to come from owning a gun," Louis said. But Alex was intrigued by the sight of the gun and wondered what it would feel like to hold one. I'm not going to shoot anyone don't be so soft, said Alex to his lifelong friend, laughing at the magnified level of concern in Louis's voice.

Later that summer at the local park a fight broke out on a basketball court between Alex and a group of boys he'd never seen before. As Alex and Louis were packing up to leave the boys appeared to be charging in their direction and Alex instinctively reached into his gym bag and pulled out the weapon firing three shots. Instantly killing one of the boys plus an innocent bystander who had nothing to do with their altercation. And just like that, the boy voted unanimously as the most likely to succeed had been turned into a "prison lifer." Alex thought often about the events of that day. The mistakes he made leading up to that day, and his ultimate mistake. His thoughts haunted him and caused him great pain while sitting in the seclusion of his prison cell, but now they seemed to taunt him.

Now thirty-eight years old Alex was still a young man with potentially a lot more life to live, and a lot more prison time to serve. Early on in his prison sentence, he went into a deep depression shortly after arriving at the Huntsville, Texas state penitentiary. He was told by the prison psychologist who had seen many come "inside" before Alex that it was a "natural thing", and that it happens frequently with "lifers" as the hope of a future once bright and full of potential gives way to the dim reality of prison life.

Alex was engaged to his high school sweetheart at the time of the shooting, and she was pregnant with their first child when he got here. She at first came to visit him often, but over time the visits became less and less frequent before coming to an end. Alex didn't blame her knowing that she had a life to live. Life goes on and so will the people in your life he thought to himself. Last he heard she was now married and living in California. "Just because you've thrown your life away don't expect others to stop living," he told a young gang member one day.

Alex, to his credit, did mentally recover and go on to college while he was in prison. Taking classes through an online prison college program. Something to pass the time, he told himself. He continued to be a straight-A student. Instructors marveled at the level of academic brilliance displayed by Alex most privately shaking their heads saying, "Wow what a waste of talent." The classwork would have been relatively easy for Alex even if he'd gone to college under normal circumstances, but for him to take classes while being incarcerated and with nothing but time on his hands the classes became "too easy" for him. Alex soon saw the classes as unfulfilling, unsatisfying, and even discouraging. He needed more.

One day while sitting and staring blankly in the prison library he received an email message from his online college professor asking if he'd be interested in becoming a teacher for a new program for GED and high school students in prison. A pilot program for inmates in the Texas state penitentiary. This was the start of the "second chance" Alex had prayed for. Alex would eventually become the head instructor in the state program and even some of the other programs they had. Alex grew to love teaching so much that he started teaching in the bible school programs as well and became an ordained minister while incarcerated. Ministering to hundreds of young men each year Alex became well known throughout the state of Texas. Men young and old would always come to him for advice and mentorship, especially those soon to be released.

Hector Rodriguez a two-time felon was one of those young men. Hector had spent the last three years as the "cellmate" of Alex, and he tapped into the wealth of knowledge that flowed freely from his mentor. Hector received his high school diploma the week of his pending release date which was a great honor for him, and he was grateful to Alex for his tutelage and mentorship. He didn't believe that he would be able to accomplish it at first, but he persisted, and he was proud of the achievement.

Hector had grown up in the gang lifestyle. Ever since he was old enough to remember everyone he knew was a part of one gang or another. To him, there was no other way of life. You had to be hardcore to live in Houston's 5th ward he thought, and he rarely saw men who went to work every day, to school, or to church. It seemed only the women were doing "that type of thing" and it became a natural way of life in his community. He never envisioned himself as being anything else, to him he'd be lucky to live past the age of 25 anyway so why bother with school? He was destined to become a statistic, a label, the reason for the explosion in the building of prisons throughout America.

It was 2 am the night before Hector's pending release later this morning after three long years of incarceration and he was laying in the top bunk of the two-person cell, staring at the ceiling, contemplating his life. It was Hector's "second strike," the judge threaten him at his sentencing with a stern warning that just like in baseball the American judicial system had a three-strikes and you're out rule. Hector thought back to that day three years ago. Alex lay in the bottom bunk. The room was black as the night and the sheer silence pierced loudly through the darkness. Although neither man made a sound both men knew that the other was not sleeping. An air of intensity gripped the room as the pending moment crept through the night. They could feel one another as if in communion together spiritually. Alex knew that Hector was feeling anxiety, a nervous apprehension about his uncertain future. Hector albeit relieved to be getting out of prison within a few hours was uncomfortable with the uncertainty that lay before him. Even though he hated being incarcerated it did provide him with a sense of security, a peace that he hadn't had while on the streets.

"I'm determined to give myself a fighting chance for a better life and get my family back once I get out of this terrible place," Hector said to Alex breaking through the deafening silence. Man, you don't know how much it means to me to get that high school diploma while I was in here. It made me feel like I came here for a purpose. Something positive in my life for a change. I couldn't have done it without all the help you gave me. Hector said a hint of emotion in his voice. Congratulations on the diploma I knew you could do it. You put in the work, and you deserve all the credit I didn't do anything. Replied Alex. Bullshit! Hector shot back. I was a mess when I got here, and you know it. Hector said. They both gave in to a moment of laughter. Pausing for a moment Alex continued. It's not how you start it's how you finish. Alex replied regaining a serious tone.

Hector took that in for a moment, contemplating it. He was always told that he would never amount to much growing up, that he never completed anything he started. You're a loser! A quitter! Good for nothing! He quietly remembered his mother shouting at him as a child over and over. The words seem to echo in his ears even to this day. I'm a little nervous about going back out there tomorrow not knowing what this new chance at life is going to bring.

Yeah, I know. Alex replied. But you'll be ok just remember to put God first and you can handle whatever the world brings your way. Making better choices starts with God, do that and you'll be fine. Sometimes you must embrace the unknown and move forward by faith.

I just don't want to make the same mistakes this time that I've always made, like I've done for most of my life that would be my "third strike."

You've accepted Christ as your savior now. That means that God has implanted His spirit on the inside of you that the world can't overcome, you just have to walk in that.

You make it sound simple, but I don't want to keep going in and out of jail, I know that. This system doesn't work. For people like you and me at least. Hector said reflectively.

This system does work! It works the way that it was intended to work. Do you see how many new prisons

America has built in the past twenty years? Do you want to know how they determine how many prisons they are going to build? How many jail cells they'll be needing?

They simply look at the birth rates of Blacks, Hispanics, and "people of color", or people who grow up in neighborhoods like ours and apply a predetermined percentage to that and it tells them how many jail cells will be needed. Because those are the people that prisons are built for. America would rather invest in prisons than in transforming those communities. I guess prisons are more profitable in the long term than education and training. Alex said shaking his head.

Both men fell silent again as they thought about what the future may hold for them. Having spent the last three years together in this 10 X 10-foot cell, although not ideal for anyone it did create a bond that had grown stronger over time. And although excited that he was about to be released in a couple of hours Hector began to feel dejected about leaving his friend behind. He felt that it was unfair that Alex would have to spend the rest of his life in prison for a mistake that he made as a teenager, but he knew there was little he could do about it. However, Alex had proven that although this was definitely not the life that he envisioned there was still life and that he would make the best of it while he had the chance.

Hector was pondering what Alex said to him earlier about embracing the unknown and was wondering how he was supposed to do that with a future as uncertain as his. How was he going to get a job to support himself, who would be his next Parole Officer, and where was he going to live? These questions raced through his mind creating even more anxiety.

I was thinking about what you said earlier about embracing the unknown. Hector said, breaking the silence. That sounds good and all, but the odds are stacked against me, a lot of mistakes that I've made that people will be trying to hold over my head when I get out there.

Don't become a prisoner of your past or allow your mind to wander and hover over past mistakes. You'll already have the people in your life and those you have to interact with to do that. There's no need for the past to become a weight around your neck or a monkey on your back. The word of God says that you are a "new creature" in Christ.

I don't feel new. Replied Hector. And these prison guards, my new parole officer, and the world out there won't think that I'm new either.

None of that matters, and that's not what it means. It means that in God's sight, you became new. The way that He sees you is new, He's redeemed you. Your new position in Christ is a child of God. And you plus God are enough to overcome any of those things and more. Alex replied.

Hector hesitated for an instant, giving himself a time of reflection before the moment that he's been dreaming of these last three years would happen. His release from prison. It's great how you have been giving me the word of God over these past three years since I've been locked in this cell with you, but do you have any last-minute practical advice that I can take with me before they call my name to leave this place?

Yeah, I do. You already have it. Replied Alex. Remember that simple exercise I had the class to do? Write down what are your three primary goals to get accomplished when you get out of here. And then we followed up by adding the necessary activities and steps to take to reach each goal. Well now is the time to put that into practice. I wanted you to write them down because I know that it's more likely that you will accomplish them if they're written down, but you'll have to hold yourself accountable for moving into action. It's not going to happen by accident.

I still have all of that. Hector said but it seemed easier when it was just in a classroom. Now that the day is here those goals are starting to feel more like a dream than something that I can do. I've never finished anything in my life until getting this diploma but that was in the confines of this prison, soon I'll be outside in the real world with no money or support, and I can't afford to mess this up again. I'll need to make some moves fast.

Don't expect instant results! Alex said in an urgent tone to his protégé. We live in a world of right now, people want microwave results instead of baking which tastes better. Everybody want what they want immediately but they don't want to go through the process it takes to get there. Looking for instant gratification produces short-term thinking, that's the difference between successful and unsuccessful people. Short-term thinking is also what keeps this place full, and a revolving door open for prisons across America.

Also, don't give in to feelings of discouragement along the way Hector. Life is a journey, and everyone's path is different. One of the easiest ways to become discouraged is to play the comparison game. Let people have their time, you just keep working and your time will come. From the outside, it may look like someone has a great life, but you never know, suicide happens to the rich as much as the poor, maybe more.

You know how to stay away from the trouble you're in here on a parole violation just like a lot of other young men who come back here. You didn't even have additional charges you're still paying the price for something you did when you were 17 years old. Alex said. That's the system they have set up to keep the revolving door moving in prisons.

Let me guess. Alex said To Hector. Your court-appointed lawyer came to you after they had threatened you with significant jail time for a drug offense and said, "I've got a deal for you," if you want to go home we can make it happen you'll just have to be on parole, and they gave you 10 or 15 years parole knowing that you would not be able to abide by every rule placed upon you, and they can put you back in here whenever they want to. You can be on parole for 15 years, and still under their control.

People are not the same as they once were Hector, not as good as they used to be. They kill for trivial reasons and material things that have little value.

They lack substance and depth of character. Mostly because they don't have God in their lives, but not you. You have all you need on the inside.

An eerie silence hovered in the air as they both absorbed their final conversation and moments together.

As strange as it may seem the Texas state penitentiary did provide Hector with the structure and foundation he needed for his life at the time. Thanks in large part to the mentorship of Alex he earned his high school diploma and became a Christian while incarcerated. Once outside of the confines of the prison walls, Hector and Alex both knew his newfound faith would be tested. Hector was about to start a new chapter in his life. But who would be the author? Would he be able to hold on to the life lessons he's learned over the past three years? An ominous feeling came over him as if potential doom was looming, lurking in the background, watching him. Hector was about to come face to face with unforeseen, and life-changing decisions that would shape the rest of his life.

Number 120-111-141-1847-2051 A voice boomed through the silence. Let's go! Hector got up and shook hands with his mentor Alex whispering something into his ear, then he made his move swiftly out of the jail cell and into the prison hallway. Looking back at a burly correctional officer who stared at him with disdain on his face. You couldn't call me by my name just once? Even though I'm leaving huh? Hector said. You'll be back. The Officer replied laughing hysterically. Hector could hear the laughter ringing in the corridors behind him as he was leaving.

Chapter 4

Choosing Bitterness over Peace

Jamal Reynolds, a childhood friend of Conrad and Janice James was in town and planning to visit hoping to reconnect with his two childhood friends . They had all grown up on Chicago's west side and attended the same schools. Richard T. Crane high school was the neighborhood school that most in the area attended, however, Jamal decided to transfer to rival John Marshall high school after they had a falling out. Jamal served as a media executive for the past ten years in Chicago before he received what he called an "offer that he couldn't refuse." He was in town to finalize the deal and was preparing to relocate to Houston soon afterward. He hadn't been planning on leaving his hometown Chicago, but this southern station appeared to want him badly. He turned down several previous offers from this news station saying to them that it was not a good fit for him. He didn't believe in their ultra-conservative format and the incendiary commentary of the station. But he relented when the stakes got higher saying to himself "I'd be a damn fool to turn this amount of money down."

Jamal boarded the train from George Bush Intercontinental Airport in Houston and was heading towards the suburb of Sun Park, Tx. In a moment of reflection, Jamal thought deeper about the circumstances that led him to this unlikely choice of moving south. Something he swore he would never do and the assignment that was laid out to him by his soon-to-be new employer was not a pleasant one, but he was willing to do it for the "right price". I had to tell them to cut the crap and give it to me straight, I'm all about Jamal Incorporated so I don't need the fluff. He remembered saying to Paul.

Jamal remembered wondering to himself why does this WKROC news channel want him so badly? I'm sure they can easily get someone else for the position of news director and for a lot less money. There is something more to this thing I'm sure of it. I don't even believe in their right-wing, ultra-conservative politics, in fact, "I don't believe in anyone's politics, he told a friend one day. I believe in the United States of me" he said. Working in today's media is all a game of pitting one group against another. Plus, it's too damn hot in Texas, I don't like all that heat and can't stand rednecks. Jamal laughed to himself. One day he received a surprise call directly from Paul Wilson himself, the General Manager of WKROC. Can we meet I'll be in the Chicago area tomorrow and was hoping that you could spare a moment of your time. I promise it will be worth it and I won't waste your time Paul said in a professional tone.

I'm going to get rid of this guy once and for all. I'll have him meet me in a local area right outside of K-town on the west side, or maybe in Bronzeville on the south side. I'll bet that will take care of him. He won't dare to show up to any of those areas Jamal laughed. But to his utter shock, Paul answered nonchalantly to him. Which do you prefer I'll be there by 7:00 if that's ok? Now intrigued by the boldness of Paul, Jamal agreed to meet in a bar off the corner of Madison and Keeler in K-town, on Chicago's west side. This whiteboy is crazy Jamal thought to himself after settling on a time and place. "I know that he's a southern redneck because I've been checking out some of the content of WKROC news. It's the same old anti-immigrant, anti-voting, anti-liberal nonsense that they love to scare suburban America with. Catering to the fears of people and their biases against people whom they have never met or anyone who doesn't look and think like them." Now I'm really intrigued Jamal said to himself.

The meeting is all set Paul said to Rex who was sitting at the same table with him strategizing about their use of media outlets to enhance their white supremacist, turned white nationalism activities while he was speaking to Jamal about meeting with him. That's great! Rex replied with enthusiasm. Rex previously directed Paul to close the deal with Jamal no matter the cost. The thought of having another black man to replace Andre as the man in charge of the day-to-day media content, plus one of Conrad's childhood friends was too enticing for Rex to pass up. He dreamed of endless possibilities.

We must keep our plans for taking back our county in motion, and a big part of our plan is what you do in the media. Hitler himself showed us the way. We must have a firm grip on the media and be able to control and shape the messages that get reported. The media outlets that we don't control we have to work to discredit. Not everyone understands us, our white power movement, and the good that it can bring to everyone whether white, black, or brown it doesn't matter. When the natural order of things are in place, the way God intended things to be with white men in charge it's better for everyone, especially the inferior races. Rex said.

He thought that he could frighten me off with a meeting place in the nigger parts of Chicago Paul laughed. He suggested K-town, or Bronzeville as potential meeting places as if I would be intimidated by going into those areas. He doesn't know that we've targeted those areas and neighborhoods for years. That we are the source and suppliers of drugs, and all kinds of mischief for areas like them Paul said to Rex with a huge smile on his face.

Yea, Harry says those are some of his prime target areas for the carjacking initiative that he has implemented. He's paying them top dollar for the cars that they take, and it has spurred a huge surge in carjackings. The money is no object because we have a larger donor pool than ever from higher-ups who are sympathetic to our cause. They can't be directly involved in our activities because of the positions they have as CEOs, politicians, judges, and law enforcement, but they support us behind the scenes and are sympathetic to the plight of the white man in America. And besides, we get the money back on the back end anyway because we know that most of those young monkeys will end up in prison and that's where we really make a profit – by filling those prisons up! Rex said.

What time are you leaving for Chicago? I have a 7 am flight tomorrow morning. Just remember I have authorized you to offer him as much as necessary to close the deal, just be careful not to scare him off by appearing too desperate. We want to have another black man directing our news, being the driving force behind the images and stories we create that way we can't be called racist by the viewers or liberal media. It's always better to have one of their own as the face of it. In fact, I think this guy Jamal is the perfect person to use to attack this "Critical Race Theory" that these radicals are trying to have taught to our children. They want white kids to feel bad about their own race and the history of this country that we built. When you get back, I want you to make it a priority to combat the evilness of "Critical Race Theory."

Jamal Reynolds strode into the local bar that was one of his old hangouts on Madison just west of Pulaski Street with the confidence that he always carried with him. He was a man on the rise and tonight a man on a mission. He was there to meet up with Paul Wilson, the white southerner who dared come into the "hood" on Chicago's westside, and that impressed Jamal or at least "made him curious." It was a hot midsummer night in Chicago, and he hoped the place had finally gotten the air conditioning fixed. Regardless, I'm here let's see what's on this redneck's mind he thought to himself.

Entering the bar with his usual glance from side to side he made eye contact with Joe the bartender and owner who he had known for years, Joe nodded in the direction of a far corner. There sat one lone white man in a dimly lit part of the bar smoking a cigar, a drink already at his table. He was a stark contrast from all the locals who were there shooting pool and rocking to the music wondering who he was. Damn, he actually showed up. Jamal thought.

Jamal went over and sat at his table without introducing himself or attempting to shake hands. I'm glad you could make it Paul said. I'm here what's on your mind? Jamal said dryly. I've come all the way from Texas to make you an offer for a position that we have open in the Houston area. It's a position coveted by many, but we need to make sure we have the right person for it. I've admired your work and did some research on you, and it seems you are a man on the rise in the media business and I believe that you could be a perfect fit for what we are looking for.

Let's cut through the crap Tex. You could have given this job to anyone in Texas but you're coming all the way to Chicago to offer it to me, why? I've done my own research on the station you work for WKROC. It's a bunch of right-wing, ultra-conservative, bullshit. So why do you want to talk to me about it? I could care less about your platform or your audience. Anytime one of you guys "stoops down" enough to come into this neighborhood I know that it's for guns, drugs, money, or some other way of exploitation so let's cut to the chase. You said on the phone that you wouldn't waste my time Jamal said.

I've been listening to your station all week, well at least as much of it as I can stand. All you do is tell lies and stoke fear based on racial biases. So, what do you want me for? Jamal said in a harsh tone.

For your leadership and news savvy. Paul replied quickly.

Bullshit! You like to have a black face driving your racial crap that way you can hide in the background and pretend that it's not driven by racism and that racism is not the American way. I researched what happened to your last news director. The way you used him and then discarded him. That's not going to happen to me! Jamal said.

The direct approach huh? I like that Paul said. You're friends with Conrad James, aren't you he's in Houston working as some big-time CEO. I used to be, but yeah, I know him Jamal said with a sting of bitterness in his tone. Paul could sense that there was some bad blood there and he was intrigued by that. How would you like to make the type of money that he's making? That's what I'm prepared to offer you a chance to skip over some of these do-gooders who don't understand how the real world works and make some real money. I'm listening Replied Jamal sliding up in his seat.

What I'm about to propose to you may be offensive, but don't take it personally. It's the media business and I believe you to be a person who understands business. Media is a ratings game and without ratings, you won't be in the game for long. So, what we would need from you is to become the face of driving our content and the person responsible for the information that we push. You mean the disinformation and propaganda, don't you? Jamal jumped in to say. So, what I'll be expecting in my next News Director Jamal is this, "we must continue to push minority stereotypes, continue to bombard the public with black and brown faces whenever there is a crime committed especially when it's a high-profile crime, and then highlight their apprehension and capture" Paul said while smiling. You appear to be a man who can see the bigger picture, one who won't take this type of thing personally Paul said.

Jamal simply laughed. I work for Jamal incorporated Paul he said flatly. The two men sat there for about thirty seconds in silence sizing one another up. Time appeared to stand still for a moment as neither man wanted to speak next. It was as if their silence turned into a negotiation ploy as they stared at one another, each waiting on a response from the other. Look, Jamal, we don't hate your people or anyone else we're simply giving our audience what it wants, what it needs to feel better about the direction of this country. People want to be able to feel safe in America. That the "good guys" are winning and have their backs. I understand you may feel like this is an attack on your people, but it's not, it's playing the ratings game. I know this might be a tough decision for you to make and you may need some time to consider my offer. Jamal abruptly raised his hand stopping Paul in his tracks. How much does the position pay? Jamal asked without emotion. Soon Jamal will be relocating to south Texas.

Chapter 5

Coming Back to Reality

Later that day after his release from police custody, and now meeting with his legal team, Conrad couldn't help but reminisce about the last time he was arrested and it brought back to life some of the unpleasant memories he thought were buried. It was years ago but the most recent contact with them brought back those old memories of the way things were growing up on the west side of Chicago.

The police always appeared to be on edge when they came into our neighborhoods. As if they believed they were in a war zone, or at war with the residents who lived there at least. In their minds every resident was a threat, they had to be either in a gang, selling drugs, or both. The reality was that most of the people there were simply everyday people who wanted better for themselves.

During the 1980's young black and Hispanic men were rounded up in neighborhoods like his and charged with "Disorderly Conduct." That was always the fallback arrest reason when the police wanted to round up a number of men to fill their jail cells with despite no crimes being committed. Maybe they needed to reach a productivity quota. Whatever the reason, the city of Chicago allowed thousands of these arrests back then with full knowledge of the corrupt practice that produced thousands of made-up charges.

One particular moment in time still resonates from the depths of his memory. A constant reminder of his true status in America and of a time when criminals boldly held badges and disregarded civil rights with impunity. During one of the Chicago police department's corrupt 13th district neighborhood random sweeps, he was detained and his hands cuffed behind his back. As he stood there with police officers on either side of him wondering what charges could possibly be brought against him, another CPD officer walked up to him with a nightstick in hand and smashed it against his head.

Blood gushed out from the blow that came within a fraction of an inch from putting his eye out. It was struck so close to his eye that it opened a gash that blended in with his eyebrows. The blood streamed down his face and felt cool as it rolled into his eyes. Flowing freely and unencumbered as he stood there helplessly unable to prevent its advancement down his face with his hands cuffed behind his back. Somehow, the blow from the stick and the blood didn't seem to hurt him at all, it only produced intense anger and a helpless feeling of being able to do nothing. The resulting scar serves to this day as a constant reminder of his true status in America the place "with liberty and justice for all."

Apparently, there was a "war on drugs" going on in the country at that time, declared by the President of the United States himself Ronald Regan. This declaration was considered a green light for law enforcement to hassle, hound, and persecute neighborhoods like ours. A war on America's inner cities would have been more accurate since America knew the source of where the drugs were coming from yet never fought their entry into the country Conrad thought incredulously to himself.

America had invested a lot in its prison system. Prisons were becoming big business in America, and they were springing up all over the place. Large, massive structures, and complexes. In some rural and small-town areas, the prisons were more of a campus than a single building-larger and more expansive than any college campus. Those buildings needed to be paid for, and they were paid for with black bodies. Someone had to occupy those buildings. The cost of them was in the billions of dollars, however, the potential profit made them a good investment for America, and America wanted a return on their investment.

Conrad suddenly snapped back to the present. I foolishly believed I had gotten out of reach for this type of thing he thought to himself. Now the CEO of Houston Exponential Engineering (HEE) Conrad was a man well known in the business world. A graduate of the University of Chicago with a master's degree in Quantum Engineering, Conrad had "made it, so he thought." He had accomplished the American dream. At least that's what others told him. But these police officers were not a part of the business world that held him in such high esteem, nor did they have any interest in Quantum Engineering. As they turned into the police parking lot one of the officers smiled at him with a sinister look on his face. He was ready to take

Conrad into an interrogation room where he was sure he could get the truth from him.

Conrad's mind shifted to the reason he was in town today. He believed that God had given him a new mission, a calling that he needed to fulfill, but he knew that without God's help he wouldn't be able to accomplish it. The task seemed monumental, too big for one person for sure, and he knew it would come with great risk attached. He came into the city of Houston to speak with a group of corporate, political, and religious leaders to garner support for the organization that he started two years ago. This after a potential mass shooting was averted at the last second at Sun Park high school where his son Jordan attended school. Conrad was apprehensive about embarking on this journey at first, even fearful, but after extensive time in prayer, he was convinced that God was with him.

Conrad dedicated the work to the memory of his late mother and named it in her honor. The Sabrina James initiative for nonviolent change. An advocacy group committed to helping bring meaningful legislation to combat the constant gun violence in America due to the seemingly endless free flow of guns and the easy access provided to them. The organization hoped to bring about common-sense legislation and gun laws that could make the country safer from the rampant gun violence plaguing the nation, hold accountable gun manufacturers and distributors, and allow them to be held liable for their products both financially and criminally when appropriate.

He strategically chose the final week of May, as well as the city of Houston to have his kickoff meeting to coincide with the opening of the annual National Rifle Association convention.

He wanted to use the gathering and the media that revolves around them to his advantage and help to bring awareness to his upstart organization as well as call out some of the hypocrisy of some of the politicians in attendance who serve as a constant shield and armor of protection for this pro-gun group, Conrad remembered telling his wife one day as he was researching some to the NRA's activities.

All the big gun manufacturers and distributors were in town to display their latest weaponry, body armor, and ammunition products without a thought to the deadly destruction that their products produce for Americans every day. They'll be there cleansing their conscience with the all too familiar slogan "The only thing that stops a bad guy with a gun, is a good guy with a gun."

Chapter 6

Bad Motives Lead to Bad Choices

After arriving at Houston's George Bush Intercontinental Airport Jamal was now in a taxi cruising towards the affluent suburb of Sun Park, Tx anticipating reconnecting with two old friends from the neighborhood. As the car turned slowly through the palm tree-covered roads Jamal took in the picturesque sights of the beautiful homes and gardens. The homes looked stately, lawns manicured to perfection, and fruit grew organically from the trees in the area. Wow, they're a long way from the projects Jamal said to himself with a hint of envy in his voice. It's going to be good seeing Janice again. I know she still looks good he thought wistfully, a smile coming over his face.

Jamal and Janice at one time held a "teen crush" on each other which would have gone further if Jamal had his way, but Janice's "old school" parents would not allow it. They had a strict rule for her not to date anyone until she was 17 years old or a senior in high school. Jamal always wondered what might have been with his long-time crush. The truth is over the years his feelings for her grew into far more than a crush. He was infatuated with Janice from the first time he saw her in grammar school and his feelings had evolved into a love for her over time.

For years Jamal rode a rollercoaster of emotions for her as he thought about what might have been. Left unchecked his emotions would surge up and down until finally forming into an unhealthy obsession. Although it was twenty years since he last saw her the emotions seemed to have a firm grip on him even now. By the time Janice met Conrad, he was a high school basketball star and brilliant student who abruptly came into the picture and swept her off her feet. In a flash, he stole her right from under his nose Jamal always felt. Leaving him confused, brokenhearted, and resentful.

Jamal never forgave Conrad for "stealing her from him" and hoped that he'd be able to get over the past resentment once in Texas. Besides, this money was too good to pass up and I could care less about the type of work these rednecks wanted me to do. If they want me to push their anti-liberal, anti-immigration, anti-Jew, anti-black people agenda then that's what I'm going to do. As long as the money is right, I could care less I'm here to get paid and they're paying me royally. That's the only reason I'm down here in Texas. Jamal repeated the lie to himself.

The reality was Jamal's anger at Conrad for "stealing" Janice from him remained inside of him, and the "root of bitterness" was allowed to fester in his heart over the years. Unaddressed, it spread into a hatred for both Conrad and Janice. He often attempted to dismiss the secret envy that weighed heavily on him as a normal reaction, but oftentimes it controlled and tortured him. Well, it's time to meet the perfect couple, Jamal said sarcastically as he stepped out of the cab in front of the James residence.

Conrad and Janice James were at home talking about the encounter between Conrad and the police department earlier that day. He had a couple of scrapes and bruises from being thrown to the ground and soreness in his leg from police officer O'Reilly's stick but otherwise, he was physically fine. Conrad had already contacted his legal team and was going over possible actions to take against the police department. He knew that he had been profiled and that the police overreacted to the situation. His first thought was that it was only because he was black and on the wrong side of town. But he was starting to feel that there was more to this encounter with the police, especially Officer O'Reilly, something more personal, something sinister. In hindsight, Conrad believed that this was not a chance meeting at all, they had known he'd be in the area somehow and were lying in wait for him.

The atmosphere of the room grew tense and became emotional as Conrad and his wife relived his encounter with the police earlier. I've had enough of trying to convince America about the treatment and even harassment that black people have faced at the hands of the police for years in America. Conrad said to Janice banging his fist on his desk. It's time to take action and expose these people and this system for what it is. The double standard is always at play between black and white during police interactions. When a white man is out for a morning jog it's called cardio, but when it's a black person he's "running through the neighborhood." Conrad said. I'm going to act not just for me, but for those who don't have access to legal representation or the resources to do it. He said to Janice.

The racial issues in America won't get any better because we have too many people willing to lie or believe a lie, attempt to rewrite history, and change stories to fit the ideal portrayal of America in their minds instead of dealing with reality. Hell, there are news channels out there now whose sole purpose it seems is to distort the truth. Janice replied. News stations like WKROC where their prime-time host Rucker Larson tells lies constantly and could care less about the truth. There's a reason we can see the same event happen and come up with completely different versions of what we see. People don't want to believe their own eyes or rely upon common sense they just go to their favorite news channels or the internet and allow them to shape their views. They want to be told what to think is right or wrong. Why are we always the ones who have to stand up against the police, oppression, or civil rights? Janice said shaking her head.

Officer O'Reilly is a bad actor and I'm going to have him removed and hopefully prosecuted for his actions, but he's small potatoes. He and his corrupt little circle behave the way they do because they are confident in being protected by their system, by codes of silence, and corruption that runs deeper than what we get to see. It's not enough to have one corrupt cop removed, we need to take on the corrupt justice system that has protected and shielded racism in America for years. We need systemic change! Conrad said with intensity.

The divisions in our country run wider and deeper today than they did in the 1960s. People are so dug into their narrow political and racial ideologies that you can't tell them anything that doesn't fit into that box. Any information they receive that contradicts what they are being fed inside of their news silos where everyone looks the same, thinks the same, talks the same they reject it. Their minds can't receive any objective thoughts or contractionary statements. Everyone has a cult-like mentality, and politicians and news channels take advantage of it and turn it into ratings for profits. I showed one of our neighbors a video of an unarmed black man being strangled by the police, and she said that he must have done something to deserve that. Janice replied in disgust.

The reason for that is when they interact with the police, they are their neighbors, kids' little league baseball coach, boys scout leader, or even a Deacon at their church. So, they can't fathom the same people doing the things they get accused of. All of their interactions are different than ours, the police aren't on edge when they stop them or while patrolling their neighborhoods. The people making the accusations must be lying, or they had to do something to deserve the mistreatment. Conrad said. They sat in silence for the next few moments, contemplating their next moves, their thoughts and mood filling the room. Time became obsolete as the seconds silently passed by; minutes passed as the James family lost track of time.

A loud knock broke through the silence of the house and jarred them back into the present. In strode their childhood friend Jamal Reynolds, who had now composed himself, at least enough to hide his lingering envy and hatred for Conrad from them. Janice was excited to see her childhood friend and acquaintance, the boy her parents would not allow her to date because of her youthful age. She ran towards Jamal and joyfully embraced him reigniting those old feelings in Jamal that he had never gotten over. He remembered the days of his youth, the dreams, and plans he had for himself and Janice. Jamal, at least for a brief moment, was allowed to dream again. He thought about what might have been, the future they could have had together. But reality caught hold of him and brought him back to the present.

Wow! What a great surprise. Said Conrad. Where did you come from? How long are you in town? He asked excitedly. Genuinely happy to see an old friend from the neighborhood.

Jamal quickly composed himself, getting back into character. Pretending to be happy for the James family and the life they have built together in Houston. I just got in town and wanted to make you guys my first stop before I take care of some business here in town. Jamal said.

Well, come on give us all the details what's been going on with you? Asked Janice playfully. She was happy to see her old friend who was also her first boyfriend. Are you married now or still living the bachelor's life? Janice said with a playful smile.

No, I'm not married, but I wouldn't call what I'm doing living the bachelor's life either Jamal smiled at Janice. Catching himself, he needed to make an intentional effort not to stare at her when he talked. But those old feelings kept coming back and he couldn't help himself. He and Janice went back and forth for a couple of minutes with Jamal intentionally ignoring Conrad.

Well, it's good to see you're looking well. Conrad broke in. What brings you all the way to Texas from Chicago? Must be some important business we heard about some of the great work you've been doing in media back in Chicago. We hear you're pretty big up there now.

I'm just here to finalize some business today and if the final contracts and numbers look right, I'll actually be relocating to the Houston area. I love Chicago but this may be a big move for my career, not to mention my bank account. Jamal laughed.

The atmosphere was jovial and festive as the three friends sat around reminiscing about the old neighborhood, school rivalries, and people they hadn't seen in a while. What's the job? Conrad finally asked. Who's it with, I probably know someone there.

WKROC news here in Houston. I'm here to accept a position with them, tomorrow I'm going to be named their News Director. Jamal said with a wry smile coming upon his face knowing the reaction that it would elicit from both Conrad and Janice. The room fell silent, and the atmosphere immediately shifted. What had been a cheery and upbeat reunion with old friends reminiscing about the good old days, suddenly became somber and bleak. Jamal seemed to relish in how uncomfortable it made his friends feel and felt a sense of power over them for the moment.

Are you sure that's what you want to do? Asked Janice out of concern. I'm sure! Replied Jamal sternly. And I already know what you guys are thinking. Why would he choose to leave a prominent job in Chicago to work for this ultra-conservative news station that appears to always be working against black people, and all other minorities for that matter? Am I right Jamal asked rhetorically? Well, it's simple, they made me an offer that I could not refuse and one that I would be a fool to turn down.

You're not concerned about how they portray our people and spread misleading information? Janice asked. Nope. Jamal responded. I could care less about what those rednecks think of black people or even of me I'm just here to get paid and if that means driving their newscast in that direction then that's what I'm going to do.

Not every choice should be based solely on money Jamal, Conrad interjected. Choices have consequences, and some choices are harder to come back from than others. That's easy for you to say Conrad while you're sitting up in this big house, on this secluded road, in an area where no other black people live. Jamal responded with a hint of contempt in his voice.

It's a corporate property owned by the company I work for and one that I've earned based on the position I obtained, and it has nothing to do with no other blacks living here. We've always lived around our own people, and you know that, where is all this coming from Jamal? Conrad asked.

Never mind Jamal said. I just wanted to stop by and visit some old friends from Chicago's westside that have “moved on up” like the Jeffersons, and wish you guys the best. I have already made my decision and I’ve chosen the direction I want to head in so I’m going to leave you guys to your evening Jamal said as he stood up to leave. It’s been great seeing you again, he said looking directly at Janice. A sinister smile came across his face as he turned and walked out. I hate them, Jamal thought to himself as he left. The heavy burden of hate and envy weighing heavily on him appeared to be shaping his personality and guiding his decisions more than he could know.

Chapter 7

The Weight of Some Choices Gets Heavy

Hector Rodriguez, an ex-gang member, and newly released inmate from the Texas State Penitentiary was on his way downtown for his state-designated monthly meeting with his parole officer. Out of prison for over three months now and times were getting harder by the day for him. Unable to find employment, Hector was growing increasingly frustrated as each passing day went by. Hearing the word no said to you over and over for an extended time period has a way of eating away at you, tearing you down. It felt like people were slamming a door in his face every single day. People weren't designed to receive rejection constantly without any positives to balance it out. And Hector was hearing no almost daily it seemed since becoming a "free man." "I think some of these people can still smell the scent of prison on me when I walk in the front door for these interviews, nobody's advertising jobs for ex-gang members fresh out of prison" he remembered saying to his frustrated girlfriend Maria.

That self-assessment Hector made of himself was not too far off. He did look the part on the surface. While in prison he worked out and lifted weights daily like a lot of the other inmates simply because it helped him to pass the time and take his mind off of his predicament. He also had gotten both arms heavily tattooed years ago and even had one on his neck so his appearance could be seen as striking at first sight. Prison had given him a hard exterior, a look of toughness that developed over time. He was a walking billboard and stereotype for some if you didn't take the time to get to know him. Hector looked at himself in the mirror, "Damn I even look like I just got out of prison" as he was about to venture outside for another day of knocking on doors trying to find a job.

Hector applied for at least thirty jobs since his latest release from prison and completed his third interview of the week just yesterday, but still was unable to find a job. He allowed himself to have a glimpse of hope about his job prospects in this last interview because it was his second one with the same company. A job as a machine operator, a trade he learned while in prison and was certain he could do the job if given a chance. "If only they would give me a chance," Hector said to himself. The first interview went well, and he made it to the next step in the process. A second interview was to be conducted on the same day, this time with Mr. Lux. Hector walked down the hall and knocked on his door as directed. Come in he heard the voice inside say and in strode Hector; he was cleaned up, dressed in what they used to call his "Sunday best" in his neighborhood, but his appearance could still be striking for someone who was quick to judge others as Mr. Lux was prone to do.

And there it was, that look. Hector saw the familiar look on the face of the interviewer as soon as he walked inside. He had seen that look before. It was given to him in the four previous interviews and generated in him the same sense of guilt, contempt, and shame. Only now he was feeling the extra pressure from making his home life with Maria work.

Hector did his best to change the mind of the interviewer. Although he could see the apprehension on the face of Mr. Lux, he wanted to highlight to him some of his past accomplishments. He didn't attempt to hide his past or the fact that he was recently released from prison but wanted to show that he was attempting to put the past behind him and was ready to work, eager for society to give him another chance. He talked about finishing school while in prison, and the Christian program that he got involved in while incarcerated hoping to demonstrate who he had become since his original conviction 12 years ago. However, as the interview came to an end "that look" came back on the face of Mr. Lux. A look of condemnation, disgust, and judgment. Hector left knowing he wouldn't get that job.

Later that morning Hector got off the bus downtown and walked towards the government building where the parole offices were located. This was his third meeting with his parole officer Thomas Ray. Mr. Ray, he demanded to be called by the parolees, was a very unpleasant man who appeared to relish these moments. He was also an abusive man who loved to threaten, look down on, and mock parolees especially recently released ones. The meetings seemed to give him satisfaction, a sense of self-worth, and power.

He was a man who wasn't happy with his own life and needed someone else he could look down upon to feel better about himself. He took joy in being in a position of power and he exploited this power abusively, and for his own pleasure. His position gave him the authority from the state to "violate" any parolee, meaning to accuse them of violating the terms of their probation and having them immediately sent back to prison until he decides if they committed an offense or not. Although working in the "justice system" in the department that was originally designed to help former convicts reenter society, Mr. Ray didn't believe in the concept of redemption, nor was he willing to give them a "second chance." He thought once a criminal, always a criminal, and investing in them was a waste of time and money. "Prison was the solution, the only solution for these animals" he told a co-worker.

Hector entered the building and walked slowly onto the elevator regretting every step he took and dreading the thought of meeting with Mr. Ray. "If things weren't bad enough already with me not being able to find a job and my girlfriend on my back about it, now I have to sit and listen to this fool." The three months since he was released from prison had not gone the way he hoped. Hector wanted to walk the straight path and do the right thing this time, but the odds were stacked against him. He wanted to do right by Maria his girlfriend and mother of his son because she had sacrificed so much for them in the past and he promised her "this time things would be different".

However, Maria was growing impatient with him by the day and started to complain to him more and more about not carrying his share of the load. Damn! She's right though. Hector said. I'll have to deal with it and make things right for a change. I'm not going back to jail! I know he's going to start threatening me with going back to jail if I can't get a job, yelling that

I'm not trying hard enough. This man loves to talk down to you like a dog or something. The elevator door opens, and Hector takes a deep sigh "Man I don't need this." He says as he heads to the office of Mr. Ray.

Come on in Hector and shut the door behind you. Mr. Ray commanded. This is our third meeting, and I would like to see that you are making some kind of progress now that the state has graciously allowed you to be released again. You know that this parole time that you have can be turned back into jail time instead, don't you? He asked. Yeah, I know. But I haven't done anything wrong, I'm just here for our monthly meeting. Don't get sassy with me boy, I'll decide if you've done anything wrong or not by the way you answer my questions. It's my job to keep our city safe from people like you and to get you on the right track. Mr. Ray said.

People like me? Hector asked. I'm a law-abiding citizen, I haven't committed any crimes. Mr. Ray laughed in contempt. Not yet or none that I know of Mr. Ray answered.

As a condition of your parole, you are required to obtain gainful employment, and pay the monthly fee that it takes to maintain this service, are you able to do that now? I have the money for the fee. Hector said. I have not been able to get a job yet though. I've applied for about thirty jobs and been on eight interviews, but my luck has not been good with these people. Hector said. Do you have any job recommendations or know of someone who will hire me?

It's not luck. It's your appearance you look like a criminal, talk like a criminal, and probably think like a criminal. I can smell the odor of prison on you. It's not my job to find you a job and I wouldn't recommend you for a job even if I knew someone. Nobody wants your kind around, lifelong criminals in the workplace with them. People like you are a cancer to society, like garbage that needs to be put out of the way.

In fact, I have a good mind to violate you right here and right now because I feel that you are not giving your best effort. Probably back hanging out with your fellow gang members, right? This went on for several more minutes, but by now Hector had tuned out all of the negativity that was being thrown at him. His mind started wandering, going back to more pleasant times and even some of the conversations he and Alex would have in prison brought him some relief from Mr. Ray's onslaught of verbal abuse.

Snapping back from his daydreaming, he could hear Mr. Ray's voice, do you hear me, answer me boy. Yeah, I hear you. Hector responded having no idea what he was being asked. The next time I see you I want to see a check stub from a job or some kind of evidence that you're working, and if I find out about you running with those gangs again back to jail you go. Now get out of my office and leave the monthly payment in my mailbox out front. After Hector left, Mr. Ray laughed uncontrollably to himself, picked up the phone, and called Harry Jacobs who was one of the leaders of his white supremacist group.

Chapter 8

New Choices with Old Thinking (a bad idea)

Harry was sitting alone in his office at home relaxing on his favorite chair and reminiscing about a time in his life when the world didn't seem so complicated. Back in the days of his childhood when his late mother would take him to church every Sunday morning, and Wednesday evening. He was a much different person then, happy, and enthusiastic about what the future held for him. Growing up in southeast Texas, part of the "bible belt" of the south he was always taught it was God, family, and football on Sunday mornings. Tragically his mom died of cancer when he was 15 years old and that would be one of the first events of his youth that would start to shape his thoughts and beliefs on life and even shake his faith in God. Harry strayed a long way from those early Christian teachings input in him by his mother. Back then he was being taught things like "love your neighbor", we are all God's children, and that "all men are created equal." Equal? Harry shook his head in contempt. That's ridiculous!

Harry laughed to himself and shook his head at the path that his life had taken, the choices he's made since then, how different he had become. Now he was one of the leaders of his white nationalist movement, which believed and embraced the superiority of the white man and that only by having a white man in charge could there be peace and development throughout the world. "That is the way God intended things to be, the natural order of things, the world God created he said to himself. Our forefathers conquered this world, conquered America, and bequeathed it to us for an inheritance and our future." He thought to himself. And that the purity of the white race must be preserved above all else has been adopted as our doctrine and 1488 has become our rallying cry. "We must secure the existence of our people and a future for white children," Harry repeated to himself.

I wonder what my mother would think of me now. Harry said to himself shaking his head already knowing the answer. Despite his racist activities and friends Harry still considered himself a Christian, a man of God and so did the other members of his white nationalist movement. They believed in the sanctity of the white race and that separation was best for all races. "Our forefathers were Christians and they owned slaves" he reasoned. What our organization is doing is for the betterment of America, and even the world. I'm doing this for the love of the white race not hatred of another one. Harry lied to himself as he sat alone in his office. He had been given multiple chances to get off of the spiraling down road he was on, but he chose to continue down this path convincing himself that he had "seen the light."

Back in his youth when Harry was still able to dream, his biggest dream was to become a football player at the University of Texas, following in the footsteps of his father and grandfather. However, their athletic abilities and traits seemed to skip a generation when it came to Harry. At only 5ft 10 inches and 165lbs he didn't possess the size or the athleticism of his father and was told the disappointing news by his father that maybe football wasn't for him, that he simply wasn't good enough, and that he should focus more on his books and school. Harry took this as a rejection from his father and he carried the burden of it around like a weight on his back. This became another one of the key moments in his life that would contribute to his evolution into the person he was now. As life moved on it seemed to Harry that he was always being told to wait, never quite good enough, always finishing in second place. He cussed to himself.

Harry was jolted out of his trance-like state by the loud ringing of his telephone, instantly perking up when he heard the familiar salutation from one of his "white brethren". 1488. Mr. Ray said. 1488 Harry replied with enthusiasm. He sat listening to the voice on the other end, "I think I may have another one of those niggers for you, he's a loser like the rest, he'd be a good candidate for the carjacking ring you have been financing. This one's Hispanic, but they're all the same. He just left my office for his monthly Parole Officer meeting and is fresh out of the joint. Let's put him to good use before I send him back to prison."

Harry smiled to himself, listening intently as Mr. Ray spoke. Great Harry replied after a pause, "I'll depend on you to seal the deal, maybe you can have him reeled in soon. Give me two more months of working on him and he'll be so desperate to stay out of the joint that he'll agree to anything. Mr. Ray replied. Keep me posted. Harry said flatly, hanging up the phone. That guy is kind of a creep, but at least he's useful to our movement, and I have to deal with him because he's one of the brethren.

Harry gathered himself and turned his attention to what he and Rex talked about at their last meeting. Harry was elevated to second in command of their sect within the white supremacy movement in south Texas and he needed to keep his mind on the bigger picture. Rex wanted to make sure they were on the same page and that Harry was all in with the direction of their movement.

"Our friend is back on our radar," Rex said to Harry that day knowing the depth of hurt and pain that time in his life caused Harry. Conrad James, a black man was given the position of CEO that was rightfully his Harry believed. Not long after that came the sudden loss of his 18-year-old son Harry Jr. who was badly in need of a bone marrow transplant before succumbing to bone cancer, and soon after his wife left him because of his involvement with the white nationalist group. Rex was aware that simply mentioning the name Conrad James was enough to fuel Harry to carry on with his mission. Rex's words echoed in Harry's mind. "Our friend is back on our radar." Harry cursed to himself.

Conrad has started some type of liberal anti-gun movement Rex told him, he has no idea who, or what he is up against. Harry thought to himself, displaying a sinister smile. We have gotten to the point here in America where we have people thinking of guns and the second amendment as sacred. Guns have become a new religion in America, in fact, people are more committed to guns than they are to their churches, and we aim to keep it that way. How else can we reap chaos in inner cities, keep prisons filled with blacks and other minorities, and make tons of money at the same time from the sale and distribution of guns? Guns are a gold mine and I'm not about to allow Conrad or anyone else to stop the free flow of them.

Harry called up one of his organization's political operatives, a gun lobbyist who has considerable power and influence to apply pressure on those legislatures to make sure that no gun laws are passed that could hurt our gun distribution. And that's both legal and illegal guns. Either way, we get our cut Harry said. The way we can now even use the internet and have people get around background checks, or simply order the parts separately and create these untraceable "ghost guns" was a brilliant idea on your part. Harry said to the Gun manufacturing executive on the other end. Thanks Harry, but you know that I must remain anonymous, right? I can't allow our partnership to become public knowledge that would hurt our movement, but you can always count on my devotion to our "white brethren" and our cause.

Anytime you need more guns or investment from our companies just let us know and we'll be more than happy to get those guns and the funds to you at once. We know that your work takes money and resources and that it costs to buy political influence in Washington. Thanks, I will Harry replied. Of course, I'll be expecting the monthly allotment of guns from you so that we can continue to deposit them into our targeted inner-city communities throughout America's cities. But there is one other thing you can do for me right now, check on this new anti-gun group that met here in Houston during our NRA convention, it's called the Sabrina James initiative for Nonviolent Change. It's run by Conrad James, see if you can find out who was at that meeting. If there was anyone of significance there taking an interest in it or that maybe a part of it. Harry said. Will do Harry, I'll let you know what we find out.

After what you helped us get accomplished by outlining and guiding us through the passage of the "Protection of Lawful Commerce in Guns Act" (PLCAA) that gives us gun manufacturers and distributors complete immunity from any accountability or liability for our products, that's the least we can do. Now we can produce guns on a mass scale with impunity without any worries of legal liability, toy manufacturers and pharmaceutical companies can be sued if their products hurt someone, but they can't touch us. They both laughed hysterically as they said goodbye.

Harry's thoughts turned back again to his childhood, reminiscing about those joyful Sunday mornings spent with his mother, going to church, leading bible study, and singing those old church hymns. Wow! Times are certainly different he laughed to himself. I wonder how my life would be now if my mom had not died when I was 15 years old. Damn cancer! Harry said with a hint of bitterness. First my mom, then my son Harry Jr. Cancer took both of them out and left me here alone.

It seemed after the death of my mom it changed my dad, and he never truly accepted me after that.

Harry, now fully convinced by his own inner voice, and bitter reasoning fully put aside the Christianity taught to him by his mother and walked into his own version. A religion that would allow him to live according to his newfound beliefs that prioritized his white nationalism. I'll show my dad and everyone else who has ever rejected or looked over me, because God has given me a new mission, He wants me to fight for the survival and dignity of the "white Christian man" here in America. "People are trying to make us white men extinct, to replace us with immigrants, Jews, and niggers and somebody has to stand up for us". I could have turned out to be a totally different person Harry said to himself. If only my mother had lived, if only my son had lived, if only I had gotten that CEO position, if only…

There has always been a struggle in the hearts of men and women in America between racism, spirituality, God, and the church as they each fight for dominance in the hearts of its citizens. Using Christianity and the church as its buffer and self-proclaimed righteousness has allowed for the violent aggressive imperialism of Europeans throughout Africa and America all done in the name of God and world advancement. With convenient reasoning, used as a shield to block against their own shame.

Convincing themselves that God ordained them to seize America from the "savages" who were native to the land and called themselves Indians, a mission they named "manifest destiny" to signify that God was with them. Soon after came the kidnapping and enslaving of Africans on the same land where they declared their freedom, but someone had to work all of this "new land." All done with the knowledge and approval of Pastors and church leaders who were often active participants themselves. They used religion to cleanse their conscience while performing their evil deeds. A large number of blacks and other minorities find their brand of religion offensive and absurd. Believing that their actions speak a lot louder than their empty words and they serve as a constant barrier to any talk of America being "one nation under God."

For centuries racist behavior and attitudes have been a part of the American fabric and church while among its members who have referred to themselves as Christians, racism never has been a "deal-breaker" inside its congregations. Slaveowners, Ku Klux Klansmen, and members who have actively participated in the suppression of human rights, and the violent struggle of the civil rights movement in the heart of the "bible belt" of the American south have all sat in their church pews worshipping, praying, and singing hymns to God.

American Christians were able to feel good about themselves due in large part to a popular theory taught in their churches known as the "curse of Ham", the wayward son of Noah, which was used to justify and co-sign their racist actions, attitudes, and beliefs. This theory taught in white churches claimed that God destined descendants of Africa to be subservient to Anglos and was a convenient justification for whites to justify everything from slavery to segregation. Armed with church-sanctioned racism, and cruelty they were free to live out their depravity with a clear conscience.

Absolved by their "religion" the "curse of Ham" allowed them to justify and coddle racists within their congregations as well as their own inaction on the most pressing and omnipresent issue still in America today, race relations. Harry now personified this erroneous and willful misinterpretation of scriptures as he proceeded down his path of destruction, the road to perdition, without a hint of guilt or shame.

Chapter 9

Life is a Series of Choices

Conrad James was back at work performing his duties as the CEO of Houston Exponential Engineering Inc. or HEE Inc. He laughed to himself as he contemplated the meteoric rise to his current position in the company and his standing in the community. I guess that quantum engineering degree paid off after all. He thought back to the days when he first walked onto the campus at the University of Chicago, how the people stared at him and assumed he was there as a basketball recruit or maybe a track and field athlete. But Conrad always went against the grain, wanting to smash stereotypes and self-induced limitations. His late mother instilled that in him early in life and always taught him to be different, to set his own standards, and live free from the stifling opinions of others. She named him Conrad because she knew that as a black man, it would stand out and be contrary to his meager surroundings and neighborhood.

But now Conrad had to deal with the reality of everyday life and work along with the inherent scrutiny that came with being the first ever African American male to lead a large engineering company in the heart of south Texas no less. He also now faced the additional burden of getting his new organization off to a good start. The organization made the manufacturing and distribution of high-capacity guns and their easy access a top target in bringing about the company's mission of stemming the direction of gun violence in America. This goal created some instant adversaries for the new organization that viewed any attempts to stop the free flow of guns as a threat to their enormous profits and bottom line.

After having some early momentum, the upstart organization began to experience a little turbulence over the last few days. There were three defections in the past week from potential allies in the business community on three consecutive days. Also, a couple of potentially large donors who at one time seemed excited about being a part of what the organization stood for had suddenly dropped out. Followed by the resignation of a board member. "Wow! I Was counting on those donations." Conrad said to himself. Well, I have to keep on going, keep fighting for what I believe in. Nothing worth having comes easy most progress comes about through struggle. God never promised us a life without hills to climb, but He does give us mountain climbing faith. He said encouraging himself.

As Conrad sat alone in his office taking a break from the grind of the day, a news segment coming across his television screen caught his eye and immediately grabbed his attention. He was watching WKROC news not because he was a fan of the news channel, but because he was intrigued by their hiring of Jamal Reynolds, and wondered what the hiring would mean for the ultra-conservative format of the station. I know Jamal doesn't possess those beliefs Conrad said. I wonder what the hell he's up to though, he said they are paying him well enough to get him to come down to South Texas for a job. Jamal always said that he would never live in the South because of its history of slavery, segregation, and lynching. Conrad exhaled deeply in a moment of private reflection.

Shockingly, he saw his name come across the bottom of his television screen. What is this? He said while turning up the volume to the news channel, now listening intently. “A Chicago outsider arrested and charged with assault on a local police officer,” the anchor said while displaying a picture of Conrad. His name is Conrad James, and he rode into town with much fanfare a couple of years ago, he has been hailed as a black messiah to the local black community here by some who had never seen an African American lead a Fortune 500 company.

But now we see another side of this outsider from the north. Is he here to make trouble, and cause commotion with his liberal antigun views, maybe he’s even anti-law enforcement. He’s also the head of some supposed nonviolent anti-gun group. Whatever the case, this CEO turned anti-constitution, turned anti-gun owner has now been arrested and charged with an assault on one of our heroic law enforcement officers and we’ll just have to wait to see how he explains this one.

Wow! What in the world is going on? It seems to me something sinister is at work here behind the scenes. Ever since I went down to Houston for our kickoff meeting during that NRA convention it appears that things have started to unravel around me. This cannot be a coincidence, there is something or someone at work here that is attempting to stop our progress and prevent us from pursuing any and all gun laws that could help turn the tide of violence in this country.

Conrad called his wife Janice to go over all of the recent events with her, and to receive her feedback and her prayers. He knew that she would want to pray because she wants to pray about everything. But I need it right now, she can usually uplift me and help me get through any situation. “That's the power of a praying woman” Conrad smiled to himself.

At about that same Jamal Reynolds was in his own meeting, going over his expectations and activities with Paul Wilson Jamal knew that Paul was a racist but was yet unaware that he was a key member of his local “Alt-Right” white nationalist movement.

Remember Jamal, the key points of emphasis for our station and what your activities should be focused on in the short term are fighting against this un-American anti-gun movement with people attempting to blame the guns for all of the mass shootings and gun violence in this country. It's not the guns, it's the people holding the guns Paul said.

You can just give me the issues that you want to be pushed and spare me the pollical talking points Jamal responded in his usual blunt manner. That's not my thing, it's simply a job to me and I came here because you're playing me well and I intend to do my job well.

Great! Also, I want you to push against this racist “critical race theory” or CRT that all of these bleeding-heart liberals are attempting to infiltrate into our educational and school systems. We can't let all of the lies that they want to tell about our great American history get out and hurt our white children and their future. CRT is designed to make white children feel bad about being white.

Jamal laughed out loud. So, we want to keep the current system of lies in place about all of the great American slave owners and segregationist and their "Christian" beliefs is what you're saying right? Jamal replied sarcastically.

Is this going to be a problem, Jamal?

No not for me, I told you before I work for Jamal Incorporated and I could care less about all of the political and racial rhetoric.

However, I do my best work when all of the cards are laid out on the table. You don't have to sugarcoat things with me. I like to know who and what I'm working for. Exactly who is it that you are getting your orders from Paul? The more you talk, the more this seems like part of a broader plan at work here. You're starting to sound like one of those Alt-Right, white supremacists, Nazis, am I right?

I don't care one way or another mind you Paul as long as I'm getting paid, I just do my job better when people are completely honest with me.

Jamal, I have given you a choice between principles and money, racial pride, and career advancement, so let me know which side you will choose so that we can be sure we're pulling in the same direction.

I've made my choices Jamal replied. You can save all of the rhetoric and patriotic speeches for some of these naïve people you have working for you. I'm only here because of the money and your motives and the motives of people like you don't concern me at all, I know what you're all about, believe me.

Jamal smiled and thought about his next move. I'm going to use this redneck in the same way that he think he's using me he thought to himself gleefully, looking ahead with joy at the choices that he'd made. The money wasn't the only thing motivating Jamal although he repeatedly stated that. It wasn't even his primary motivation; although not fully aware yet he was being pulled by something that was much stronger than money - hatred, envy, and the need for revenge against Conrad and Janice was directing his actions. Emotions that have taken down many men and women through the years.

The news segments about Conrad and his anti-gun work were coming in daily as the conservative news channel WKROC led by Jamal Reynolds set its sights on him. They blamed his beliefs on him being an "outside agitator" from Chicago who was here to make trouble. Each day for the next ten days the station aired some type of conspiracy story about Conrad and his new organization saying that its main purpose was not safety in America but that he wanted to get rid of the second amendment and take away the guns of American citizens. Jamal at first questioned Paul Wilson about the strategy of conspiracy theories and rumors about Conrad, wondering if he and the station could be held liable for the news segments, they were running on their evening news channel. Paul assured him that he did not have to worry.

These are "opinion segments" Paul said to Jamal. We don't need to present any evidence or even be factual about anything that we are saying. The fact that we are calling them opinion segments gives us the license to say whatever we want about any issue without even a shred of evidence. That sounds kind of far-fetched Jamal replied, your lawyers have ok'd this. We've been doing this for years Jamal, running these opinion segments are in fact our highest-rated shows, they've made stars out of some of the news anchors and politicians while allowing us to get our message out unburdened by the need for being factually correct.

So, you basically have no respect for facts because you have no respect for the level of intelligence of your own audience is what I'm hearing Jamal said. You know that you can tell your viewers anything and they are willing to believe it simply because it's coming from your news channel. You've developed a cult-like following from everyday Americans, you've turned them into a bunch of groupies, robots waiting to be told what to believe and think, or what's the next conspiracy theory to believe.

It's not about their level of intelligence, we have all types of people listening to us. It's more of a matter of them wanting to believe in something, we have shared values and beliefs Paul said.

Sounds like a cult to me. Replied Jamal I could care less.

I do have one last question for you though. What does Conrad James have to do with all of this? In the broad scheme of things with this gun battle debate, he's small potatoes. He's just an idealistic dreamer from Chicago. Why do you care so much about attacking him?

Let's just say that I have a friend who shares a mutual disdain and hatred for him as you do. Paul said, getting up from his seat to signify that he was done with the meeting.

Conrad and Janice were finishing up their family prayer time and were reviewing their day's activities they believed would help with the direction of the Sabrina James Initiative for Nonviolent Change. Janice was to play a more active role in the group's planning and fundraising efforts in order to lighten the burden of Conrad who seemed to be getting bombarded from all directions. They were committed to doing something to help with all of the senseless gun violence that is plaguing America and has been for years.

You know with all of the excuses we hear from people who say they are pro-gun, and pro-second Amendment despite the epidemic of gun violence it never occurs to them that other countries have the same issues. Conrad said to Janice.

Yeah, except without all of the gun violence. They have video games in other countries, music with violent content, and movies that dramatize violence, but only in America is there rampant gun violence on the streets. Janice said.

That's because what those other countries don't have is politicians who are bought and paid for by the gun industry, or its gun lobby the NRA with its propaganda machine always at the ready with a carefully crafted message after each “mass shooting.” Conrad said.

That’s true Janice replied. Don’t forget the news media and their “spin doctors” that help them with all of their lying and with providing distractions from the real issues.

The gun industry always have their ”spin doctors” at the ready with a distracting message for pro-gun enthusiasts. They say that gun regulation does not stop gun violence, that it's a mental health issue, but Japan has strict gun regulation and there were only five gun related deaths in Japan all of last year.

That’s right five! Janice said. So, what we need to do is get the truth out to law abiding and responsible gun owners is that their message is being hijacked by people who carry out these mass shootings, as well as the gun lobby and news media.

As Conrad and Janice sat in their living room engrossed in their conversation discussing goals and plans of action for the organization suddenly there was a large commotion outside, creating a spectacle that broke through the quiet of the normally peaceful Sun Park subdivision. Outside there were a group of protesters chanting pro-gun and second amendment slogans, waving American and Confederate flags, honking car horns, and shooting through bull horns. “Outsiders go home! Get your hands off of our guns! We love the second amendment!” They shouted repeatedly from in front of the James residence.

Conrad and Janice looked out of the window in amazement at the group, which looked to be about thirty people outside of their home.

Shockingly Conrad spotted a familiar face that arrogantly stared back at him from the crowd of protesters. He at first was not really looking at the faces of the people, but more so at the signs they were carrying while trying to discern what they were shouting about. But one face stood out from the crowd and commanded his attention. It was police officer O'Reilly, who had arrested him a few days earlier using excessive and out of control police illegal tactics derived from the 1960's during the shameful time of legalized segregation in America. O'Reilly was an obvious racist cop who circumvented the law at every opportunity and secretly belonged to the same white supremacist group led by Harry and Rex.

As Conrad peered out of the window, he made eye contact with officer O'Reilly who gave him a wry smile, his way of letting him know that he was there and would always be watching Conrad. Conrad shook his head at the level of hypocrisy of the corrupt police officer marching for rights and the constitution.

Janice, that is the Officer who was the ringleader of those rogue cops who arrested me the other day when I was in Houston for the NRA convention. A blatant criminal who's out there wrapping himself in the American flag and pretending to be some type of patriot standing up for the constitution.

You mean the one with the evil looking smile who seems to be enjoying himself out there? This is a police officer? I'm sure he must be off the clock at the moment and now he's found the time to harass a person that he recently arrested and also used excessive force on. Janice replied.

You can be certain it wasn't his first time doing that to someone, because of how brazenly obvious he behaves when he's committing his crimes. He's confident in the people and the system that has shielded him throughout his corrupt career. He's enjoying disrupting the lives of the people living in this quiet community and I've seen firsthand that he cares very little about whatever he's shouting about the constitution.

At the same time as if choreographed by a skilled planner the same thing was happening at HEE Inc. headquarters. Protesters lined the street in front of the offices of the company to demand the resignation or the firing of Conrad James, the company's CEO. Shouting anti-American slogans, fire Conrad, and leave our guns alone. The protesters intentionally made a public spectacle of themselves to send a message to the company's board of directors and its customers. They were operating under the direction of Harry Jacobs who planned the protest against Conrad and his former employer knowing that the company did not like adverse public opinion.

Harry thought back to when he and Paul were planning the protest and the role that their media person would play in it. "Be sure that Jamal is aware that he needs to drive WKROC's programing to focus on the call for protest and the protection of the second amendment" Harry said to Paul Jacobs the station's manager. He's your guy and you are the one who likes to work with these low life immigrants from another continent. Don't worry about one thing Harry. Paul replied. I have that boy right where I want him, we'll use that darkie to do our bidden in the same way that we did with Andre who actually thought I was his friend and cared for his lowly people.

Yeah, but this one is Conrad's childhood friend, you are sure that he won't get a conscience on us when things get rough and side with his friend? Harry asked. I'm sure! Paul responded emphatically. He's not his friend, he hates Conrad just as much as you do if not more. He's got some type of deep-rooted hatred for the man. All he wants is to be paid well. This one is not like Andre he's a man without any moral compass or principles, he's our kind of nigger. They laughed hysterically at what was about to go down.

The protest grew in number and intensity over the next week in front of the James family residence as well as at his place of employment. WKROC under the leadership of Jamal ran daily segments against Conrad and became a driving force behind the protest. Daily they encouraged their viewers to participate in the protest and help to "save America".

Conrad and Janice immediately started receiving threatening phone calls, mail, and social media posts continually targeted them. The Sabrina James Initiative for Nonviolent Change was experiencing some turbulence in its efforts to combat gun violence and were seeing firsthand how the power of the gun industry and its gun lobby can galvanize against any perceived attacks against its bottom line. Conrad received a phone call from Steven Lawrence, a member of the board of directors at HEE Inc. who had been contacted by Rex Rutherford, his white nationalist leader, to put extra pressure on the board to get rid of Conrad.

The board wants to meet with me as soon as possible regarding all of these protests in our community and in front of their building. Conrad said to Janice. I believe they are going to ask me to cease all of my outside activities and simply concentrate on being the CEO.

That's going to be a hard thing for us to do. Janice said. We've put in a lot of tears, hard work, and prayer into starting and organizing this thing. Don't forget that we named it in honor of your mom. We have to keep going!

Well, we didn't go into this thing with short-term thinking, we knew that there would be some bumps in the road, and some hills to climb. But we know that with God all things are possible. So, we'll just have to keep trusting in him and keep on climbing. I'll meet with the board in the morning. Conrad ended.

Earlier that day Rex Rutherford the leader of the white nationalist movement in SE Texas, and Steven Lawrence met to go over their next move regarding Conrad. Our plan worked out perfectly to get Harry on our team. Our movement needed a man with his talents and in order to do that he needed to experience for himself the plight of the white man in America, how they are attempting to replace us with all of these immigrants and illegals. Rex said to Steven. Passing over him for CEO and putting an African American in his coveted position and one that he rightfully deserved was the final blow to push him over the ledge and to embrace our movement.

Yeah, it was a great strategic move, but I'm sure it must have been painful for him. Steven replied. Anyway, so what now? What's our next move?

I know it was painful for him, but the pain was necessary. It's the most bitter pill that heal you from your illnesses. Besides he needed to feel what our everyday brothers and sisters on the front lines have to deal with each and every day in America as these people try to replace us. Getting preferential treatment, Affirmative Action, and other government handouts to help them bypass hard working Americans.

The front lines? You make it sound like we're at war or something Rex. Wake up Steven! We are at war and it's time for us to awaken as many sleeping troops as we can so that they can be prepared to fight when the time comes!

I think it may be best if we proceed carefully with Conrad, you know he's one of those sly ones. We don't want to arise any suspicion with him.

Remember who you work for and who owns this company, he's used up his usefulness to us, I'll admit that he's made me a ton of money the last couple of years, but now it's time to remove that nigger from my company. Rex said. I'll give you some leeway to proceed with your caution, but my decision has been made and it is final.

Chapter 10

Pursued By My Choices

On a typical blazing hot summer day in the city of Houston's 5th Ward, Hector Rodriguez woke up with his mind in a state of turmoil. Throughout the night, all types of different nightmare scenarios ran through his mind, and they all ended up with him back in prison. It was a restless night, and he didn't really sleep much. Faith and worry can't occupy the same mind Hector said, attempting to encourage himself. Three months had gone by since his latest release from state prison and the harsh reality of life as a recently released convicted felon was starting to hit home with him. He got out of prison energized with a new enthusiasm for what the future would bring for him and Maria. While in prison he accepted Christ as his Lord and Savior like Alex and the preacher said he should, so he believed his newfound faith would help things be different. That his Christian faith would be a road to a smooth transition back into the outside world. Hector also completed his high school diploma and started taking some college-level courses while in prison.

Surely people would be able to see that he's a changed man ready to commit to a new way of life he naively thought to himself. But the potential employers didn't see it that way, all the job interviews appeared to be going well up to the point where they looked at the checked box on the application. Have you ever been convicted of a felony was the question that it asked. Seeing his answer, they kept telling him no and the bills kept coming in. Hard times were here, options were few, and he didn't know what to do about it. As Hector stood in front of the mirror attempting to groom himself preparing for another day in the "real world," worry and depression both fought for space in his mind, and he took a hard look at himself. "Damn, I even look like I just got out of prison no wonder I can't find a job".

Hector might have stayed in bed this morning as the weight of his burdens grew stronger and stronger, but today he woke up with a purpose. He was about to go back to a place he would not have otherwise gone back to, at least not voluntarily. He was going to visit his friend and mentor Alex Alvarez. This put Hector in a contemplative mood. He thought about his time in prison and his current station in life. He remembered how he prayed and asked God for another chance while in the dark place of a jail cell and his mind. Also, the words of his mentor Alex who told him how God was a forgiving God, and that once God forgave you for something He would not hold it against you anymore. Hector remembered the promises he made to God during this time of uncertainty, "if you just give me one more chance at freedom God, I will turn my life around and never come back to this place or torment again" he promised.

God may be a forgiving God, but these people out here in these streets are not nor are these human resource departments either when I go looking for a job Hector said dejectedly. How is a man supposed to be a man out here if he can't provide for his family? He was faced with a grim present reality of unemployment, a home life falling apart because he couldn't help his fiancé with the bills, and a Parole Officer who was threatening him with violating his parole and sending him back to jail if he couldn't find a job soon and begin to earn some type of income. "Gainful employment is a condition of your parole," Mr. Ray said to him with a gleeful look on his face, obviously relishing the power he wielded over him.

Hector made his way to the local bus station to visit Alex and to get some much-needed support and spiritual guidance from his friend. These last three months of freedom have been rough, He said to himself shaking his head. I had a lot less to worry about while in prison and a lot less stress he said as he climbed aboard the charter bus for the loneliest one-hour ride in Texas, driving to Huntsville, Tx the site of the Texas state penitentiary.

This system seems to have been set up to keep those prison revolving doors open. I think I have about a month of freedom left he said to himself as he reclined in his bus seat on his way to see Alex who was serving a life sentence in the state penitentiary for a bad choice he made as a 17-year-old kid. Wow! I don't think that it's fair that Alex will never get another chance at freedom Hector thought to himself as the bus pulled onto the prison compound. "A place where dreams come to die, and a new life begins" Alex called it.

Entering the visitation room brought back unpleasant memories that he hoped he would never have to relive. The room looked unkept and like it had been unchanged for the last 20 years. Hector looked around to see all of the inmates intentionally confined by iron restraints to their tables. Scanning the room for a familiar face Hector couldn't help but notice what had become the norm for most prisons in the United States. All of the inmates were either black or Hispanic. That figures they got to feed the system and we are the prey he said. Then he noticed a young white inmate in a corner also in prison garb meeting with what looked like his parents. He must have done some crazy shit for him to be here with us. Hector thought to himself.

Then he spotted Alex waving at him from the corner of the room chained to the bottom of a steel table, the two men greeted each other with enthusiasm, but Alex could see that Hector was carrying a heavy burden. Thanks for coming to see me my friend we don't get many visitors down here Alex said managing a laugh. How have you been getting along? Is everything all right?

Things have been rough, but I'm managing to stay out of trouble. I have not been able to find a job though and it's kind of affecting everything else. My home life is falling apart because I have not been able to help out Maria with the bills around the house and she's letting me know about it more and more with each passing day. It gets depressing man. Makes you feel like you're not a man when you're unable to carry your own weight. I want to help her out. I've just been unable to find anything, nobody is looking to hire any ex-cons out there. Nobody's been willing to give me a chance. Hector said dejectedly.

Remember we talked about times like these coming up, that it was going to be hard out there at first, and that the time would be challenging. Just remember that you have been equipped to handle this. You're an overcomer! Alex replied.

But I do have a question for you. When you go on these job interviews are you dressed the way that you are now? Alex asked. This is the way that I dress, so you are saying that the people can't take me the way that I am. Hector replied.

No, I'm saying that they don't have to. You already have multiple strikes against you, a tattoo on your face, and you're just getting out of jail. If you think that people are not going to attempt to size you up or make some type of judgment about you at first sight then you're simply not being realistic. You're going to need to change your look some on these interviews. And if you need some help with that, I can put you in touch with some of the people who come here for prison ministry because they have a clothing closet for this type of situation, and they've started a program where they give away free suits to men getting out of prison.

Suits? Hector said with skepticism. I've never worn a suit in my life. That's a part of changing Hector, doing things that you have never done before. Maybe it's time to start dressing the part, it certainly won't hurt you, and it will show the employers out there that you are serious. Besides dressing up makes men feel better about themselves, and if you feel better about yourself, you'll have more confidence and perform better in the interviews Alex said. But you have to see yourself differently before anyone else can, like it or not the way you dress does reflect how you see yourself at times. Proverbs 23:7 “For as a man thinks of himself, so is he.”

They both paused and bonded together in a silent moment of reflection on Hector’s situation.

I’ve actually been praying for you a lot lately as God has placed you on my heart Alex said. He’s been telling me that you’ve been struggling with discouragement and disappointment out there because things have not been happening for you as fast as you wanted them. The lesson that I’ve been teaching this week is from Luke 22:31-32 and it made me think of you. It says “Satan has desired to have you, that he may sift you as wheat. But I have prayed for you that your faith won’t fail.” I believe that God dropped that in my spirit for you and for our visit today. Alex said.

The two men met for almost an hour until a burly-looking correctional officer came over to their table to break things up. Times up you two, it’s time for your reality check, enough with all of the religious stuff he said with a hint of disgust in his voice. Besides, you’ll have plenty of time to finish off your conversation soon enough because we all know that Hector over here will be back home soon, where he belongs. What about him? Hector asked pointing at the white kid in the corner who was there fifteen minutes before Hector, “he was on that visit when I walked in.” The correctional officer laughed loudly as he escorted Hector out of the visitation area, and Hector could still hear the echoes of him laughing as he walked down the long corridor to the prison exit. The laughter rang in his ears again.

Later that same day Hector was back in Houston's 5th ward, to outsiders it was seen as a dangerous place, a place to avoid, but for him, it was home, a place where he could find peace. He was happy to be back in his old stomping grounds where he could be himself and not worry about prison systems or parole officers. It was like fresh air to a person who couldn't breathe, and water to a thirsty man. Hector walked freely through the neighborhood that he called home. He was known there, a former gang member who had enough street credit to move about freely. The talk with Alex helped him to see things in a different light and gave Hector the spiritual boost that he needed. The talk put his mind at ease for the first time in a long time since his release from prison, now he was using the time to relax and take his mind off of the cares of the day.

He walked down Lyons Street just taking in the sights and sounds of his city, appreciating its history. When he got to the corner of Lyons and Schwartz Street, he stopped to look at the mural of one of the "points of pride in the neighborhood." The Fruits of the Fifth Ward. A mural depicting 21 notable individuals who were from the neighborhood and had distinguished themselves. It was created by students from Wheatley High School. Hector stood there for a moment looking up at the sight, taking in the names and some of their accomplishments. He read some of the names, Senator Barbara Jordan, former boxing heavyweight champion George Forman, and blues musician Lightnin Hopkins. Pride in his community welled up inside of him. Damn, we can do anything if we choose to put our minds to it and decide that nothing's going to stop us.

Suddenly, a car pulls up to him inside he sees three members of his old gang from the neighborhood, one was his former best friend growing up - Darryl was his name, but he went by Little-d, and the other two he was locked up with recently. What's going on Hector, one of them yells from the car. Glad to see you finally got out of that hellhole man we were wondering where you've been. Little-d said looking him up and down as if sizing him up. Hector stared inside the car seeing some of his old crew inside. He knew the car wasn't theirs, no way they could afford something like that Hector thought to himself. A brand-new Mercedes Benz being driven by a car full of criminals? No way, he thought.

Hey, get in man, Little-d said holding open the door to mischief for Hector. Naw man I'm good. Hector replied. I'm just hanging out here for a moment. Maria will be coming to pick me up in a minute he lied, needing to avoid them. Okay Little-d said, but I'm going to come by your place later though, I need to talk to you about something important. I have some business to discuss with you. I know you can use some money in those empty pockets you got just getting out of jail. And they all laughed in unison as they sped away.

Business to discuss huh? Hector said. I know that it's illegal business if he's involved, but he's right about my pockets being empty and times are getting rough. I'm sure I'll be seeing him again soon, at least I passed that test. I'm not riding in no more stolen cars, as a matter of fact, I'm not riding in any cars with people who are still in the game. Nothing good is going to come of that. Alex was right when he said that half of the people in this jail were arrested either inside of a car, trying to take a car, or wanting a car that they can't afford.

Hector knew that in order for him to stay out of jail he would need to avoid hanging out with his old crew. He wanted to make a change and become the man that Maria deserved for him to be, but also someone that their three-year-old son could look up to. But it would have to start with making better decisions, especially about who he would hang out with. Little-d was the only one of their inner circle who has been able to stay out of jail since they were all arrested together as teenagers five years ago. Man, he's the craziest one of all and does more dirt than anybody. Hector said shaking his head. But he's been the lucky one, and hasn't been back inside since, maybe I should at least listen to what he has to say.

Little-d was a young black man who also grew up in Houston's Fifth Ward. He was a product of the system that makes pockets of America's cities into what is popularly known as ghettos. These communities were originally intentionally engineered by the federal government to contain a segment of society inside of a well-defined area of America's cities. From a single-family home, no job prospects in the area, poor and under-financed schools which lead to underperformance, most of the residents relied upon welfare or some type of public assistance that gave you just enough to keep you alive, but not enough to ever leave the area, so he never got to see any other way of life which led to a lack of vision or hope. Drugs were allowed to permeate the area that came from places that most of the people who lived there had never seen or even heard of. But that didn't stop the police from holding them responsible for the abundance of drugs that freely flowed there from the outside. Police only went after the street-level drugs never at the source. This provided the cities the steady supply of people to fill their prisons with that they wanted.

Little-d became a statistic early in his life along with Hector and their friends. Succumbing to a common practice of the American legal system of chaining young black youths to the system for most of their young adult lives. After being arrested as a teenager he was told by his public defender "I have a deal for you." If you want to get out of jail today, I have an agreement in place with the prosecutor to allow you to plead guilty and go home, but you'll be on probation for the next 15 years. All you'll have to do is plead guilty to the lesser charge and you'll be a "free man" today.

Little did the youths know that the promised freedom would be paid over the next 15 years of state supervision, and by turning the prisons into a revolving door for them as they were constantly being violated by their parole officer and taken back into custody for any minor deviation from the strict terms of their parole, or at the Parole Officer's discretion. And that any complaint against them by anyone requires the parole officer to have them arrested.

Little-d now, however, appeared to be free from all those restrictions.

Later that evening, Little-d was on his way to see Hector, still rolling around in the black Mercedes Benz he was in earlier. Little-d seemingly had the green light to do almost anything he wanted, and he committed crimes with impunity with little fear of law enforcement, and the police never bothered him. He pulled up in front of the modest home where Hector and Maria were staying with his music blaring, always wanting to make a spectacle. Hector came out to greet him, not having to look out the window to see who it was.

What's up Little-d I see you still haven't changed much since the last time I saw you. Hector said. Well, if it isn't the gang leader turned preacher boy. Little-d said laughing. Change? What the hell do I need to change? Little-d responded. We're running this area right now, it's our time to shine. And that's why I wanted to talk to you. I heard about your "religious conversion" while you were in prison and all of that. Little-d said shaking his head in disbelief. But now that you've fooled the parole board and are back on the street you need to look at the harsh realities of life as a convicted felon, with no job prospects, or connections. You're a walking statistic man.

I became a Christian while in prison, God is changing me from the inside out. Little-d laughed. I heard about the religious scam you used to get out of jail, but I know you man so you can drop all that religious bull shit with me.

I'm here to help you, to give you an opportunity to put some real money in your pockets and help get the man and his systems off of your back. Little-d said. Opportunity? Man, you've never worked a day in your life, except for this street work that you've been putting in all these years. Hector replied.

Little-d smiled and pulled out a wad of money. This says that I've been working and there's plenty more where this comes from, he said reaching out his hand attempting to give the money to Hector. Hector taking a step back. I'm good man, I don't need that kind of money He said. Good huh? Does Maria think that you're good? How about the bill collectors, or even your parole officer, do they think that you're good? Little-d said. Attempting to get a rise out of Hector like he's always been able to do. Don't worry about me, Hector said in anger don't forget I know how to take care of myself. Hell, I took care of you when we were younger out here! Hector snapped back.

Now that's the Hector I know, not this new soft religious one. I'll get down to business then. We have a new connection out here on the streets these days that is paying our carjacking crew top dollars. I mean dollars like you wouldn't believe, and he's promised to keep the dollars flowing like that as long as we stay active and keep bringing him at least two cars a week. He's some big wig from out of town I believe but he pays us at least three times what we had been getting for the cars. All we have to do is keep jacking the cars and soon we'll both have enough money to do some things on our own. Little-d said.

Carjacking! Hector said in amazement. You want me to join some petty carjacking ring that you guys have going on? How long do you think that's going to last? You guys will all be in jail or worse soon and I don't want to have anything to do with it. I'm choosing to go in a different direction, to live my life for God. You're throwing your life away for some chump change from a distant stranger.

It's not small change man is what I'm telling you we get paid a lot more than we used to and my connect says that if we keep up the good work there's other things he may have in mind for us. Little-d said.

Hector took a deep breath, we've known each other since the third grade and been friends for a long time, so I'm telling you that you're headed for destruction, it's the blind leading the blind. And look at the hurt that you're bringing to the fifth ward, to your own community just so that you can live "hood rich" while someone else is making the real money off what you're doing. No thanks man. And I'll be praying that you will stop this madness as well.

Ok fine. Little-d said, but maybe you need to pray more for yourself while you walk around here broke and begging these white folks for a job that they've already disqualified you for. That's part of the prison system's end game, it's how they keep the money flowing into the prisons, into the legal profession and prison jobs. Lawyers, judges, law enforcement, and prisons need criminals, and they won't have them if they allow people like you and me to become part of the outside economy. It's the new segregation my brother. You still don't get it, we pay for their houses, their cars, and for their kids' college education, that's why there is mass incarceration, but not from the masses it's from us. Little-d said displaying a sudden infusion of wisdom. Laughing as he walked away.

I'm tired of people laughing at me, that's for damn sure! Hector said walking back inside of the house. He's right about one thing though, it looks like nobody is going to hire me for a real job. I'm getting close to the end of my rope and only have a couple of hundred dollars left in the bank. I'm going to have to do something soon.

What Hector didn't know was that earlier that day Little-d was in another meeting with a mutual acquaintance of theirs, Mr. Ray who was the Parole Officer for both men. Mr. Ray was the real reason that Little-d was the only member of their crew who had never gone back inside. Little-d was secretly working for Mr. Ray who was funneling the funds from an unknown source to them to finance the carjackings. He was ordered by Mr. Ray to help recruit Hector into the gang. Little-d at first resisted not wanting to work against his old friend, but he was in too deep with Mr. Ray. "I own you boy" You'll do what I say, or you can go back to jail to finish off those ten years of probation from a jail cell, the choice is yours. Mr. Ray said to him. The threat of going back to prison to serve out the rest of his ten-year probation was something he was not willing to accept.

Chapter 11

Holding on to a Choice

Conrad arrived early in the morning at HEE corporate offices eager to meet with the board once they were all in place. Walking briskly and unseen pass some of the protesters who were still assembled outside he wondered if these people had been there all night. It's only 8 am and they're out here already. He thought to himself. Apparently, they don't have jobs or families to keep them occupied, they have such passion for gun ownership, but no compassion for the thousands killed by gun violence each year in America Conrad said as he entered through a side entrance that had been blocked off from the view of protesters.

I'm here! And ready for whatever they attempt to bring my way this morning. The Sabrina James Initiative for non-violent change has clear goals and a clear mission and it has nothing to do with taking guns away from lawful gun owners. That is the message they get from the biased media and social media silos people live in today. They are constantly being fed a stream of lies and deceitful messages from the gun industry, their powerful gun lobby, and their news media all in the name of ratings and profit. There's nothing patriotic or righteous about owning a gun, the gun industry has turned gun ownership into a religion for most of these people. That's a carefully crafted message they've been fed. As he sat down and engrossed himself in his work blocking out the chants from outside. That was one of his strengths, the ability to focus, blocking out the noise for the tasks at hand. He remembered his mother saying to him one day "The difference between successful and unsuccessful people is their ability to focus."

His phone rang breaking through the self-induced silo he was buried in. It was Steven Lawrence the chairman of the board. Fresh off his meeting with Rexnord Rutherford. Only a handful of people seemed to even know that was his full name. Not originally from Texas, five years prior Rex seemingly appeared from nowhere. He was a mysterious character who liked to work behind the scenes and in the shadows. Armed with tons of money to spend, which he skillfully converted into power and influence, and although his wealth was great, no one seemed to know how he came to possess such a vast fortune. Highly educated with advanced degrees in psychology and human behavior, Rex possessed a Southern charm and charisma that quickly advanced him in "the movement." Rex secretly owned a majority of HEE's stock and liked the power it enabled him to weld from the background. His hiring of Conrad for the position of CEO was all part of the plan to lure Harry over into his organization and demonstrated his strategic approach to his White Nationalism advancement. The board will meet with you now Steven Lawrence said to Conrad and hung up the phone.

The meeting with the board started off with the board questioning Conrad about what he planned to do about all of the protests and the bad publicity that the company has been getting because of him. "Your protest has disrupted the peace in our small community of Sun Park, Tx, they're calling you an outside agitator from Chicago who wants to tell us what to do and take away guns from law-abiding citizens," Steven Lawrence said combatively wanting to turn up the heat. What do you plan on doing about this, you're hurting the company with your outside activities, another board member said. You know that you can't come down here talking bad about the gun industry and gun owners' people down here believe in the second amendment and their constitutional right to bear arms came from another.

You've also been charged with assaulting a policeman and resisting arrest. Mr. Lawrence said. And you're all over the WKROC news every day. They're running a news segment on you constantly and tying the company in with you, we can't allow this to continue. And what were you doing hanging out near the NRA annual convention anyway?

The questions from the board grew more and more contentious and the atmosphere grew intense as they came at Conrad from all angles. Mr. Lawrence in particular appeared to be more on edge than all the others. He wanted to make sure he lived up to the expectations of Rex who would be updated about the meeting soon afterwards.

Conrad sat back and absorbed the rapid fire of questions, comments, and accusations that were coming from the board of directors. Especially Steven Lawrence before deciding to speak on his own behalf. Conrad was aware that the board was made up of mostly card-carrying NRA members, but he believed that most of the members of the NRA have grown tired of mass shooters, and kids at schools with AR-15s hijacking their message of lawful gun ownership. However, he was getting more and more upset as he listened to the list of complaints and accusations.

I've made this company millions of dollars in the last couple of years and at the first sign of any trouble, you guys are in an uproar after a few news headlines Conrad retorted back in anger. If the CEO of a company can't express his own beliefs and rights freely in this country, then who can?

The Sabrina James Initiative for Non-violent Change is simply about doing something to combat the everyday senseless violence that happens in America all too often, and we believe that can be done by stopping the free flow of guns in America and making the gun manufacturers, and distributors liable for the products that they produce just like all other industries are for theirs. There are too many people who have taken the warped and twisted position that gun violence is acceptable as long as their Second Amendment rights are protected and they're against common sense when it comes to any type of gun legislation because they've been led down that rabbit hole by their propaganda machine - the gun lobby. We've become so casual about guns that parents are buying AR15s for their kids on their 18th birthday and as Christmas presents. Conrad said defiantly.

America is the most violent nation in the world when it comes to gun violence and it's not even close. We have been bombarded by violent images in movies, video games, and music, but so has every other industrialized nation. But what doesn't happen in other countries is people who attempt to solve every argument, disagreement, or problem with a gun. What's the difference between us and other countries? Easy and plentiful access to guns allows criminals, kids, and people with mental problems to walk around with guns. The gun industry and gun manufacturers from other countries target America because they know that we have people who are profiting from the violence, legislators who are in the hip pockets of the gun lobby, and Americans who have been sold a bill of goods in regard to gun laws. Guns are like a religion to these people.

Despite your lectures, I will remind you of your position here at HEE and within your own community. Steven Lawrence said to Conrad. You are the first black CEO ever in this company and I'm sure that you are looked up to in the black community and if it wasn't for this board allowing that to happen you would not be here. We had the power to make you the first black CEO and we also have the power to take it away. He said looking to get a rise out of Conrad as the meeting became more combative.

So, I'm a black CEO? I know where I've come from and where I've been, and the reason I've been able to reach this level is by striving to be the best at what I do while at the same time making good choices in life. That's how I was raised, that's what my mother taught me all my life. God gives gifts to all people, and He is the one who has allowed me to use those gifts to elevate to this position, and if I lose the position, I know that I still have the gift because I'll still have

God. No man has given that to me, and no man can take that away. Conrad said his voice reverberating throughout the room.

We're going to have to ask you to cease and desist all of your anti-gun and anti-police activities if you intend to remain in your current position. Steven Lawrence said moving to fulfill his orders from Rex. We're not prepared to move on it right now, so you have a little time to think about what you are doing and your commitment to this company. Also, keep in mind that the house that you're living in is corporate property so if you lose your position then you lose the house as well he said, hiding the sneer that had formulated on the side of his mouth. We'll get back to you in one month on this matter, already knowing what he wanted to do and closing the meeting.

Conrad was already mentally preparing to leave the company that he had taken to new heights in the two years that he'd been there. The company was worth more now than at any previous time, but he was being given an ultimatum. He had a choice to make, would he give up his role on the Sabrina James Initiative for Non-violent Change which he and his wife Janice had been planning and praying about to keep his current lucrative position as CEO?

Conrad was at a tipping point in his life, facing a moment of decision that he knew would have far-reaching ramifications for hm and his family. He had obtained a highly sought-after position, a height rarely reached by a person who came from where he came from. Meeting with a board of directors of a large corporation, he was a long way from the Westside of

Chicago. He did feel an obligation to his past to make it work and be someone they could point to as an example of what is possible in life. Conrad wasn't ashamed of his past or upbringing, in fact, his mother was the most principled person he had ever met, he often said.

"No suburban mom could implant for integrity into a child as my mother did for me," he told a friend one day. He considered it a badge of honor to represent her, and his people, and it allowed him to generously give back to his community. But now he was at a crossroads and the clock was ticking and the weight of his choice would only grow heavier in the next few days.

Leaving the meeting, Conrad immediately called his wife Janice to inform her of how it went, and the ultimatum that was given to him by HEE's board. Janice seemed unsurprised as if she expected the result. But she was also unfazed by it. Janice always put her faith ahead of worrying. Don't worry about it she said to Conrad we knew that there would be some obstacles to taking on the issue of guns in America. To a lot of people, it's their number one concern, but to some guns are as American as baseball and they feel like any restriction on gun ownership is an attack against them and constitution. At least that's what they've been told. She replied.

I've got Jordan on the other line he called because he's been hearing about all of these news headlines that we've been involved in here in Sun Park, Tx all the way in Florida at his college campus. He was worried about us and was wondering if he should come home right away Janice said. Absolutely not! Conrad responded quickly. I knew you'd say that and that's exactly what I told him. He says the football team is doing great and that he scored another touchdown last night, they are coming up on homecoming week and there's a big party planned on campus for them. That's great Conrad said tell him to have fun and remember to keep his head clean and don't get into anything that he couldn't tell us about.

At about the same time another meeting was about to take place at WKROC news station involving Conrad's childhood friend turned secret enemy Jamal Reynolds and his news anchors. Jamal was a man gripped by bitterness and fueled by a need for revenge that even he could not explain nor was he fully aware of the power that it possessed over him.

Jamal kept repeating the same lie to himself that he was in Texas because of the amount of money he was being paid by WKROC and that even though he knew that Paul was a racist he could care less because his money was green just like everyone else's, and that was the only color that mattered to him. However, the "secret envy" that he's held against Conrad through the years, along with the anger of him "stealing" Janice from him now overwhelmed him and grew into hatred for them both.

Jamal received his instructions from Paul Wilson and was armed with the authority to carry them out. "Remember I need you to push our agenda constantly about the inner-city violence that is happening every day, protect gun rights and gun ownership, and make sure that we call out this Critical Race Theory for what it is. We can't have white children made to feel bad about being white" Paul told him. He's never given a damn about the effect of America's lies on black children I'll bet. Jamal laughed to himself.

Also, when you meet with your staff you are going to receive some pushback from one of the news anchors when you get there, her name is Pricilla Prescott and she's one of those bible-toting, self-righteous Christians. She's an annoyance, Paul said to Jamal. Oh yeah then why is she still on staff, why not just get rid of her? Jamal wondered. She's still useful and has an audience that likes her, but I've already scouted out her replacement and I want you to implement the plan to remove her. Pricilla's about to turn fifty years old and that's the time when we start to move in another direction around here.

Aren't you older than she is? Jamal asked with his usual boldness. Yeah, I am, but that only applies to the working class in America Jamal not to those of us in upper management, the people at the top, we get to set the rules for those at the bottom, you know how the game is played.

They both let out a sinister laugh as they thought about the situation. Who is that staring at us from the other room? Jamal asked as he spotted a very attractive twenty-something-year-old over Paul's shoulder sitting in his office. That's Laura she's going to be Pricilla's replacement once you put her in a position to learn the job, she's already learning the way we do things around here and teaching me a thing or two Paul said winking his eye. Laura walked in with a mischievous smile and shook Jamal's hand.

I'm sure she's a quick study Jamal said with a sneer on his face leaving the room.

Walking confidently into his meeting with the news anchors Jamal laid out the direction of the station in the short-term, letting them know in the next 90 days what the main tenor of their stories ought to look like. That they were to drive stories that presented the violence of the inner-city, especially the black and brown criminals that are involved. Especially highlighting their capture so that Americans can feel safe in their own homes. And we want to be certain to let the people know that we are for protecting their second amendment right to bear arms. Lastly, this evil CRT cannot make its way into the American mainstream educational system.

Pricilla Prescott abruptly stood up in the meeting, "this sounds exactly like the last person who was in your position Andre, and his family ended up paying a heavy price for this type of thing. You can't expect to participate in lies, racial profiling, and conspiracy theories and not have it impact those close to you. I'm here for the conservative agenda when it comes to the news but not for the race-baiting. Andre wanted us to highlight criminals when it came to the inner-city and people of black and brown skin, while giving out these vague and obscure descriptions for white criminals. That came back to haunt him as one of those white criminals who could have been captured ended up killing his wife. He had no idea that the crime he was trying to sweep under the rug would come beating down his own door.

Also, can I ask why are we so focused on this Conrad James person? We've been running news stories on him daily about his new anti-violence organization. He's not a major player when it comes to the people of influence in the gun debate. I hear that you and he are childhood friends or something from Chicago. Is this some type of personal vendetta or agenda you have against this person? Because I'm here for the news, not personal agendas. Pricilla boldly said to Jamal.

Jamal laughed, unfazed by what he thought was a challenge to his authority from Pricilla. He was, in fact, expecting some type of pushback from her because he was already pre-warned by Paul Wilson. "That self-righteous do-good-er Pricilla will have something to say and will attempt to challenge your authority but don't worry about her because we already have her replacement here. I want you to introduce her to the staff at the meeting and have her work under Pricilla for a while. We'll have Pricilla to mentor her own replacement." Jamal remembered Paul telling him. This is not propaganda Pricilla this is the news we are just giving it from our perspective and giving our audience what it is they want to hear. They're ultra conservative so we're giving them the news with extreme views, that's all. Jamal said.

In typical Jamal fashion he thought this was the perfect time to introduce the staff to a new employee. He waved in Laura who was standing in the doorway watching and wondering if she should make her entrance or wait. In walked in a 28-year-old Texas beauty with typical southern charm and manners.

Politely smiling and waving to the room of about 10 people.

I want to introduce you to Laura everyone. She's new to our station and was hired by Paul, she's been working closely with him, and he's been bringing her up to speed on how things operate around here. We expect her to be a great addition to our news anchor team. Jamal said. Great, what's her background, has she worked as an anchor before? Pricilla asked, skeptical of the surprise visitor.

No, not specifically as an anchor but she shows great potential Paul assured me, and we believe her to be a quick study. But she has worked in the news business before? Pricilla asked now highly suspicious. That's where you come in Pricilla, Jamal responded ignoring the questions. We believe that you could be a great mentor for Laura, you know teach her the ropes and bring her up to speed. With your great amount of experience, I believe that she could learn a lot from you in a short time. As Pricilla was about to respond Jamal jumped back in. In fact, she's already been assigned to the small office right next to yours and been given the title of your assistant anchor. Jamal said standing up and ending the meeting without any more questions or comments.

Pricilla Prescott grew up in the southern tradition. A white woman from a conservative evangelical background and was a proud daughter of Texas. The daughter of a southern preacher who had conservative morals incessantly drilled into her by her father. He would emphasize the importance of news over politics in her job, truth over popularity, and God over religion. She understood some of the past racist teachings and southern traditions accepted in the church, but she rejected them at an early age and wanted to help make a difference. The "curse of Ham" theory that she heard as a child in an effort to justify everything from slavery to segregation taught in some white churches was never compatible with this woman of the highest level of integrity and loving spirit. She was the person who always believed in doing the right thing, always living her life according to her faith, and wanting to be judged by her deeds and not simply by her words.

Because of these core principles and beliefs that she held, there was constant conflict between her Paul, Andre, and now Jamal. Pricilla had been at WKROC since graduating from college at twenty-one years old and was approaching her 30th anniversary at the station. She was recruited to the station by the previous owners while a communications major at the University of Texas and had seen the station grow from a fledgling small station with a small audience to one of the biggest and highest-rated stations in Texas.

But things started to change around five years ago when new ownership took over and started to make drastic changes to the station's format making it one of the most far-right, conservative stations in the country. Pricilla still today has yet to meet the station's new owner, Rex preferred to remain in the background and influence changes in silence, but he learned from previous Nazi movements that he would have to have some semblance of control over the media. That the Neo-Nazi movement he was orchestrating would need a voice and influence in the media, a propaganda machine to distribute "alternative facts" to the public. Pricilla chose her path in life a long time ago and was not about to become a part of that type of movement, and Paul Wilson the station manager understood that and started to implement the plan to have the long-time anchor with the largest audience at the station removed. The hiring of Laura was intended to be the beginning of her end.

Chapter 12

Choosing A Side

Harry was sitting at home taking in a quiet morning reminiscing about his childhood that for him appeared to be such a long time ago. The good times watching football with his father and talking about his dad's days on the football field at the University of Texas.

A fleeting memory of a past life that seemed a long time ago, when he was still able to dream, still had faith, and still believed in the promise of America. These were the type of days that his mother used to warn him about when she would recite the old adage "an idol mind is a playground of the devil."

The disappointment Harry felt at not being able to walk in his father's shoes, and the sting of rejection he felt from his father who told him it was time to give up on his dream of football and concentrate on school never left. It became an albatross around his neck, an inescapable emotional burden and he carried the heavy burden around like a weight on his back.

Harry now lived alone; his wife having divorced him soon after the death of their son Harry Jr. Thoughts of his son would dominate his mind on days like these and send him down the road of regrets, loss, and what ifs.

Those early days of his youth were the best. Harry reminisced nostalgically as the quiet stillness inside the house pulled him back into a simpler time. Back when he could still dream, back when he still had hope for the future. Odd thinking for a man with a degree in engineering and the former executive of a huge corporation like HEE Inc. Harry was only 40 years old, educated, and experienced, and appeared to have a bright future in store for him, yet the disappointments in his life consumed his mind and always dragged him back to the past. Peaceful quiet mornings like this one always got the best of Harry and his mind took him down dark roads. The quieter the moment the darker his thoughts became, someone had to be the blame for his predicament, and someone would have to pay Harry thought. A ping came from his phone breaking through the silence, Harry picked up the phone and glanced at the message. 1488 it said. 1488 Harry replied back. He knew it was Rex and that he wanted to meet. This had become their familiar salutation. Code speak for Neo Nazis and white Nationalists all over the world.

Harry was continuing his downward spiral of going down this dark road with his newfound beliefs in Nazism. He was handpicked and chosen for recruitment by Rex as someone who would be an asset to "the movement" he called it. Harry wasn't really a racist, he was a man who did not know how to process the perceived rejection he got from his father, his disappointments in life, and his dashed dreams that fell short of his lofty expectations. Rex sensed and used those emotions in Harry as a means of recruitment of him to their sect just as he's done for hundreds of other young white men and women, urging them to "take back our country", and you're not going to have a country unless you "fight like hell." The spirit of rejection that Harry carried around with him made him easy prey for Rex, his psychological recruitment methods and Nazis propaganda were a tried and proven recruitment tactic.

Rex and Harry met up at their usual spot in a local park. It was a secluded area where the large number of trees provided both shade from the oppressive Texas heat and cover for them not to be seen by too many people. They greeted each other with the familiar 1488 salutation. Our friends send they're thanks to you Harry for all of the help you've given in the gun industry and the way that you've helped to keep the politicians on our side.

We see the violence and lawlessness taking place in the country. This plays right into our message of taking back the country, you're doing a great job with the gun legislation and using free speech to our advantage. Social media has been like a gold mine to us, it's a recruitment playground for us now thanks to your leadership. Rex continued. We know that most whites in our country don't believe in our white nationalism movement, but that's because they don't really understand it. They've been brainwashed by all of this America as a melting pot nonsense for years. They just need to be enlightened to the truth; diversity is not a strength it is the enemy of America. Our people just need to have their eyes opened to the truth of how all of these illegal immigrants are trying to replace us.

Look how they gave your job to Conrad James. A nigger from Chicago, you were supposed to have that job, he used affirmative action to skip over you, replace you. How else do you think he could have gotten that position? Always the manipulator, he knew the answer to that question because he was the one who gave the position to Conrad as part of his plan to recruit Harry. Rex always wanted to get the name Conrad into any conversation he had with Harry to serve as a reminder of the disappointment he experienced because of him. The hate that it produced in him.

Harry sat and listened to the familiar message from Rex, the passion in his voice for the "movement". Finally, Harry spoke up. What's our long-term goal here Rex we put guns into America's inner cities and turn them against one another, but how is that really going to help us make things better for the white man in America?

What about the millions of whites that don't agree with our message of white nationalism and white superiority? What is the message that we have for them and those of us who still profess to be Christians, we may be far-right Christians, but we still consider ourselves to be Christians. Harry said.

I believe in God as well Rex replied. I just believe that he's given me a different message to deliver to the masses. I also believe that he's given whites a special place in his heart, and that he wants us to rule over the inferior races. Remember they're all descendants of Ham and God cursed them to be subservient to us.

Our friends in the prison system also send their thanks and they have something special for you that's why I wanted to meet with you face to face today. Rex said, handing Harry a briefcase as a token of their thanks. The work you do with the gun industry and its effect on the prisons is enormous. You're helping to keep America's prisons full of these niggers, illegal immigrants, and criminals. People whine all the time about "mass incarceration" in America, but that's how we keep these niggers in check, keep their numbers from multiplying too fast. And it prevents them from voting Rex said and they both laughed hysterically.

Yeah, Harry replied I know the relationship between the influx of guns and the filling of these jail cells. I know that it results in heavy profits for our friends so I'm glad to do it. But also, we couldn't keep the cells full without the help of judges that have seen the light and understand their primary mission is to protect America and our way of life. They've played a key role in releasing criminals back into their neighborhoods when they know they'll commit more violent acts and keeping lock up the darkies who have tried to "turn their life around" as they say. Those kinds are of no use to us.

One last thing Rex replied and the main reason I wanted us to meet is we have a friend that needs our help, and this needs to be a high priority, I want you to get with Paul Wilson at WKROC and make sure that a news story is killed. It's one that could prove very damaging to one of us, he's one of our members who sits in a high place. He's a big contributor and financier behind the scenes of a lot of our activities. Paul has a news anchor working for him that is looking into some things that are best left unseen and unsaid. She's swimming in some dangerous waters.

Paul knows about the story he has an informer close to her, but I just want you to make sure he understands that the story can never see the light of day. Rex said in a tone that stressed the urgency of the moment.

Harry stood quiet for a moment wondering what the story could be and waiting to see if Rex would say who the friend was, but he didn't. I'll be meeting with Paul later today and we have to go over some of the media direction and news coming out of the station. Plus, I want to see how it's going with that News Director he brought in from Chicago, one of Conrad's friends no less. Harry said in disgust. Speaking of I want to be there when he's finished at HEE, I want him to see my face on that last day he's forced to resign or is fired.

You've earned that much. Rex replied. Is there anything else I can help you with before I go? As a matter of fact, yes. Harry said. I've been thinking a lot about my son Harry Jr. lately and what happened to him two years ago. I wish that other bone marrow donor had come forward, it may have saved his life. Do we have a connection with the hospital system that could possibly find out who it was and why they never came forward? Harry asked.

I'll look into it Rex said, but that system is buttoned up pretty tight. Ok, thanks, Harry replied as they left.

Harry had no idea that he was speaking with the person he was looking for, and that Rex put his own selfish ambition before the life of his son. Rex didn't want the appearance of having the same blood type as James Jordan a young black man who was the donor that they encouraged Harry to reject. Saying "you can't taint pure white Christian blood with that nigger blood, God will provide a better solution." That was two years ago, and Harry was continuing his downward spiral from a series of choices he made during that time period. Rex sized him up perfectly when he recruited him to the white nationalist movement.

Chapter 13

Confronted by Life's Choices

Hector Rodriguez was at home going through the mail handed to him by Maria, his fiancée who asked him "What are you planning to do?" with a look of disgust on her face as she walked out the door. Notice of past due amount one of them read, your account is past due you have to call us immediately to avoid shut off, another read. This is your final warning was stamped outside of another envelope. Hector didn't even open it, he simply tossed it and all of the others to the side for now. Immediately afterward came a text message from his parole officer Mr. Ray "I need to speak with you about your job search activities and what you are planning on doing soon" it read. Hector felt like the weight of the world was on his shoulders without any signs of letting up.

Just three months earlier Hector left Huntsville State prison with a newfound excitement about the future. He believed that this time would be different from all of the other times. Although he had been in and out of prison since he was a juvenile and never been able to walk down the straight path before, this time "I have God on my side." Hector excitedly told a friend, so I'm ready for anything the world can bring me! But now Hector was feeling the sting of disappointment as it appeared to him that God was not answering his prayers; that God was rejecting him in the same way as these jobs were. Even God has given up on me Hector dejectedly said to himself in a moment of intense discouragement.

He thought about the wad of money Little-d offered him with a promise to get him much more, a wry smile on his face. And the corrupt parole officer Mr. Ray looking down on him, calling him names, and taunting him, using the system to flaunt his superiority over him. Then Maria giving him the look that felt like a warning as she left this morning. He got up from off the couch feeling weighted down and almost stumbling as he moved, he went into a private room he set up for prayer and he stayed there for the next 45 minutes crying out to God for help. Half praying, half venting.

Dropping down to his knees Hector began praying. "Dear Heavenly Father, I know that I have not been perfect, but I have been faithful. I know that I have committed sins in the past and even now I probably still commit a few, but I'm trying my best God. I don't know all of the fancy words and terms that other people use in church but I'm here, ready to learn if you would teach me. I've been praying for a job and help so that I can provide for my family, and stay out of prison, but it's been hard on me since I've gotten out of jail. People judge me by my appearance, my past, and look at me funny, but I thought you were going to be with me, to help me, and make a way for me! It seems like you have deserted me. I hear all of the talk from people saying that you have done this and have done that, and I've read all of that stuff in the bible about rescuing people from the fiery furnace and stuff, and my grandmother used to always say that you were a miracle worker, but where are all of your miracles now?"

Hector went back and forth in his prayers to God, at one moment expressing his strong faith and confidence in God, but in the next showing frustration and a defeated spirit at the condition of his life. He wondered why God would not simply give him the needed help. Am I doing something wrong? He asked, what is it that I'm missing? His emotions teetered up and down, swaying back and forth. At one moment he appeared to be full of confidence, and in the next fear of the unknown crept back into his mind. It was as if there were two different people there praying at the same time as his emotions swayed from one side to the other like a pendulum going from one extreme to another at a moment's notice. As both faith and doubt fought for supremacy in his mind they collided in his prayers, and his praying became discombobulated.

Hector emerged from his prayer closet feeling better for the time being. He was always told to be honest with God about his feelings and to express them with sincerity. He needed to regain his confidence and he needed to make some moves quickly, he thought to himself. Looking at himself in the mirror as he dressed to go out for another day of job hunting, he said "I feel better now, but my situation has not changed." Hector knew that the bills were piling up and that he needed to respond to his parole officer Mr. Ray today. This man loves to talk down to people and throw his power around, it makes him feel like a man I guess, he's one of the most despicable, and vile persons I've ever met, and I've spent half my life in prison. Hector said shaking his head. But I have to call him back to keep my freedom.

Calling his PO before he left for the day Hector took a deep breath and said to himself, it's a good thing I've been praying this morning, you have to be prayed up to talk with this person. Mr. Ray answered the phone in his usual way, displaying a bad attitude with a level of superiority. It's about time you called me back, when I tell you to call me, I mean right away not when you feel like it, ok boy! He said with contempt in his voice. Hector didn't answer.

Anyway, I don't feel like meeting with you convicts today so I wanted to get an update from you over the phone. Did you find a job yet boy? No. Well the clock is ticking, and the sand is almost out of the glass. If you don't show me some results soon I'll be forced to revoke your parole and send you back where you belong. I have a good mind to do that anyway we both know it's only a matter of time before it happens. Mr. Ray laughed. Are we done Mr. Ray? Hector asked sarcastically. No boy we're done when I say we're done.

Have you talked with Little-d lately? Mr. Ray asked. Little-d? What does he have to do with you and me, or me finding a job? Surprise! He's under my supervision as well, you didn't know that did you? How do you think that criminal has been able to stay on the streets for as long as he has? I'm the one who makes that possible, I have the power over you and him one word from me and you'll both be gone back to that hell hole called prison where you belong. You got three days to find a job. If not, I've made an offer to you through Little-d, and I suggest you take it. Either you take the offer that Little-d has for you, or you're gone. And besides, it pays well, more money than you're worth, that's for sure. Mr. Ray said laughing as he hung up the phone.

Hector immediately called Little-d. We need to meet. Are you at the spot right now? I'm on my way. Knowing where Little-d was Hector made his way there quickly to a neighborhood pool hall in Houston's fifth ward, he needed to get to the bottom of what was going on with his parole officer and Little-d and he needed to know now. He had known Little-d from school since the third grade, Hector used to cover up for Little-d when kids tried to bully him because of his small size, and they became good friends as a result.

Arriving quickly, he walked intently right up to Little-d, why didn't you tell me you have been working for that corrupt parole officer Mr. Ray? How long have you been conspiring with that racist punk to get me involved with this mess? Hector said with anger in his voice. I'm not conspiring with him. I'm good whether you get involved or not I was just trying to help you put some money in your pockets. Little-d said.

Who is he really, and what does he have to do with this carjacking ring? Is he the leader of it? Hector asked emphatically as the room became intense. I don't think he's the leader, but he funnels the money through to us. He's some type of racist white boy who likes to use blacks and minorities to do his dirty work near as I can tell. Little-d said.

And he's your parole officer to when were you going to tell me that? Hector replied trying to control his anger. I don't like him, but he keeps us well-paid, and out of prison. That's why I'm able to do my business and not worry about the police he's the reason my pockets are full and yours are empty. I don't care about how racist he is as long as that is the case, he can think what he wants. I'm not here to please white people, black people either. Little-d said.

So, he's a bigger crook than anybody in the fifth ward but likes to talk down to us and treat us like criminals to make himself feel better and superior. Why does he want me in the gang? Hector asked, finally regaining his usual calm demeanor.

Little-d took a sigh and lit a cigarette, I don't know, but he wants you bad for some reason it's something personal he has against you I can tell because every time he brings your name up he gets red in the face and riled up for some reason. He has this weird look on his face like he hates you or something. Brings my name up, how often does he do that Hector asked.

A lot since you've gotten out of prison, he's been asking me about you because he knows that we grew up together. I just figured he believed you could be as good as me at this carjacking thing. It's not just the carjacking, because of him the police allow us to do a lot of things we would not have been able to get away with around here. They just look the other way as long as we stay down here and do not venture too far into other neighborhoods.

He told me to give this to you today, attempting to hand him an envelope with 1500 in it I've got another 3500 later this week for you once we finish a couple of jobs later this week, but I need you to ride with us on them I'm going to need somebody I know I can trust on these next ones with me.

Hector froze for a moment, staring at the cash, he was in a desperate situation and badly in need of the money. Times were hard, and his life and freedom were being threatened. He remembered the last thing Mr. Ray said to him "You got three days to find a job, if not either you take the offer Little-d has for you or you're gone." Hector stood there as if in a trance for a moment he could hear the voice of Little-d encouraging him, tempting him to take the much-needed money. Here man this money don't know where it came from he said. Hector's hand started moving almost unconsciously towards the envelope in the tempter's hand.

Hector! He heard a booming voice in his head calling his name, but he didn't recognize the voice, it didn't come from Little-d or anyone else in the room, it was a voice without a face or body, coming from within him, and it jarred him back into reality. Man, I can't take that Hector said. I need to go home and process some of this stuff. I need time to think and pray he said as he headed toward the door. Little-d turned to a friend nearby and smiled, he's going to do it.

Hector was filled with turmoil and confusion as he made his way back home, he was under great pressure with the bills mounting up at home and the threat of being sent back to prison. Walking briskly his mind was racing, going back and forth over the situation and the options that were before him. He couldn't believe that his life had come to this point. He was a newly freed man and thought this time it would be different, that he was out of jail for the last time. Believing he'd be able to put his past life of crime behind him, and he and Maria would be able to work towards the life they hoped for. "I thought God would make a way," he said shaking his head. Mr. Ray was using his position and the authority granted to him by it to pressure him into remaining in a criminal lifestyle. The system was set up that way, to have the parole officer keep in line recently released inmates and those under legal restrictions, they were given the sole discretion, and power to incarcerate at a moment's notice whether the person has committed another crime or not.

Hector started to think about the money Little-d offered him and the long list of bills waiting for him when he got home. Damn $5,000 he said, I could use that right now. Maybe Little-d was right, and I am being a fool thinking that this system is going to get its foot off of my neck. I Could pay a couple of months' rent and a few bills with that money and buy myself some time. Maybe if I did the job and explained to Mr. Ray that I would do it just this one time and be done he would leave me alone for a while at least until I can come up with something better. I could use temporary peace of mind.

Believing he'd be able to put his past life of crime and the gang life behind him, Hector suddenly felt almost as if he'd been deceived. Remembering the bible teaching he received while in prison and the aspiring words from his teacher and mentor Alex, Hector had put his trust into his newfound faith and belief in God. Now, it looked like nothing was going the way he'd hoped, and he was feeling boxed in, caged like an animal. Trying to overcome a system that was set up for his failure, the bitter pill of defeat was hard for him to swallow. Continuing his brisk walk home Hector felt a single tear rolling down his face, feeling distraught Hector broke out into a full sprint as he raced home to be alone with his thoughts.

Life's choices can lead us down some strange roads at times and Hector was coming to yet another "fork in the road," facing a key moment of decision in his life this new Christian was being pulled back into an old way of life. One that was more familiar to him than the ways of God. Alex had warned him while he was still in prison that his faith would be tested. "The enemy is not going to just leave you alone when you're trying to turn your life over to God, if you stay on the path of destruction, he'll leave you alone," Alex told him on their last visit.

At about the same time, Mr. Ray was meeting with Harry who didn't care about the stolen cars it was simply a great way for them to continue to cause mayhem and murder across America's inner cities. It served the dual purpose of violence among the Negros in those cities as well as helping to keep the prison system stocked with the young black men it needed to maintain its lucrative profits. "Mass incarceration was like gold to our network and movement," Harry told a friend one day.

Harry considered Mr. Ray a creepy and grimy individual, beneath him even, but he served his purpose with passion. To Harry, he was the perfect individual to deal with the lowly Negros and Hispanics in the cities. He reminded him of the old slave overseers in the good old days of the old South. He worked for the master of the plantations but wasn't allowed much direct contact with the plantation owner, they never socialized or were seen together in public. However, the institution provided the otherwise poor slave overseer to feel good about their own destitute situation.

Mr. Ray attempted to shake Harry's hand, but he simply nodded in Mr. Ray's direction. 1488 they greeted each other. I just wanted to give you an update on the carjacking rings. We have them here in Houston, Chicago, and Los Angeles everything is going according to plan, Mr. Ray said. In fact, we have some big things planned for this weekend, so we're going to be busy with this crew for a while. That's good, Harry said, handing Mr. Ray a case containing a large amount of cash. Keep the natives well-fed with this and they'll do anything we ask them to do even to their own people. Harry said. Be sure to try to contain it as much as possible to the inner city though. We want to keep the news media focused on the crime there and label it a black-on-black crime. We want to show that these animals don't belong here.

You still have that same person as your lead? Little-d or whatever he calls himself. Harry asked Mr. Ray. Yeah, he's been good for business, and he knows how to recruit his own people to the party. He's been with you for about three years. Right? That's Right. Well then, his time is up, Harry responded. Huh? Mr.

Ray said. You heard me. He's outlived his usefulness; I have a three-year limit that I'm willing to allow one of them to be connected to us. At that point, he may begin to figure some things out and pose a threat to our movement. Get rid of him it's time for a new batch of niggers.

What do you want me to do with him? Mr. Ray asked. I don't care. You can have him killed or arrested it doesn't matter to us as long as it doesn't connect back to us. Is that clear? Harry said in a stern tone. Clear, It's fine with me. The little monkey was becoming a little too uppity for me anyway. Maybe you can have this new person you've been recruiting to take his place. He's fresh out of prison and probably desperate for money, Harry said. Do you mean Hector? No, I'm going to have to take him down along with Little-d he's a nigger with a conscience, and he's actually trying to turn his life around we have no use niggers like that. Mr. Ray said. Get it done Harry said walking away.

Chapter 14

Holding On To Choices, Good and Bad

Conrad James was on his way home from a long day at the office and there was a weird aura in the atmosphere. As he left, an ominous feeling came upon him as if something was about to happen. Being given an ultimatum from the HEE board of directors to cease all of his anti-gun work was not a surprise to him nor was it the cause of his present anxiety. The board told him that his outside work was un-American, hurting the company and that he could no longer engage in this type of disruptive behavior while being the CEO. He was threatened with a choice of the work he felt God was leading him to do to help stop the flow of guns which led to violence and his lucrative position with the company.

Conrad had been working later than he normally did and by the time he got on the road it was very dark, a slow but steady rain was falling that was a refreshing diversion from the Texas heat that night. However, it did make visibility a little tougher on some of those dark highways in south Texas. As he drove along, he noticed a vehicle behind him was approaching at a high rate of speed, Conrad signaled and moved to the other side of the two-lane highway to allow it to pass. The vehicle behind him came over to his side of the road, Conrad again moved to the other side to allow the oncoming vehicle to pass but instead, it moved over to get behind him again. Not knowing the intentions of the other driver, he simply remained in his lane glancing down at his speed which was set to cruise control at the speed limit of 70 MPH.

Suddenly, red and blue lights flashed behind him. It apparently was an unmarked police car now moving in on him. Conrad pulled over to the side of the road wondering what possible reason they could have for stopping him. He knew what he had to do; his mother had done what parents of young black men have done for decades now in America. She gave him "the talk" meaning to keep your hands visible in a 10 and 2 position on the steering wheel at all times and don't move until commanded to do so. The relationship between black men and police is unique to them and unbelievable to those outside of the two groups. Two men got out of the squad car with flashlights that appeared to be ultra-bright pointed at his face, intentionally temporarily blinding him to their identities.

He heard a voice coming from the officer now standing right outside his window which was already let down. What are you doing out here? And why are you traveling at such a high rate of speed the voice said. Is there a problem officer? Conrad responded. I'm the one asking the questions. You got any identification on you the voice said keeping the light shining in his eyes as the officer on the other side remained quietly in the background. I got ID in my wallet Conrad replied, but he didn't move, sitting there with his hands still clasped around the steering wheel.

You trying to be a smart boy huh? The voice said and both officers laughed. You can move now and hand me that ID boy. "OK, I'm moving right now reaching for my wallet he said, grabbing it from the seat beside him and handing it to the officer. Don't move, the officer said I'll be back in a few minutes. After about 15 minutes where they simply sat in their squad car talking not even calling in the driver's license because they already knew who Conrad was. They also did not want a record of contact for an official stop. The officers wanted to make him sit there waiting, squirming in his seat attempting to increase his anxiety.

The two officers came back shining the lights in his eyes again, everything checks out, the voice said handing Conrad his wallet back. Can I ask you why you stopped me, you never answered my question the first time Conrad said. Is this one of those stops that you guys are always saying don't happen in America? You're that anti-gun person from Chicago the voice asked through the light, come down here to take away the rights of law-abiding citizens huh? Just make sure you slow down on these dark and lonely Texas highways you never know what can happen to a person out here they could easily get lost and never found the voice said through a sinister smile. The two officers walked away laughing together.

Conrad recognized the perverse laughter of one of the officers, the one who wanted to remain unseen, and never said a word to him during this traffic stop. It was that of Officer O'Reilly who arrested and assaulted him during an earlier encounter for "running through the neighborhood," and who was also part of the protesters who were chanting in front of his house. This is getting weird; this man must have some type of obsession with me. Conrad said starting his car back up. But I could sense that something was about to happen as I left the office this evening, I better start listening more intently when God is telling me something, he's never steered me wrong.

To Conrad, this was another one of those moments that he debated with some of his white and well-meaning friends, co-workers, and acquaintances. They always offered logical reasons for why blacks were stopped and frisked at such an alarmingly higher rate than whites. They wanted to hold on to their own idea of America and its commitments to "truth, justice, and the American way" Conrad said to himself shaking his head. Black families know all too well about those differences because we've had to live them, but I'm done trying to convince someone of a truth that they'd rather not know about. If the police or anyone can't control themselves when they know that they are being video recorded, how bad do you think they were before we had cameras all over the place?

Driving on towards his Sun Park home he was mulling over in his mind all of the things that have happened in his life since he started his organization. Ever Since I started this anti-gun violence organization, I've been stopped by the police twice, beaten up by them once, arrested and charged with assault on the police. Also, I now have protesters at my home and job daily, plus a childhood friend of ours takes a job down here where he said he would never live and runs negative news segments about me every day and encourages people to protest against me. What the hell is going on? Maybe I should just go back to being a CEO and just mind my own business I don't need all of the extra stress of going up against this system set up for gun industry profits.

That cop said something about me attempting to take away guns from law-abiding American citizens before he walked away that must have been the real reason they stopped me. And if he's working with that corrupt officer O'Reilly then he's probably just as crooked as he is. They think that by harassing me I will give up on our organization and give up the fight against all of this senseless gun violence. This is not the first time and probably won't be the last time that they've tried to intimidate someone, I'm sure of that. He grabbed his phone to call his wife Janice but saw that he missed a call from his son Jordan who was in Florida away at college he called him back instead. I'll see Janice in a little while anyway.

Jordan answered hurriedly. Hi Dad, I'm on my way out the door, we are trying to get to football practice before we have to run extra laps for being late. How have you been? Jordan said. I'm great I saw your football game last weekend and you made some great catches it looks like you're getting better by the day. Hard work pays off Dad that's what you've always taught me.

I see that you've been paying homage to Harry Jr. after you score your touchdowns with his name inscribed on your gloves and shoes, I think that's a great thing you're doing Conrad said. Yeah, dad, I figured that it was the least I could do in remembrance of someone who gave so much. Jordan replied. They both sat in silence for a moment thinking about how Harry Jr.'s last act on earth before succumbing to cancer, helped to avert a mass shooting at Sun Park high school. While on his death bed, he reached out to the parents of one of the two kids who were being mercilessly bullied to help them just as they were about to enter the school armed with multiple guns including AR15s. Jordan believed a lot of people may not still be here if not for Harry Jr. including himself.

Jordan gathered himself before continuing, I've been seeing all of the stuff on the news, and the protests and things are you in trouble Dad? Are you sure you're ok? Jordan asked with concern in his voice. Nothing I can't handle, don't worry about me Conrad replied, you just make sure that you're taking care of your studies, handling your business while you're down there, and being smart. I don't mean in the books I mean with your life, just remember it takes a lifetime to build a good name Conrad said. But you can ruin it in a second with one bad choice. Jordan jumped in and said beating Conrad to the punch. It was a familiar refrain that Jordan heard seemingly thousands of times growing up from his father and it was now ingrained in his heart.

They both laughed at the constantly repeated use of the phrase in the James home, but it was one that Conrad wanted him to keep in his heart at all times. Your homecoming game is next weekend right? Your mother and I will be coming down for that, and I know you'll be having the homecoming party that weekend, we'll be out of the way by then. We know you don't want us around for that Conrad laughed. Yeah, it's going to be a big weekend down here with a lot of excitement and there is a big party planned we can't wait. Jordan replied. I've got to run before I'm late for practice. Ok have fun but be safe. Conrad said.

Hearing Jordan talk about his friend Harry Jr. made Conrad think about his dad Harry Sr. a former neighbor and colleague at HEE. I wonder what he's been up to these last two years, he's been off of the radar in the business world, the last time I talked with him he was still heading down that dangerous dark tunnel with his white supremacist friends. What a waste of time and energy, hate blinds people to the truth, makes them easy prey for lies, and produces nothing but misery and loneliness, I hope he's been able to pull himself together before it's too late.

As Conrad finally made it home and was about to pull into his driveway he couldn't help but notice what looked like an off-duty police car parked conspicuously out front with the engine running. Conrad reluctantly got out of his car and walked over to the vehicle although he couldn't see the occupants. They shined a light in his eyes as he approached. You Conrad James? He heard a husky voice cracking through the night air. I am, who are you and why are you sitting in front of my house? Conrad replied. It's a nice house, they let boys like you make a lot of money down here, times have really changed. Welcome home the voice said as they sped off into the night.

Conrad stood there for a moment trying to get a glimpse of the car for possible identification but was unable to as his eyes were still attempting to refocus from the glare of the bright light. Damn! That's the second time in one night I've had a light shinned in my eyes this is getting dangerous. More obstacles to be put in my way, I guess. Now they're at my home and I can't allow them to endanger my family.

At about the same time, Janice James was having a meeting of her own, she recently reached out to Jamal after their awkward reunion at the James home to see what was going on with him. Janice could sense a weird vibe in the atmosphere that day, the room felt strange, something was not right about Jamal, and she was concerned about her old childhood friend. Janice wanted to know what was really behind all of the negative news coverage Jamal was giving to her family and why he seemed angry with them when he came to their home.

The two were childhood sweethearts growing up, but this was in their early teen years and Janice's parents were not about to allow her to start dating someone at that time. But she felt they had remained friends even through high school and when she started to date Conrad a few years later and eventually got married to him Jamal appeared to be genuinely happy for them.

They were meeting at a local coffee shop in Sun Park, a quaint spot that was frequented by many of the locals. Jamal was surprised when Janice called him to ask if he'd meet up with her alone, but he couldn't help but be excited about the possibilities. Had she somehow come to her senses he thought to himself. "Janice was supposed to be my wife," he said. But that conniving Conrad stole her from me from right under my nose. I've been playing second fiddle to this guy since we were kids and I'm tired of being the guy in the background. It's my time to shine. Even when we played on the same basketball team as kids, he got all of the attention, and then he turned around and stole Janice from me to cap it off." Jamal grumbled to himself as he drove towards the meeting with Janice.

Jamal had been holding on to a grudge against Conrad for years now and it had gradually grown into bitterness against him. Jamal's "schoolboy crush" he held towards Janice evolved into an infatuation over time, and when his childhood friend Conrad started dating her in high school, he secretly became enraged by it. The unresolved feelings of jealousy and envy engulfed him at times. He thought that Conrad was always getting things his way. Things seemingly came too easy for him, and he hated him for it. In fact, he now hated Janice as well for going on without him and living the life that they had planned to live together with someone else.

But as he drove towards their meeting Jamal's mind was thinking about the possibilities. Why had Janice reached out to him? And why did she want to meet with him alone? Had she come to her senses and had a change of mind? Maybe she was ready to come running back to him and beg for his forgiveness, while expressing her undying love for him. Jamal daydreamed as he drove robotically seeing the road without seeing the road. Pulling up to the coffee shop he attempted to snap himself back into reality. Stop it! He scolded himself, "I'm down here in Texas to work and get paid and that's all not to live out some juvenile fantasy" he lied to himself. Let's get down to business, he thought as he strode into the coffee shop.

Janice was already there sitting at a table in the corner, and she enthusiastically waved for Jamal to come over with a joyous smile on her face. Jamal came over hiding his emotions and calmly sat down intentionally not returning the enthusiasm.

Thanks for coming. I hope you're doing well and adjusting to life down here in the big T. How have you been? It was great seeing you again after all of these years. Janice rambled off quickly. I've been fine, I'm just down here working, I haven't really been up to much else since getting here. Jamal said coolly. There are some great places to visit down here and a lot of single ladies, if you want, I can probably hook you up with one Janice laughed wanting to keep the mood light. I don't have time for that right now but thanks for the information, maybe someday I'll take you up on that.

Janice started to reminisce about the "good ole days." Remember how we used to run down to Union Park and go swimming in the summer back on those hot days in Chicago? You guys loved to play softball all day or that game where you pitched the ball against the wall like a one-on-one baseball game what was that called? Strike'm out Jamal said dryly wanting her to get to the purpose of her calling for the meeting. Jamal glanced down at his watch intentionally showing impatience.

I have another meeting to get to in a little while, so I appreciate the trip down memory lane but I'm going to have to ask you to get to the point of the meeting Jamal said coldly. Janice looked at him with a surprised look on her face. Ok, but you seem a little agitated or angry about something, did I do something wrong? What's going on with you, I'm just trying to catch up with an old friend. You know we were pretty close at one time. Janice said. Yeah, I know, but that was then.

When you came to our house you seemed a little angry, hostile even, and I just wanted to clear the air if that's possible. Janice said. There's nothing to clear up, I have my life and you and your husband have yours. We used to be friends back in the day, but time, and people move on and that's what I had to do. So, we're not friends, is that what you mean? That's how you made it Jamal replied. An awkward silence fell over the table as they sat quietly for a moment. But I guess we're still friends Jamal finally blurted out.

Can I ask you then why you're attacking my family? Janice asked. I'm not attacking your family. I work in news media and what you and Conrad are attempting to do with guns is important to our audience. Maybe you guys should re-think what you're trying to do. Jamal said.

You may work in media, but not in the news, WKROC is not news it's propaganda, just a bunch of people who attempt to create news based on their biased opinions. In fact, that's what they hide behind is saying that they're opinion segments and not meant to be news, but your audience accepts what they are saying as facts.

How much are they paying you to be the News Director at a place like that? Janice asked with contempt in her voice. A lot! Are we done here because my time is valuable, he said standing up to leave. It's not enough for you to lose yourself or to sell your soul. Janice replied. I don't believe in that soul and eternity stuff, how long have you brainwashed black people been praying for deliverance and equality in America? Not me, for me seeing is believing and I believe in the power of the "all mighty dollar" Jamal said as he walked out the door.

Immediately, Jamal's phone rang, and he heard Paul and a voice that he recognized but had never met the person behind the voice finishing up a conversation. Paul always seemed to become secretive when he talked with this person, respectfully, almost reverently as if the mysterious voice was in authority over him. Yeah what can I do for you, he said after a brief pause. We need to meet today I'm getting word that Pricilla has been working on an unauthorized story that I need you to get rid of. One that can never see the light of day Paul said in an urgent tone. Jamal remained nonchalant, unbothered by the urgency in Paul's voice. I'm on my way back to the office right now so just let me know when you get there, I can see that you're in another meeting right now. Jamal said as he hung up the phone.

That other voice is the person calling the shots I'll bet you, probably one of Paul's white supremacist friends. Whatever these white folks are plotting it's their business and I could care less about it or them. If what he wants from me is something big, he's going to have to pay me more money I know that.

Jamal made his choice long before he sat down with Janice, allowing his unresolved feelings for the hurt he experienced when she moved on from him and later started to date Conrad to become his burden. He now attempted to soothe the hurt with career success and financial gain. Chasing the bag became his slogan, and the more he could get the more he was able to justify himself. Money became a quick temporary relief from the hurt and pain. He was not yet able to recognize that the more money he obtained the less satisfying it became, and the less satisfying it became the more he chased it. He was unaware of the pull that the hurt had on him; he only knew that he was being driven by something he could not control.

Paul was talking with Harry who was the one pulling the strings, directing from the background, and making sure that whoever this big contributor to the movement was that Rex wanted to be protected was covered. That nigger is kind of uppity Paul said to Harry hanging up the phone, but he knows how to get the job done. Well for now that's enough, if we have to put him in his place in the future, we'll do that, but as long as he's useful then use him. Harry replied. It's always better to use one of their own to get our work done for us. He's useful, all he cares about is money, so we don't have to worry about him getting a conscience like that Andre my last News Director. That nigger actually thought I was his friend. Paul said and they both laughed in unison at their grand manipulation.

Jamal's meeting with Paul was short and to the point. Paul wanted to move the process forward of replacing Pricilla a popular longtime anchor who had a committed audience, with Laura whom he was having an affair. She was already in the position as the young protégé for Pricilla. Paul didn't go into any details about the story Pricilla was working on but wanted Jamal to know that his own job security could rest on the fact that he killed this story. And if he did get rid of it there would be a huge bonus in it for him. Paul wrote down a number on a piece of paper and showed it to Jamal which induced a smile from the usually stoic Jamal. It was the "huge bonus" part that intrigued Jamal he cared little for what the story was about that Pricilla.

This meeting was easy it was the one with Pricilla that he dreaded "that bible-tooting do-gooder" Jamal said shaking his head. I wonder who, and what the hell is that story about, it must be something big, and about someone of importance the way Paul was talking, the worried look on his face, and that dollar amount he wrote down as a bonus.

But it doesn't really matter, I didn't come down here to get involved in these southern problems, I'm here to get paid and go back to Chicago. Jamal said as he picked up the phone to call Pricilla, but still, he couldn't help but be intrigued by the mystery.

Chapter 15

Trapped by My Choices

It was a bright sun-kissed Saturday morning and at 9 am it was already 88 degrees, the time of day in south Texas where if you had outside activities to do you did them before the unrelenting heat of the day started beaming down. The neighborhood was already awake with the sound of children outside playing, lawnmowers roaring, and people out walking and greeting each other with cheerful smiles. Sun Park was alive with activity and the hope of a new spring filled the atmosphere as nature turned the page on winter and blossomed fully into spring. Sun Park residents were enjoying its fruits as most of them already had their windows open to receive the fresh air and sunlight of a new day.

However, one house seemed out of place. A stark contrast against the backdrop of the rest of the neighborhood. Harry Jacobs sat alone in his stately mansion on the outskirts of Sun Park, Tx with the windows closed and shades drawn, and all the lights turned off inside, giving the house the look and feel of a mausoleum. A large, gloomy, and depressing building that contradicted the surrounding neighborhood of finely manicured lawns, welcome signs on doors, and children playing outside. In his early 40's Harry was already a rich man who possessed all of the material wealth that he would ever need. However, none of those things provided him with the contentment, peace, or fulfillment he needed. As he sat staring blankly in the dark, Harry finally opened the briefcase he received from Rex a week prior, and he could see that as per usual it was full of $100 bills.

Harry walked over to his fireplace to start a fire not because he needed heat, but it had become a place of comfort, sometimes it helped him to think, to remember the "good ole days" when he and his wife Judy used to sit around the same fireplace and plan for the future. Harry grabbed a couple of the bills and lit them with the cigar he suddenly realized that he had in his hand and threw them in the wood attempting to ignite the flame. Small puffs of smoke emanated from the fireplace but no fire. Harry grabbed a hand full more of the $100 bills and threw them into the fireplace, the fire kindled so he grabbed some more and tossed them in as well.

The money meant nothing to Harry as he sat alone in his empty house, Judy had left him after the death of their son Harry Jr. as she watched the change come over Harry soon after his "conversion" to this white nationalist movement that she blamed on the destruction of their family. Judy to her credit did accept some of the blame for sitting idly by when Harry started down this dark path that would eventually destroy their home, "I have to take some responsibility myself" she said to Harry. However, she could not bring herself to remain with Harry because the pain of her son's death became unbearable.

Not Harry. He never took any personal responsibility for his own actions, instead he always seemed to blame someone else. Unable to face the magnitude of his own decisions Harry has been going through a downward spiral of his own making ever since. A past too painful to face and a uncertain future needlessly burdened down by his own inner turmoil.

Harry never went through any type of grieving process after the death of Harry Jr. He attempted to simply keep going by committing even more to the "white power movement" that led to him being in this position. Sitting in front of the fireplace he thought about how he believed his dad rejected him as a kid, then meeting Rex who introduced him to the movement. It was the white nationalism members and Rex who convinced him to not allow his son to receive the blood transfusion from Jordan James because he was black. "You can't taint pure White Christian Aryan blood with nigger blood God will provide a better way" they told him. Harry, an engineer by trade rose quickly up the ranks of his white nationalist sect in Texas and was now the number 2 person in rank there behind Rex.

Being alone again was becoming Harry's worst enemy. It became a time of darkness, when his mind would take him down the dark tunnel again, back into that place of anger, hurt, and now revenge. "God allowed my son to die!" Harry angrily proclaimed to the empty room. I put my trust in him, and he allowed my son to die! He repeated. Lost in his own thoughts Harry suddenly felt the need for revenge, but revenge against who he wondered. At that moment it struck him again. The second bone marrow donor never came forward to help us. That's why we rejected Jordan James I was expecting the second donor match to come forward and they never did and allowed my son to die. Harry lied to himself to relieve the pain. The real reason he rejected the James's offer was he was blinded by the racism that had filled his heart and controlled his decision making.

He had been further radicalized into the movement in the early days of his recruitment by Rex by going into the dark cave of irrational websites on the internet. And the constant bombardment of the extreme news channels that he watched. In those early days of his recruitment Harry watched little else on television. Once a passionate football fan he now only watched the rightwing extreme news channels and those with extreme views. Conspiracy theories replaced reality and logic for him.

I've asked Rex if he could help me find out who the person was that stood by and let Harry Jr die but he hasn't said anything. I may have to find out for myself, and when I do that person will pay a high price. Harry said. He grabbed his cell phone to text Rex their familiar meeting code 1488. Then he thought about the meaning of 1488 and wondered how it helped him now that his son was dead. The 14-word phrase they often used "We must secure the existence of our people and a future for white children" now seemed irrelevant to him with his son dead. And the 88 which signifies the 8th letter of the alphabet H, and denotes Heil Hitler, which is a tribute to the Nazis tyrant and mass murderer Hitler now rang empty because it would not bring back Harry Jr.

Was this all worth it? This was a hefty price to pay to have my eyes opened to "the movement" Harry thought shaking his head and heading out the back door to meet with Rex. An isolated man, not interested in being a part of the vibrant community he lived in, Harry would always use the back door these days. When I find out who that second donor was, I'll find out why they never came forward and I'm going to take out my revenge on them for letting my son die. Harry said. Revenge gave Harry a new purpose, a new reason to live.

By the time Harry reached the local park and designated meeting area Rex was already there sitting alone waiting on him, a phone in his hand he was finishing off other business. Thanks for coming. Harry said to him. Of course, you know the "brotherhood" has got to stick together, and look out for one another Harry what's up?

Have you got any information for me on that second donor for Harry Jr, have you been able to get anything that could help me identify who the person is Harry asked. No not yet, it's medical information so it's not easy to access. Rex said now getting worried about the persistence of Harry to pursue this thing. Knowing that he was the person that Harry was looking for and that it was information he could not allow to get out. Yeah, I know it's difficult to get, but that's why I asked you. I thought wc had connections everywhere, or people that could hack into any system all over the world. Harry said. I'll follow up with our people on it, Rex said with a hint of nervousness in his voice that Harry couldn't help but notice and make a mental note of.

Rex attempted to buy himself some time by changing the subject back to "the white nationalist movement." I have a new list of judges that we need to get into the legal system so that we can keep things in check. We have to keep the jail cells well stocked; mass incarceration has been a great weapon for our people. Why do you love talking about the prison system so much? I don't think we've had a meeting without you saying something about the use of the prison system. Harry replied.

That's because a great piece of our plan revolves around the prison system, and a lot of our top people are heavily invested financially in the prison system. Hell, we own it! Rex said emphatically with the return of his usual confidence. Not only do we own the prisons themselves but most of the related businesses that come with housing millions of these darkie criminals each year. Most people don't think about the level of contracting done via the prison system, but we also make money off the food being bought, the hygiene products, and even the telecommunications. Do you have any idea how much we make by charging the inmate's families extra high rates for telephone calls and even emails? We sell these people e-stamps in order to send emails for crying out loud. Rex laughed hysterically.

Keep in mind also that a number of white families now rely on the incomes from the large prison campuses that we have in some of America's most remote towns. For a lot of these towns, the penitentiaries that we've built are the main employer and source of revenue for these small-town whites and without them, there would be no jobs. Most of them are second and third-generation employees in these prisons, half of their families work there or have related businesses that contract with the prison. Don't you get it? Prisons are the new modern-day slavery. Rex was on a roll.

I get it prisons are big business and these judges you want to put on the bench will help us keep them stocked. Is there one name in particular that you want us to help? Harry said. No, they all know that we want to release some of the violent ones back into their own communities, and the ones that are attempting to turn their lives around we'll have them locked up until the system can get a hold of them and make them the hardened criminals they were intended to be. Rex said. I have to go but let me know about the second donor I asked you about as soon as you can.

For the first time, suspicion arose inside of Harry while he was around Rex, somehow he felt different being around him. The man who had personally recruited him into the White Nationalist movement. Something inside of him made Harry question the motives of his leader whom he once revered and who hung unto his every word. Harry thought about all that he had sacrificed to appease Rex and "the movement" that he preached. His son Harry Jr. was dead, his wife left him, and he hadn't spoken to his dad in years. "The movement" had now detached him from his family and engulfed him in a false reality.

Chapter 16

Disappointed While "Doing The Right Thing"

Hector Rodriguez burst through the door of their modest two-bedroom house and immediately fell down to the floor, his eyes filled with tears, and his heart with disappointment. He was a man filled with hope and optimism about the future just three months ago believing that God had given him a new life. He had been in and out of prison since he was sixteen years old and knew no other life but gangs and prison. But not this time he thought, this time would be different. Armed with his newfound faith Hector was ready to take on the world.

Now immense disappointment weighed him down and was overpowering him, and his once enthusiastic faith was waning fast. Hector was in a confused state of mind as he sat on the floor in a daze.

Hector finally summoned up the strength to pray, but just like his previous prayers the prayers soon morphed into a list of complaints as a distraught and dejected man laid out his list of grievances before God. "You said that if I turned my life over to you everything will work out for my good, I've been attempting to finally do what's right in my life. I've been praying every day for your help and guidance, looking for a job with honest work and not going back to the life that you have brought me from. Yet I'm still without a job, all of these bills are piling up, and we're about to lose our home. I believed that you would be with me to help me, to make a way. And besides all of this, it looks like soon I'll be back in prison because of this racist Parole Officer Mr. Ray and this broken prison system. How can you let all of this happen to one of your own? And where are all of the miracles that I hear people bragging about?" Hector cried out.

Hector remained prostrate on the floor for the next thirty minutes lying there sometimes crying, other times in complete silence. Life seemed to be taking another bad turn for him and his options looked bleak. Time stood still for Hector at that moment, and he was lost in his own misery, reliving his own past mistakes in his mind as each scene played over and over again. Now felt like a time of reckoning for him as he believed that all of his past mistakes were catching up to him. He had paid his debt to society for the crimes he committed, but now it appeared that society wanted even more. God may have forgiven him for his mistakes, but people will always hold on to them, using them at convenient times as a weapon against him. He thought to himself.

Damn, I was 16 years old when I first went to prison, and "the system" will be holding this against me for the rest of my life I see. Hector paused for a moment of reflection, thinking about his time in prison. Had he been lied to by Alex, the parole board, or even by God? Am I playing the fool to believe in second chances? He was a man with many questions, but few answers were coming.

Finally, rising up from the floor, this time not driven by faith, but defiance. With a newly discovered strength, "If I'm going down, I'm going down swinging, and since no one will help me, I'll have to help myself." Picking up the phone he called Little-d to get more information on what he had in mind, what was the plan, and mostly how this is connected to Mr. Ray.

Little-d answered the phone with a laugh. Seeing his childhood friend Hector's phone number on his screen it was as if he'd expected the call and this frustrated Hector even more. It's about time you called me. I've been sitting here waiting for you. I knew you'd be calling me today. It's time for you to stop dreaming, believing in fairytales, and make the right choice. It's time to get paid. Little-d said. What do I have to do and how soon will I be paid? Hector replied. I still got that $1500 for you today, and like I said I'll get you an additional $3500 after we do these few jobs that are being set up, I'm just waiting for a word from our sponsor. Little-d laughed at his own attempt at humor.

Who is our sponsor and what does it have to do with Mr. Ray? Hector asked. Don't ask too many questions man, I've never met him I just go through Mr. Ray I've heard his voice in the background though he sounds kind of weird, like one of those numbers geeks in school. Little-d said. Hector wondered if it was the same voice that he heard giving commands to Mr. Ray as well. You don't have to worry about getting put back into the system anymore brother I'll connect with Mr. Ray and let him know that you're in and he'll leave you alone, you won't even have to go to the monthly visits anymore. I'll call you later, Little-d said and hung up the phone before Hector could respond knowing he had many questions running through his mind.

Damn, Hector cussed to himself this system is all screwed up, and I'm the one who's the criminal? There are criminals running the criminal justice system for profit and people wonder why it's so messed up. Alex was right when he said, "The system does work, it works the way it was designed to work." One thing was for certain though, his corrupt PO Mr. Ray would try to use his circumstances against him to send him back into the system. I'm still in "the system" out here anyway he thought. It may be worth playing the game just to not have to deal with Mr. Ray anymore. Hector laid back and waited for his instructions.

Hector was now experiencing a "crisis of faith," his faith was teetering up and down like a sea saw, and he had no idea what he would do next. The things that he said he would never do again, he found himself being tempted to do. The life that he said he would never go back to he was now back in, and the clock was ticking on the time that he had left as a free man. Hector's choices were driven by frustration, financial and family pressure, and disappointment, but where they would lead him was yet to be discovered.

Chapter 17

When Conflict Chooses You

The headlines kept coming, each week in America had the feel of a recurring nightmare, a bad rerun that would not stop playing, over and over again similar scenes played out across America. A mass shooting in California kills 11, a gunman in Texas kills 17 children and Chicago sees another violent weekend. Conrad and Janice James sat in front of the television watching the evening news attempting to unwind from a full day of activities. They were both busy in their personal lives and careers but the events unfolding before them made that all seem frivolous. That they were just wasting their time, holding on to a false hope of change.

All of this violence has happened on our watch, it's the legacy that we are leaving for our children in America. It's almost like we're beyond the point of redemption Conrad said to Janice while turning off the television in bewilderment.

Life as we once knew it has changed right before our eyes, with our generation. Janice responded. What used to be the unthinkable has become routine. The shootings are more frequent, and more random. Some of these "mass shooters don't even have a criminal past. These shooters who believe that they can no longer cope with life or were easily offended by a perceived slight all come to the same conclusion as to what action they need to take. Pick up a gun and hurt as many people as they can, let others feel the pain of what they were feeling inside. Guns have become the new cry for help, the way to gain attention, notoriety, or even relevance. "My 60 seconds" of fame. Janice continued.

It hurts Conrad replied. Places once considered a refuge from the violence of America are now the primary targets of those who carry out these despicable acts. It's as if they want to inflict as much harm as they can, for maximum impact with their expressions of violent outrage against the world. For a lot of them they know that it'll be their last acts in this life, how they'll be remembered, and they want to go out with a bang! Get maximum publicity and attention.

Notice how their weapons of choice Semi-automatic and military style guns are in the hands of "ordinary citizens" as they attack places once thought off limits such as college campuses, grammar schools, parades, and even churches. These "ordinary citizens" unleash their rage into areas they consider the most vulnerable and least likely to have ample resistance. Their goal is to attack the unarmed and strike fear into the hearts of people, while bringing outrage among the media, "thoughts and prayers" and little else from political leaders, and sorrow to those afflicted.

Easy access to guns is what we don't need, Janice jumped back in. Guns can now be purchased along with a package of bubble gun or a carton of milk at local department stores, or to those who want more specific artillery local gun shops have sprung up all over the place "ready and willing to serve all your gun needs." She said in disgust. If still not convenient enough, or if you're living in a state with gun restrictions there's usually a gun store strategically placed by gun distributors directly across the state line of a neighboring state. Plus, you can simply use the internet if that's still too much trouble to go through the process to buy a gun. America's gun culture is strong and apparently, we've decided to live or die with the consequences.

Ghost guns! Conrad replied. That's what they call these gun parts that you can buy over the internet and assemble your own gun in 30 minutes. You don't need a license, there's no background check, and the guns are completely untraceable, and there is nothing preventing anyone from buying and assembling one. Plus, the gun lobby has the legislators in their back pockets so that no type of regulations are made to prevent these types of guns from criminals. Despite all of their talk about the second amendment and sport shooting, they profit off of violence.

"This is what people are defending to have the right for people to do?" Conrad said to Janice. I got stopped again by the police coming home from the meeting with the board and I'm sure one of the cops was my personal watcher, Officer O'Reilly. I couldn't see him because he stayed in the background while the other policemen approached me, but I recognized his sinister laugh as they left. The officer mentioned something about the anti-gun work before he left.

This is going to be an uphill battle Janice and I'm not sure it's worth fighting. Putting our family at risk, or careers on hold, and for what I'm not sure that it's worth it. Watching the news makes you feel like you're wasting your time trying to do something about it. Guns are too engrained and the gun industry too powerful. The gun industry has been crafting its message for years, now people believe that gun ownership is a sacred right.

It's worth it! Janice replied emphatically, remember we prayed about this, and God told us to go forward, but He didn't say that it would be easy. Janice paused for a moment and then went in another direction. How did the meeting go with the board?

They've given me an ultimatum either I give up this anti-gun violence organization or I'll have to step down as the CEO. I wasn't surprised though I kind of thought that the board would feel that way, but one board member in particular seemed to be making an extra effort to get rid of me. They gave me 30 days to decide. It's been the fulfillment of a lifelong dream, but the dream may be ending abruptly. Conrad said. It'll be hard to give up, we've uprooted our whole family to come down here for this position only to come to another crossroads.

Life is a series of crossroads and where one road ends another will open up, we just need to stay true to ourselves Janice said. I know it'll be hard, but we have some time maybe they'll change their minds, or something else will come along we just need to keep God first in all of this.

I met with Jamal earlier today to see if I could get a sense of what's really behind all of the media attacks and the animosity, he has towards us. He's holding on to some bitterness because of our past relationship I believe and he's using getting paid as an excuse. I think it's more personal, either way, it's probably not going to end soon. She said.

Jamal has really changed a lot since our days as kids. Where we grew up may not have been under the best of circumstances, but we were given a foundation of how to treat each other and were taught right from wrong. He's now being guided by nothing more than anger, revenge, and money. It's not going to help him in the long run, those are only short-term bandages to cover up whatever his real problems are. Janice said.

Bitterness will do that to you Conrad said. It sounds like he has a lot of bitterness inside of him. He kind of reminds me of Harry, carrying around a weight that he does not have to carry will get too heavy for anyone. It'll change a person from the inside and will come out as anger trying to fill a void that only God can fill.

He blames me for you and him not being together and holding on to his anger is just a reflection of how he is feeling on the inside. That "root of bitterness" doesn't just go away, if a person does not address it somehow, it'll come back and overtake you without you even knowing it.

I hope he gets the help he needs, but we have to get on the road. We're driving to Florida this evening to see Jordan and we need to be there for the homecoming football game. I know that he's excited to play in his first one as a freshman in college. He's had a great season so far! Janice excitedly said. I can't wait to see him.

Jamal was on his way to meet with Pricilla whom he summoned to his office about an urgent matter. Jamal had no idea what Pricilla was up to or what story she was working on, but whatever it was he knew that it had wrinkled some feathers higher up, and Paul appeared nervous about it. "I heard that voice on the phone in the background when Paul wanted to meet and whenever I hear that voice Paul starts acting weird" Jamal said. This story must be about someone important if "the voice" is involved, Pricilla's swimming in some deep waters with this one. I don't care either way the number that Paul wrote down on that paper as a bonus for killing the story is motivation enough for me.

Pricilla walked into Jamal's office with her usual stoic look on her face as if she was a skilled gambler playing a game of poker, she spoke without breaking character. You wanted to see me, Pricilla said, not knowing what was going on or what to expect, the only thing Pricilla had to rely on was her distrust of Jamal.

I hear you've been moonlighting around town, working on some unauthorized stories that we have not sanctioned Jamal said. Oh yeah, where did you hear that? Pricilla answered her face expressionless, but she correctly assumed that Laura was probably the source. Come on Pricilla, we all have our sources this is the news business. So, it's true that you are working on some unauthorized story then is that correct? I've been doing some investigative reporting if that's what you mean, I've been doing what I've always done, what I've been trained to do. That's what the news used to be before all of this opinion segment news came about, where people are too lazy to do investigative work, and devoid of facts, like you who could care less about journalism can thrive Pricilla said bluntly.

Jamal laughed at her brutal honesty, he would never say it to her but in a way, he admired her for the directness of her speech, her unfiltered style. But he also thought of her as naïve, her kind was a thing of the past, and that she belonged to a generation that was dying out.

What's the story about? Who are you doing a story on? Jamal asked. You know I'm unable to reveal my sources Jamal, which must remain confidential until I'm ready to do the story, but you can be sure that they are reliable. Pricilla said.

I can't allow you to do the story Pricilla, it's been getting some pushback and I'm told it could harm some very reputable people around town. Reputable people? I doubt you even know any reputable people Jamal, you're only here to do Paul's bidding you don't care about the news or those "reputable people" you spoke of. Jamal simply smiled, even so, the story won't see the time of day and I hope you don't intend to waste any more of the station's time or resources on a dead story.

Pricilla just shook her head. You know Paul is just using you, right? He likes to have a black person pushing his extreme conservative agenda he believes it somehow justifies some of the rhetoric, and racist stereotypes that this station spews out while he hides in the background. Andre was a young black man who had the position before you, but he was not like you, he actually wanted to do some good. He wanted to help his people and bring in more minorities. But not you, I sense no type of good motives coming from you, it's all about money, power, and position.

You know me well Pricilla and you're right about the power that I have in this position, so you can now go back to your office and work on the list of stories that my secretary will send to you. By the way, Laura will be handling your segment this evening, she'll be in the first chair, and you'll be backing her up. I trust that you've trained her well.

What's next getting rid of the news altogether, there is an attack on the news in this country, an attack on journalism, on facts, on the truth and I'm not about to play a part in you and Paul's dismantling of the news. You guys just want to cater to people with narrow minds and views because you make money off of it, but I still believe in the news, I still believe in the truth. Pricilla said as the intensity rose in the meeting. And my story is the truth, and I don't care about some high up person paying to cover up their lies and hypocrisy.

You're one of those preacher's kids, right? Jamal quickly shot back. You're a thing of the past Pricilla, about to become extinct but will be the last one to realize it. Nobody wants to hear all of your morality on television anymore. These are different times, and they require a different approach. The truth has gone out of style. People want to be told what the truth is so they can live in their own reality Jamal said.

The truth is not a style or a fad that will fade away. The truth is the truth, and "a lie is still a lie no matter how many people you can get to believe it." The truth will always stand the test of time. You and Paul are fooling people into believing they're watching the news on this station when in reality it's entertainment. That's why your opinion segments have such high ratings, it's become an addicting entertainment Pricilla said.

This was very enlightening Pricilla, even entertaining as you put it. I've already informed Laura that she's in the first chair tonight. Let's see how it goes, see if she's ready for primetime and we'll play it by ear. That will be all Jamal said turning his back to her and typing on his computer.

By the way Pricilla, Jamal said as she was walking out. You were working for the station at the time when you did that interview so that makes it our property so I expect you to give me all of the notes from the interview and email me the story you're working on so that I can close the files properly. Jamal said, but Pricilla didn't answer she was already out of the door before he could turn around again.

This was the next step in Jamal implementing the plan to replace Pricilla with her young protégé Laura. Although Paul cited her age as the reason for wanting to replace her, the truth was that Pricilla's moral standards and unshakable views on integrity and the truth in the news were the true reasons Paul wanted her ousted. Paul was taking the station down a path in stark contradiction to the characteristics that Pricilla possessed, and he knew that there was no changing her.

Pricilla knew that Laura was behind Paul finding out about the story of the McMasters family and could see the writing was on the wall. Her time at the station was probably coming to an end. She had been there for almost 30 years, but she saw the changes in direction as something she couldn't be a part of anyway. The reality of leaving the only news job she ever had saddened her, but she had a choice to make. Conform to the way the station was going or be forced to leave, which for Pricilla was no choice at all. She thought about what her late father Pastor Prescott told her when she first took the job all those years ago. "Always chose the news over politics, truth over popularity, God over religion."

Chapter 18

Choices Under Duress

Madsen County Florida was alive with anticipation and excitement as they were kicking off the local homecoming weekend in this football-crazed Florida county. They were in the midst of the preparations for the annual Friday evening parade when Conrad and Janice arrived from Texas and they were anxious to participate in the festivities, but first, they wanted to see their son Jordan. He was one of the prized freshman recruits and a rare first-year starter for the football team. The James headed straight to the campus and were directed to the athletic dormitory where Jordan stayed. Unable to hide how overjoyed they were to have the short reunion, but regrettably knew that they would not be able to stay long, there was too much pressing business to attend to at home.

Jordan joyfully hugged his parents as they entered the building, sharing a long two-minute embrace and wanting to take in every moment. It's so great to see you! Janice said with excitement I know it's only been about six months, but I feel like it's been a couple of years. How have you been getting along? How are your classes going? I see you've gained a few pounds his mother rattled off. Yeah, we have to do extensive weight training here to get ready for the season, but I'm actually about the same weight I just look bigger he laughed. I wish we could stay longer we've missed you so much. That's ok, I'm glad you could make it in time for the parade and the game tomorrow. Jordan said.

I've been telling your mother you'll be fine this weekend without us, that you have all types of activities planned for this weekend, and that none of the players want to be hanging out with their parents all weekend. Conrad and Jordan both laughed. It's ok dad, I've missed you guys, missed being at home, but they've made us feel right at home down here this is a great college and a great little town with extremely nice people. Jordan said.

They met for about an hour and a half before Jordan had to leave and prepare for the Friday evening parade later that day, the football game would be early afternoon the next day. There would be the usual sellout of over 70,000 fans in attendance for the traditional Saturday afternoon college football game with a festive atmosphere and all of the local dignitaries will be in attendance. Including the Mayor, members of Congress, and businesspeople.

The game would end in high drama with Jordan scoring the game-winning touchdown with a great catch and run in the last ten seconds to pull out a victory as the crowd roared in unison. Sending the stadium crowd into a frenzy and rocking and rolling out of the stadium. The entire town was ready to celebrate the big victory of the local college as the game capped off a big weekend. After the game during a rare private moment away from media and the camera, Jordan sat alone with his parents.

The proud parents wanted to take in as much of the moment as they could before they got back on the road and headed back to Sun Park, Tx. This was a great weekend for them that provided them with a temporary escape from the chants of protest in front of their home as well as the media attacks and they wanted to cling to every second. The road back to reality would come soon enough.

Jordan knew about some of the troubles they were experiencing back home and asked "Is there anything I can do to help, are you guys going to be all right? We'll be fine son you just concentrate on your studies while you're here and don't worry about us. Janice replied. Is all of this anti-gun stuff worth it though? Do you guys believe it can make a difference? He asked. We're not anti-gun we are anti-gun violence, and allowing anybody who wants to go out and buy one to have easy access to them just for profit. And making a difference doesn't always mean some drastic shift, small steps can make a big impact on someone's life, be the difference between life and death. Conrad said.

Everything will work out the way God intended them to work out we just have some decisions in front of us, some choices to make, but like we've always done we'll let God guide us in those choices' son. You do the same while you're down here and keep putting in that work. Conrad said, handing him a wall plaque for his dorm room. It's a housewarming gift from us he said. It's not much of a house Jordan said as he reached for it. A beautiful handcrafted wooden plaque with a message engraved into it. Conrad read the message as he passed it to him "It takes a lifetime to build a good name, but you can ruin it in a second. Jordan jumped back in and said that last part in unison with his dad like he's done so many times before and they all laughed together.

Also, Under this family mantra it has your grandmother's favorite scripture Proverbs 22:1 "A good name is more desirable than great riches; to be esteemed is better than silver or gold." This is great Jordan said, I'll be proud to display it prominently on my wall where I can see it every morning. They hugged for one last time before they had to get on the road. Have fun at the homecoming party, but not too much fun Janice laughed only half kidding as they said their goodbyes for now.

Madsen County Florida was alive and in a celebratory mood. It was the highly anticipated homecoming week in this normally slow and easy area of South Florida, but not this weekend. The football team had just completed an historic comeback win, the parade was a great success luring in people and money from across the state and the local shops were buzzing as the downtown streets were packed with visitors. The entire weekend exceeded all expectations to this point and the parties were just beginning as the evening gave way to Saturday night.

Jordan James and another freshman Mark, an 18-year-old from northern Florida were headed for the campus party ready to enjoy their first homecoming weekend on campus. That was a great game Mark said to Jordan, but now it's time for the real fun to begin he said laughing. We have a couple of days off so we might as well enjoy ourselves and take in the festivities of our first homecoming and I'm looking forward to it. Jordan said nonchalantly. You sound like an old man! Mark exclaimed while laughing at his freshman teammate.

You made the play of the game and you acting like it was nothing, loosen up man it's time to party. I'm here aren't I, let's go to the party and have a good time. Man, I met your dad, and you are a younger version of him, but I have a surprise waiting for you at the party hopefully it'll help you to loosen up a little. Mark said. A surprise? What type of surprise? I don't like surprises. That figures Mark said shaking his head. Man, you'll see when we get there he said as they drove to the party.

By the time they reached the campus party, it was packed with a mixture of teenagers and young adults, the music was blaring, and the big celebration was going full throttle. The state's legal drinking age of 21 was obviously being violated by hundreds of people as the light mood turned that into an inconvenient formality.

Jordan was handed a beer which he accepted with some hesitation, having never had a drink of alcohol before. Jordan thought to himself I may as well celebrate with all of the guys since it's homecoming weekend and the biggest party of the year. "I'll just have this one and that'll be it" he naively said to himself. However, the party atmosphere lured him in, and before he knew it that one turned into three. Jordan feeling a bit tipsy sat down on a nearby couch for a moment to compose himself. This stuff sneaks up on you he said to himself.

Mark came over to where Jordan was and was accompanied by 3 or 4 women. Hey man what you over here sitting down for there's a party going on all around you. I know I'm just taking a quick break, taking it all in. Jordan lied, not wanting to admit that he had gotten drunk off of the beer. Why can't you handle your liquor? Mark asked laughing along with the girls he brought over with him.

Hey, man remember that surprise I was telling you about before we came got here? Well, we're about to enter into the room of surprises, we're about to play a game and it's one that will set this party off right. Some of my guys brought over the surprises and they promised that they will bring delight to any party. Let's go man we're about to go into the other room where the real party is going on these are just the nerds out here man. In the back room is where the real party is going on.

Mark and his newfound friends turned and started walking towards a rear door, but then he noticed that Jordan was still sitting down. Are you coming man? Nah you go on ahead I'm just going to sit tight right here for a moment and then I'll catch up to you later. Mark walked back over to Jordan and urged him to come along with him. So did the girls that Mark had with him, he encouraged the girls to persuade Jordan to come, and they all pleaded in unison for him to come along. You're going to miss the best part of the party, one of them said, it'll be fun, said another.

Jordan was in a precarious position one that he never faced before. He was a college freshman away from home for the first time. A big-name football recruit who was used to the spotlight that local fame can bring, but this spotlight was different, all eyes seemed to be on him, and internally the pressure of the moment was growing more and more intense. The festive environment along with the consumption of alcohol made him more vulnerable to the peer pressure he was experiencing, and he did not want to let his friends down.

One of the girls reached out her hand as if to help him up, she smiled at him with an enticing glance. "Come on let's go Jordan it'll be fun" she promised, it's homecoming weekend don't be a downer plus all of the cool kids are on the other side. She said laughing. Jordan obliged, standing to his feet. Ok, I guess you're right we've been working hard all semester we can have some fun once in a while.

Walking into the next room Jordan began to feel better as the movement helped him to regain his equilibrium a bit, he thought ok I feel better now I'm not as drunk as I thought I was. The room was vibrant with its own personal DJ playing loud music almost at an ear-piercing level, it appeared to be bouncing off the walls.

The drinks flowed freely on this side, and someone handed Jordan a drink of hard liquor the first one he'd ever had. They danced and shouted in rhythm with the music and got lost in the aura of the party. "I could get used to this, if this is how it is for every homecoming weekend," Jordan thought. He yelled at Mark thanks for bringing me out to the party man I'm having the time of my life. You haven't seen anything yet, now it's time for the big surprise. What big surprise? Jordan responded. We're about to go to paradise Mark said with a mischievous smile on his face.

The place of paradise he referred to would come from the pills that an acquaintance of Marks brought to the party with the guarantee that when you take one, you'll be taken to a place you've never experienced before he promised. "It's time to ride the OX" Mark said, ride the OX? Jordan wondered, what are you talking about?

"The ox," As in Oxycodone, the new heroin of the day, a prescription drug that had become popular in America's suburbs without the negative stereotypes of what were considered "inner city drugs" like crack and heroin. Despite the fact that most of it was being obtained illegally through fraud and theft, politicians and the legal system were pushing to treat the abuse of this drug as a medical problem and not a crime. That treatment was the solution for this type of drug abuse and not "mass incarceration" like the "low-level" drugs done in America's cities. These were the sons and daughters of upright people who deserved another chance. The decriminalization of drugs has come at the same time as its rapid spread across American suburbia and the disappearance of the negative stereotyping of drug treatment.

These were "good kids" politicians argued and we don't want to ruin their futures by sending them to prison and allowing the prison system to prey on them, and they proved it with legislation to decriminalize "small amounts" of these drugs in their communities. They need our help, and they need treatment became the consensus of those in the political and legal professions. There was no need to treat them like the "low-level" drug abusers of America's cities who were given the slogan "just say no" as their help.

The place of paradise that Mark referred to was happening in an adjacent room next to them and they made their way over as they danced to the music. Mark said it was a gift of the host to have a package delivered their special for them. He poured out the package on the table and they all looked at one another. Time to go to paradise he said, a pill poppers paradise I promise.

Caught up in the ambiance, and festive mood of the room, intensive peer pressure, and the influence of alcohol Jordan's decision-making became more and more uncharacteristic. To the point that he became unpredictable, unstable, and his choices more erratic.

Mark then led a countdown from ten to zero and when the count reached zero each of them would take a shot of the liquor and swallow one of the pills. "Riding the OX" he called it became part of the drinking game and the festivities. Mark went first, followed by one of the girls, then another, then another with each countdown. Others who were already in the room and not part of their inner circle joined in as the countdowns became louder and louder. The countdowns became a show unto themselves and the center of attention. Each one grew louder and more intense, and so did the peer pressure, the need to participate, and conforming to the flow of the room.

Jordan was the last of their group to receive his "OX" and he was up next. All eyes were locked on him, the moment grew with anticipation as the big-time college football recruit everyone knew who he was, and they were eager to have his participation. The countdown started loudly and in unison. 10, 9, 8… Jordan stood there as if frozen in time seemly powerless because of the atmosphere of the room.

Four states removed from all the commotion going on in Jordan's life and not consciously aware of what was transpiring Janice James was in prayer. Having returned home from the trip to Florida earlier in the day she was uncharacteristically unable to sleep that night. Janice was normally a very sound and easy sleeper but tonight was different and she couldn't find rest, she kept thinking about Jordan for some reason, and was unable to calm her spirit. So, leaving her husband in bed alone she got up for a moment and gave in to the urge she was feeling to enter the prayer room that she had recently set up in their home.

At that very moment, Jordan was teetering and swirling down as the party had taken on a life of its own. A number of the students in the room were now "riding the OX" and the countdown was on, and Jordan was at the center, as all eyes were fixated on him. 7,6,5 went the count. It was as if they were celebrating a New Year's Eve countdown and Jordan was a prisoner of the moment, powerless against his circumstances the count was coming to a crescendo, a thunderous ending of loud celebrating.

Caught up in the festive environment of the homecoming celebration and under the influence of alcohol Jordan appeared destined for a fall, but prayer was being made on his behalf at that precise moment from a small prayer room at his home in Texas. Janice was interceding for him as she was being prompted to do without even knowing what was happening to her son Jordan at the time. He was potentially facing a life and death choice and he had no idea what he would do or what direction to go in. 4,3,2,1.

Chapter 19

Hector's crisis of faith, What Choice will He make?

Hector was still trying to wrap his mind around the workings of the prison system and how it continues to hold you down long after you've "paid your debt to society." He'd concluded that it was a debt you can never pay off because of its high interest rates. They want to be paid back with your name, your dignity, and with your life, Hector said to himself in disgust. Once they get you in "the system" you're there for good. Being "on paper" is a form of control that the prison system has been using against people from my community for years. I've been on some kind of system control since I was 16 years old, I'm almost 30 now and I haven't been convicted of another crime since. Hector said to himself.

How corrupt is the American criminal justice system when people like Mr. Ray can be in control of whether or not people are going to remain free or go back to jail once get released from jail. He's about the biggest criminal that I've ever met. Well, I can't just sit here and wait for this system to swallow me up, I'm going to do something about it. Little-d was right they're never going to allow me to be free of this unless I play by their rules.

Hoping against hope Hector decided to reach out one last time to one of the jobs that he applied to earlier in a futile attempt to live out the life he believed God wanted him to live. Maybe there was still a chance, he thought as he reached for his phone to call the company's human resource department. I'm sorry Mr. Rodriguez the lady on the other end of the line said, but you are no longer under consideration for that position because we have a new policy that states that anyone with a past felony on their record regardless of how long ago is ineligible for employment with us. The HR person said. But I was told that only applied to the past ten years Hector said dejectedly. Like I said, it's a new policy the HR person repeated, good luck with your future job search she said hanging up the phone.

I need to reach out to Little-d to see what the plan is. I'm not going to sit here and wait any longer, I'm tired of being stepped on and passed over and these bills are not going to pay for themselves. Hector then called Little-d, what's the plan, and what's our next move? Hector said in a low tone. I knew you'd see the light Little-d said laughing, don't sound so defeated man I'm going to help you get back on your feet, and don't worry about Mr. Ray and going back to jail, I already talked to him, and he won't be bothering with you anymore as long as you're with us. Little-d rattled off.

I've got that $1500 for you right now you can come pick it up, it's a front payment to put something in your pocket until we do these jobs this weekend. I don't want no front payment you can hold on to it until we do the job and pay me the full $5000 then. Hector said. Same old Hector, boy you still holding on to that pride of yours, you've been that way since we were ten years old, I would expect nothing less he said.

Damn! I've been spending the last few years while still in prison preparing to get my life together so that I could make a change when I got out of prison. I completed my high school diploma in prison and even took a couple of college classes to become an electrician. I've accepted Christ as my savior and have been going to church faithfully these last two years trying to grow and do better like Alex and those Pastors said I should and for what? Hector said in disappointment. Just to be at the mercy of criminals like Mr. Ray and even Little-d, just doesn't seem right, how am I supposed to have faith when it doesn't appear to work for me? I'm going to get this job done and make that $5000 to buy myself some time to see what I'll do next.

Chapter 20

Carrying The Burden of Our Choices

Meanwhile in a neighborhood not far from Houston's fifth ward where people were struggling with economic decisions, lack of community investment, and opportunity a meeting was about to take place under vastly different circumstances. On a street where lawns were manicured perfectly, palm trees lined the road giving it a tropical feel, while the houses were a beautiful backdrop to the area with white picket fences, and individual gardens. Children rode bikes and played carefree in the expansive yards that each magnificent home possessed. The houses were simple yet extravagant in appearance with each one possessing its own individual blend of elegance and décor.

At the end of the block sat the biggest house of all, a model of perfection for others to attempt to emulate. The house had no one living there at the time but was still being kept to perfection and cars were starting to line up there for some type of event that was about to happen. Rex Rutherford had secretly purchased the home two years ago but had no intention of living there, he need to be a part of the community and have a place of residence in the South Park area. Today he was having a meeting and reception for his White Nationalist members, and he wanted to encourage the new and potential members gathered there. Rex was happy to see people coming from all walks of life, everyday people who no one would expect to be a part of or in agreement with his movement. Teachers, lawyers, judges, political leaders, law enforcement just like he envisioned.

Rex started the meeting with their familiar greeting 1488 he said to those gathered and then led them in a chant that the code signifies and the mission statement for the movement. "We must secure the existence of our people and a future for white children" the room of about 200 people said in unison.

The presentation from Rex which he called "The White Race, A God Ordained Leadership" was a five-point plan of action that he wanted to emphasize were the keys for them to obtain their mission statement and to secure the future of "taking back America" he called it. 1. The great replacement theory. Be sure that white men understand that immigrants are being brought in to replace them. 2. Control the media. Always shed a seed of doubt about media that is not in agreement with us. 3. Control history. We are the one who make and document history so that it benefits us and our children. Fight like hell against this Critical Race Theory. 4. Control education. "Mis-educate" and under finance minority education 5. Control elections. Never admit defeat in an election and emphasis election security

After the meeting concluded Mr. Ray and Officer O'Reilly sat around in one of the quaint yet stately dining halls the home possessed basking in the message of White superiority Rex gave them. The message made them both feel good about themselves, which was something they struggled with from time to time. Each man was enjoying a drink of cognac and smoking a cigar. Feeling like they were enjoying the fruits of their labor, a moment of relaxation time seemed right to them. They both laughed about the circumstances that they found themselves in, enjoying the power that came with the positions that Harry and Rex placed them in, it felt invigorating to them.

They longed for the good old days like their parents and grandparents had. Dominate. Rex was right Mr. Ray said, when the natural order of things is in place everyone is happier and better off, even the inferior races. Yeah, their brains can't handle the power of leadership O'Reilly replied that's why we need to keep them in their places. So, what's next? What did you want to talk with me about after the meeting.

The two had been working together for a number of years now helping to carry out some of the plans that Rex and Harry developed. It was a relationship that was mutually beneficial, Mr. Ray would help officer O'Reilly with his arrest record by setting up former inmates and Officer O'Reilly would allow Mr. Ray to the wield the power of arresting any of the parolees under his care or using them to comment more crimes when it served the interest of the movement. It was time for them to collaborate again and put an end to Little-d and Hector.

I'm in need of your services again, we need to get rid of another crew of carjackers that I have been using. Mr. Ray said. You mean that nigger Little-d and his crew? Officer O'Reilly asked with anticipation. Yeah, Harry says his time has come and I need your help in getting rid of him and whoever else is with him. That's fine with me I've been waiting for the ok to take him down, he's been acting a little too uppity, parading around the fifth ward like he owns the place, like we can't touch him. O'Reilly said. The boys don't like it, we've been waiting for the time that his number is called.

Well now you have your chance, you and your team have the green light from Harry himself, so he's all yours. They'll be out doing the carjacking this Friday night I'll give you their exact location and the times then, but just be ready. Remember Harry wants Little-d taken care of, he is not to survive this he doesn't want him to be linked back to our movement in any way. Don't you worry he won't be talking to anyone after Friday night, you said that he'll have a gun right? Officer O'Reilly asked. He'll have a gun and so will the members of his crew that's with him. What do you want to do with the rest of his crew, arrest them, beat them, or shoot them? It doesn't matter, just make sure that Little-d doesn't make it out alive.

Hector woke up on Friday morning and went directly into his usual devotional time of prayer and read a couple of scriptures before taking his morning shower. Despite the performance of the routine, he still planned to go ahead with his choice to join Little-d and his carjacking crew later on that day. His situation was not changing regardless of the faith he showed, and he was intent on doing what he thought was necessary to pull himself out of the hole he was in. "I'm ready to do whatever is necessary," he said. But I'm not going back to jail this had better work the way Little-d said it would.

It was a restless and agonizing day for Hector as he spent the day being tortured by his thoughts and his emotions were swaying back and forth. Hector was still working at convincing himself that he had no choice but to participate in the carjackings with Little-d, he foolishly told himself that it was only for this one time. "I just need a little breathing room, a way to buy some time, and give myself a chance." His mind raced through possible scenarios and outcomes of his choice. Upon leaving prison Hector sincerely wanted to live a different life, one that did not involve his prior street life, but the odds were stacked against him, and circumstances were pulling him back into the only life he had ever known. "Opportunity doesn't knock around here; we have to make our own opportunities," he told himself. He spent the next few hours pacing back and forth in the house unable to relax with his mind racing.

Later that evening he received a text from Little-d, it's time! Was all it said. Signifying that they were getting everything ready and that it was time for them to meet up. I have to leave out, but I'll be back as soon as I can, he said to Maria as he grabbed a jacket despite the hot temperatures outside. Hector knew that Little-d would be handing him some type of gun for him to use on the job, so he wanted to have a cover for it.

Hector started his long deliberate walk to Little-d's house, giving himself extra time to think, or was it worry? As he got closer his heart started pumping faster and his breathing became short. With each step, Hector could feel a bead of sweat rolling down his face, gaining momentum with each successive step he took.

The last couple of years of his life started to replay in his mind like scenes from a bad movie. He remembered standing before the judge who said to him "The next time I see you will be your third and last strike, this is the last time I want to see you he said in an ominous tone," The lonely and dark times of being in prison, the renewed hope he gained from the time he spent with Alex in their cell who mentored and helped him obtain his high school diploma, his conversion to Christianity. Boy, that seems a long way off he said shaking his head, unconsciously his feet kept moving in the direction of mischief, heading toward what looked like certain ruin. Desperate times call for desperate measures he said attempting to reassure himself, so he kept on walking.

Hector was unaware of the setup that Mr. Ray was planning for Little-d that night, his only thoughts were on his survival and how he could navigate through this tough time. He finally made it to Little-d's place and went around back where he was usually parked. There he saw him sitting in his car, music blaring, appearing to have not a care in the world. This troubled Hector, here I am a nervous wreck, feeling like I'm about to pass out from anxiety and he's back here like it's another day at the office Hector thought.

Little-d seeing his childhood friend was smiling at him amused by Hector's nervousness. Why are you looking like that? I told you that everything will be set up by Mr. Ray, this will be a piece of cake, there's nothing to worry about. We're going to handle this, and you can go back to your boring family life and wait for the next one. Little-d laughed. Plus, I told you that Mr. Ray is connected with someone who has a lot of money to spend and doesn't mind spending it, he's paying a lot more money for these cars. Little-d said.

Hector looks inside of the car where he sees two kids sitting in the back seat smiling, looking excited about being involved. This would be their first carjacking and they were eager for some action. They were kids from the neighborhood that looked up to Little-d and saw how he lived around the fifth ward. To them he was like a local hero, they admired him and coveted his lifestyle, and saw Little-d as someone they wanted to be like.

Who are these damn kids in the back seat? Hector asked forcefully. Eliciting a laugh from Little-d. "We're not kids we're ready to put in work one of them said proudly pulling up his shirt to display a gun in his waist. The other kid points to an assault-style rifle lying beside him and says we're ready to put in the work and they both giggled in a childlike manner.

I see they have brought their courage with them today, one in his waist, while the other on the seat next to him. Do they think we're playing a damn video game or something? I know these kids are not going to be with us they don't know a damn thing about life or what they are talking about! Hector said in anger. Man, we need some of these younger ones with us sometimes they can't do any jail time and are willing to do whatever we ask. Enough talking brother it's show time right now we have to go Little-d responded opening the door for Hector and motioning him to get inside.

Hector, his mind in a daze walked around to the passenger side of the door to go through the door to mischief. A point of no return that we all must face from time to time. He was a desperate man, a man without strength, who was allowing his circumstances, emotions, and discouragement to get the best of him. He knew this was a bad choice to make, but It was as if he was watching another person on a screen and screaming for them to do something else, only they couldn't hear him. Or watching himself be stupid without the power to stop himself, sure destruction awaited but he had lost control of his actions.

Meanwhile about 70 miles away at the Texas state penitentiary in Huntsville Tx. Alex Rodriguez was finishing up one of his bible lessons being attended by a large crowd of inmates, and he asked if they would join him in prayer for one of our recently released brothers. "He's struggling with his decisions right now I can feel it in my spirit," Alex said. There comes a time and a place where we all will struggle with our choices and with our faith Alex said, that's why we need prayer and God's word as the foundation for our lives. If you have a strong foundation, you can handle the storms that come through, in fact, the foundation is designed for times like these.

Alex motioned all of the men to come up to the altar together so that they can petition God together, as one body, and on one accord, for one purpose. I want all of us to come together for the purpose of "Corporate Prayer." Which means to come together in unified prayer, as one for a shared purpose and goal. God responds to unity, and we must all come together as one for our brother Hector who's facing a crisis of faith right now. There's no one who has ever lived who has not faced a crisis of faith, even Jesus asked this question on the cross in Mathew 27:46 "My God, my God, why have you forsaken me?

All the men gathered together, and the room was filled with the presence of God, his Holy Spirit filled the room and prompted even the prison guards to temporarily leave their positions to participate in the gathering for "Corporate prayer." Both women and men joined hand in hand. For a moment in time all divisions were made whole, the relationship of prisoner vs prison guard was put aside, one gang against the other, black and white lines were crossed as all of the artificial barriers that are put into place to divide were torn down in a powerful moment of prayer most had never experienced at this maximum-security facility.

Chapter 21

The Choice of A Lifetime

Janice and Conrad were enjoying an easy Sunday morning, joyfully preparing to attend church services as did most Sundays and this always put their minds at peace. The sound of gospel music playing in the background provided an uplifting tone to the morning as the sunlight began to brighten their home and the optimism of a new day shined through the windows. Outside you could hear the sounds of spring as birds chirping were being carried through the air by a light breeze. A long time ago the James family learned not to allow their personal success to hinder their level of commitment to God and in fact, wanted to be even more faithful because of how grateful they were to God for all He had brought into their lives.

As Janice was getting dressed, she decided to turn on the news for a brief moment only to have the peace and serenity of the morning shattered by the headlines flashing across her screen. Nine college students suffer from an overdose of fentanyl-laced oxycodone in a small Florida college town during homecoming weekend, three have died! My God! She said reaching for her phone to call Jordan, but got no answer, she called a second time, then a third still getting no answer. Her anxiety was increasing with each successive call and was about to turn into a full panic by the time Conrad walked into the room. Seeing the look of horror on her face he became fearful as well.

What's wrong? Why are you looking that way? Look at the news screen nine kids just overdosed from fentanyl and three have died in that college town where Jordan is away at school, I've been trying to reach Jordan, but getting no answer. Janice said with alarm. At hearing this Conrad felt his heart leap in his chest and he immediately started calling Jordan's phone as well getting the same results. No answer. How could this be? And why is that stuff on a college campus? He asked rhetorically. Damn! Conrad said loudly not knowing what else to say. Has the news given any more details or any names about who the kids were? Attempting to remain calm. No, only the numbers and that they were at one of the homecoming parties going on around campus, this cannot be happening Janice replied.

Stunned silence filled the room as they sat on the bed together not knowing what to do next. They tried calling again, but to no avail. After about thirty minutes, which seemed like a full day, Conrad finally rose to his feet and mustered up the strength to pray. Let's go into the prayer closet you set up; we need to be in prayer in times like these.

Not long afterward Janice and Conrad could hear a phone ringing in the background and they both emerged from the room in hopeful anticipation. Janice grabbed her phone and could see that it was Jordan, she cried out in joy as she heard the voice of Jordan on the other end. Putting her phone on speaker so they both could gain a sense of relief from the anxious moments they had experienced.

Jordan was crying on the other end of the phone and then he started to tell his parents about what transpired at the party. He went into details about how he and a teammate Mark, another freshman, were out celebrating with some of the other students for the homecoming and how he had his first drinks of alcohol. The mistakes that he made leading up to taking those drinks, the pressure he allowed to affect his decision-making, and how the alcohol contributed to making bad the decisions worse as he went along.

Jordan stopped for a moment he began to be overcome with emotion and regret as he recounted the events of that night. Unable to continue he fell down on the floor and began to sob uncontrollably. Janice attempted to comfort him, but he was inconsolable, crying harder with each attempt at continuing. After a while, he was able to receive the comfort of his parents who were also crying on the other end of the phone. They both said to him that it was all right and that they were glad he was ok and could finish telling them the rest later, but Jordan determined that he wanted to finish.

Then we went into a back room, and someone there had those pills which were supposed to be oxycodone, I had never tried or even heard of before. Jordan said as his parents sat quietly listening. We were told that the pills were harmless, they gave you "warm and fuzzy feelings," and helped to reduce stress and anxiety. Someone started a countdown for each person to take their turn "popping the pills" and give each other the confidence to take the drugs.

When my turn came, the crowd counted down and I felt like the whole room had their eyes on me and I could not let everybody down after my friends had already taken the pills, especially Mark who I came there with. Jordan paused again for a brief moment to steady himself, I somehow started remembering those words that you say all the time Dad, and a picture of that plaque you gave me with the inscription of the saying flashed into my mind. “It takes a lifetime to build a good name, but you can ruin it in a second.” Those words echoed in my mind and gave me the courage I needed at that moment, and I was able to get up and walk right out of the door no matter what anyone said or thought. Jordan said.

Jordan then broke down again as he thought about his friends and the nine people who overdosed on the fentanyl-laced drugs. Mark a freshman on the football team was one of the nine to overdose and died from the fentanyl. They all sat reflecting on what happened and how different the results could have been. I almost threw it all away trying to fit in, plus I didn’t do enough to stop Mark and the others from making a big mistake Jordan said tearing up. I wish I could go back and help them, do more to prevent this tragedy he said.

After a long pause, Conrad asked how did those pills get on campus in the first place and into the hands of college-age kids? You can’t just walk into a pharmacy and get Oxycodone.

One of the students belongs to a group on social media where they teach each other how to obtain a prescription. They tell you all of the symptoms needed and what you need to tell the doctors to get a prescription. They even coach each other on how to act around their parents and show the symptoms to be taken to a hospital for prescriptions. The group pools together whatever information they need to keep a steady supply of Oxycodone and they even know what doctors are more likely to write the prescriptions and not bring suspicion on them.

And this is allowed on social media? Janice asked in disbelief. I'm done with being surprised by the things people are allowed to post on social media. The news report said that fentanyl and opioid have become the number one cause of death among young people and that fentanyl is being distributed by drug cartels because it's a cheap substitute for the actual drug. Also, the drug cartels know that it's highly likely that whoever takes one of their fentanyl-laced drugs will probably suffer a drug overdose. and die, but they could care less, I guess.

Who is it that allows these drug cartels to operate in this country? That's all we need in this country another epidemic to go along with the epidemic of gun violence. I guess our lawmakers are going to do nothing about the opioid crisis like with the gun crisis? Janice continued.

Big business. Conrad said. It runs the country whether legal or illegal and can get away with almost anything. There's an old saying "The business of America is business" and as long as the money is coming in you can find someone willing to look the other way and allow it.

The family sat silently for a minute feeling numb, a somber mood had overtaken the once-cheerful household before Jordan finally jumped back in. I can't believe that I was tempted to take those pills. I almost threw everything away in a moment of weakness. Jordan said with a dejected tone. Everyone gets tempted from time to time. It's a matter of how you respond to the temptation and what you can learn from your mistakes, we can work through this Conrad said as quiet fell on the room again.

Chapter 22

Hope Arrives When Faith is Turned Into Action

Hector Rodriguez was facing his own crossroads, being tempted with a life-or-death decision. He found himself in a situation that he promised never to be in again, however life after his release from prison was not going the way he thought it would. His "newfound faith" was not giving him the smooth roads in life that he naïvely believed it would, and now he was inside of the vehicle with Little-d and a couple of minor teenagers about to participate in a carjacking gang.

Feeling lost and disillusioned Hector flopped down inside of the vehicle. But suddenly, without warning, he was gripped by a feeling of power that he had not experienced since his days in prison. Hector instantly recalled the promises to God that he made while laying prostrate on the floor of his prison cell one night. "if you give me just one more chance God and allow me to get out of this terrible place I'll never come back again. I'll be faithful to you the rest of my life." Those words came rushing back into Hector's mind and lifted his spirit, bringing him back into his right mind. Like the prodigal son Hector "came to himself" and was again able to think clearly without the fear that was clouding his judgement.

Open the door I'm not going to throw away all that I have gained the last few years, all that God has shown me he said, turning to Little-d, the confidence was back in his eyes. I'm not going to spend the rest of my life as a criminal or under the control of the criminal justice system and you shouldn't either. Hector said, stepping out of the vehicle. You have time to change your mind Little-d, you don't have to do the bidding of that criminal Mr. Ray and his corrupt prison system. You and these kids have your whole lives in front of you stop this madness before it's too late.

Madness? Little-d said. If you don't have the heart for this then that's your problem, I was just trying to help you out by putting some money in your pockets, but if you want to continue to live on your knees begging for a job that no one wants you to have then you go right ahead. You need to wake up man, they'll never allow people like you and me to get on the inside. Little-d said.

I don't want to be on the inside Hector replied, I just don't want to be under their control, and that's what Mr. Ray is doing to you right now controlling you and he even got you bringing these kids along with you so that he can control them.

Little-d laughed. I'm not the one who has to report to Mr. Ray every month and tell him what I've been doing while being talked down to and called names you are. I'm not doing this for him, it's all about the money for me and nothing else, I use him as my shield to keep me out of prison and do what I want around here.

Well, can you at least get rid of these kids you have with you why drag them along? Hector asked him in a pleading tone. These kids are smarter than you are man. They understand that around here there's the haves and the have-nots, only one way to get paid, and one way out and that's what we're looking to do is get paid. Hell, they'll make more money tonight than they've ever seen in their lives and more than you have since getting out of jail. Little-d said laughing hysterically as they sped off.

Hector called out to Little-d as he and the kids drove off in a final desperate attempt to stop him, but to no avail. He then collapsed to the floor under the weight of his own guilt for agreeing to meet with Little-d in the first place. Hector couldn't believe that he almost was pulled back into a life he swore off, but the temptation of the money and temporary relief enticed him. He had no idea how he was able to summon up the strength to resist in the end. Unaware that Alex Alvarez and a crowd of other inmates were in prayer for him at that precise time of his choice to get out of the vehicle.

He lay there for about three minutes crying over his decisions that led him to almost throw it all away, and for his friend Little-d who was deeply immersed in the gang lifestyle. Suddenly Hector couldn't shake off the feeling of pending doom in the air. That something terrible was about to happen and there was nothing he could do about it. Damn. Are these feelings about Little-d and his crew or about him going back to prison?

Chapter 23

Choosing Right Under Pressure

Pricilla Prescott was a woman of virtue, honesty, and integrity. These qualities at one time made her a highly sought-after journalist and were considered essential for success in the news industry but had now turned her into an outcast. She was considered someone to be shunned and not trusted at the only job she had since graduating from the University of Texas over twenty years ago.

Times had changed in the news media as big profits and the quest for political influence have chipped away at the integrity of the industry. Primetime anchors were becoming media celebrities with cult-like followings who clung to their every word almost robotically without the need for facts. Pricilla seemed to be in isolation at WKROC, “a voice crying in the wilderness.” Paul and Jamal were fazing her out for a younger more willing replacement.

As Pricilla sat in the quiet solitude of her office, she was staring intently at her computer screen going through some of the emails from Jamal Reynolds. Mornings were normally a slow and easy time around here for the evening host, but today the peace was being shattered by the communications from her News Director Jamal. Pricilla at first tried to ignore his communications hoping that at some point common sense would take over and she could resume her duties, but at present that was not happening.

Pricilla noticed a reminder from Jamal to forward all of the documents, files, and notes from the "unauthorized" meeting and interview she did regarding the McMasters family. With an additional request that she reveals the source of this information. Jamal and Paul wanted her to reveal the name of the person she conducted the interview with and what their connection to the McMasters family was. Laura her young protégé turned informant for Paul could only provide a vague description of this "mysterious best friend."

This was the first email after the meeting she had with Jamal, then she read a second, then a third marked in red final warning. Pricilla had not been on the air the past two weeks as Jamal replaced her with Laura, an overly ambitious young lady whom Paul was having an affair with. Pricilla was certain she was the person who informed Paul and Jamal about the yet-to-be-released McMasters interview. But she kept on working from her office, tightening up timelines and confirming information, wanting to make sure of the accuracy of the accounts she obtained from the "mysterious woman" on such a prominent and connected family that the story was attempted to be buried by a major news channel.

Pricilla, who grew up the daughter of a white evangelical preacher and was brought up in the old southern Christian beliefs was about to have her integrity, beliefs, and even faith tested beyond what she could have imagined. The McMasters were one of the most powerful and influential families in Texas and prominent members of the white evangelical church in the south.

Staring intently at her computer screen Pricilla didn't hear the knocking on her office door she was immersed in reading the communications from Jamal and Paul. Her work had become a cocoon for her, a place of refuge where she could work and mentally get away from the office drama taking place around her. Suddenly, she was interrupted by a voice and looked up to see a stranger standing before her.

I knocked several times and could not get you to respond a young white man with curly brown hair said. I even knocked on your window because I could see you inside, but it seemed like you were in a zone or something, so I went to talk with Jamal, your boss and he said he'd allow maintenance to let me inside. Jamal? How can I help you? Pricilla responded in a disturbed tone. I'm here to let you know that you've been served, thank you for your time. The young man said kindly and turned and walked away.

A few days passed and Jamal Reynolds called Pricilla into his office for the second time in the last two weeks, he wanted to see if he could get a feel for what she was planning to do with the story that Paul wanted suppressed. He had fully installed Laura in Pricilla's place as the lead anchor, and she was going all in on the issues that Paul and Jamal wanted out front. Issues they believed spoke to their base like Critical Race Theory, and the great replacement theory where they stoked the fear of immigrants being brought in to replace the majority white populace of America. Keeping these issues always out front to exploit the fears of their audience. Conspiracy theories that Paul believe would rile up those who believe in such things.

Pricilla walked into his office with a skeptical look on her face and sat down without speaking, after a minute of ignoring her presence Jamal finally looked up from his phone to address her. I've been waiting on those documents, files, and notes from the McMasters interview that you unlawfully did while working for our station. Why haven't you sent them to me yet? Unlawfully? Pricilla responded. I didn't break any laws and the work that I did on that interview I did on my own time and not as a representative of this station. I was doing some investigative reporting.

Your work belongs to us, and as you can see, we've taken legal action against you to turn over that information to us. That lawsuit that you were served with outlines the legal rights that we have to work done on behalf of this station and the consequences of your actions if you don't turn over the documents immediately. Also, if any of its content is disseminated to the public, we'll hold you legally responsible. I'm the one who did the work and the investigations so it's my story. Pricilla responded.

But you were doing it for WKROC, so the work belongs to us. Jamal responded. By us do you mean the people that Paul is trying to cover for? Or those who own the station? I've already told you Jamal and you can relay this to Paul since he's afraid to talk to me himself, I'm not turning over my work so that he can gain favor with his powerful friends. I'm a journalist first, a news reporter, which means I report the news. Unlike what's going on at this station now, it's all a bunch of opinion-based entertainment looking to cater to people who think and feel like their country is being taken from them.

Paul is looking to protect someone and he's using you to do it, that's how he works. He did that with Andre who was the last News Director, and now he's doing it with you. I told you that he likes to use a black person as his mouthpiece so that he can remain in the shadows, but at least Andre was attempting to do some good, hoping to bring change to the industry. But not you. I can see that you don't have those qualities, with you it's all about the money. Pricilla said in disdain.

When you're done with your lecture, I'm still going to need those files from you. Jamal said almost laughing. I know why I'm here; I know what I'm doing, and better still I know where I am. This is America and America cares about one thing and that's the almighty dollar. How long have black people been waiting for the "American dream" to come about? So, you can spare me the self-righteous talk. Jamal said bluntly.

Are we done here? Pricilla asked nonchalantly turning away from Jamal to leave. Just a moment, I can still make this all go away you know. Jamal said in a hushed tone as if keeping a secret. Pricilla paused for a moment, her back still turned to Jamal. How's that she replied. I can get you your old anchor position back and allow you to talk about the issues you want to talk about if you give me those files right now without all this becoming public. Plus, I've been authorized to give you a nice bonus for the work that you put in on the case. Otherwise, we may just have to let you go and continue the lawsuit for the files.

So, all you need from me is my soul, and you'll give me my job back is what you're telling me? Pricilla said without turning around. Think about it, you have three days to get back to me. Jamal said as she left his office.

Chapter 24

Choosing Not to Follow the Crowd

Later that evening on a hot and steamy night in Houston, Hector lay in bed unable to sleep as he thought about the recent sequence of events, and the bad choices he was making. Choices that put him on the brink of disaster with his freedom and even his life at risk. It was almost midnight and Hector hadn't been able to sleep, he was thinking about Little-d and those two kids in the car with him. The night was still and eerily quiet for a Friday night as if nothing was moving outside. The quietness appeared to echo in the darkness like a dripping faucet, making Hector's mind wander relentlessly going back and forth to his days in prison, to Mr. Ray his corrupt parole officer, and to Little-d.

Hector couldn't shake an ominous feeling of pending doom that something bad was about to happen, and there was nothing he could do about it. Unable to find the peace needed to sleep he tossed and turned in the night, "I'm feeling nervous for no reason" he attempted to convince himself. Am I going back to jail? He thought. That's the worst nightmare I could have right now. It's like the system won't let me go, and people are always trying to be bringing up my past mistakes.

Maria lying next to him was sound asleep having worked a double shift earlier. Hector stared at her for a minute envying how lucky she was to be tired from working. “I’ll never complain about working too hard again,” Hector said shaking his head.

As another hour passed by Hector finally fell soundly asleep. His body succumbing to the weariness despite the uneasy condition of his mind, all was finally calm. The third watch of the night was always the darkest, a time between 12 am to 3 am when only the late-night partyers, people getting off work, and others up to no good would be up moving around in Houston’s fifth ward. All was silent.

Suddenly, without warning the neighborhood was jarred out of its sleep by the ear-piercing sound of rapid gunfire, followed by a number of people shouting and loud screams. The sound broke through the silence of the peaceful night with a frightening tone as the screams grew louder and more intense. The gunfire stopped for a second and then started back up again as the sound of bullets rained down on the neighborhood. Hector and Maria were jolted out of their sleep by the abrupt commotion and the ensuing mayhem.

The sound of gunfire was not new to the area, but this time it was different. It was as if a mini war had broken out in the middle of this working-class neighborhood where most of the residents, who were hard-working people, were sound asleep in preparation for another day of going to work the next morning.

The gunfire stopped again for a moment and was followed by the sound of wheels screeching from a car attempting to speed away. The car roared and the wheels turned so fast that the car hardly moved, then the car suddenly leaped forward, and its occupants were on the move at a high rate of speed. Another barrage of bullets followed, and the sound of a large crash boomed in the air as the bullet-riddled car crashed into a nearby building.

Hector and Maria, who by then had taken their cover on the floor, were in shock for a moment but were now recovering their senses. You ok Maria? He asked. Yeah, but that was crazy, it sounded like a war going on outside. Maria said. They hugged each other for comfort and were about to stand on their feet when they heard an explosion from the car that crashed. The car burst into flames and was being consumed by a fiery blaze. Screams of agony could be heard coming from the blaze, excruciating sounds that the neighborhood would not soon forget as its occupants were still alive at the time of impact and were now being tortured by the fire.

The sounds of police sirens blared soon afterward, followed by two fire trucks as the recently quiet street became the scene of chaos. Onlookers who stumbled out of bed and hurriedly dressed looked on in horror. One man who got there quicker than most upon hearing the screaming coming from the fire attempted to get closer hoping to attempt to free whoever was inside the car but was stopped by the police telling him that it's too late, and too dangerous. A peaceful night had become a tragic one while the people looked on wondering who was inside.

Looking out of his window from about two hundred feet away Hector could see the commotion and the crowd that gathered around it. Wow! It's crazy outside right now he said to Maria, and there is a car crashed into the old, condemned building on the other side of the street that has been totally gutted by fire. And the street is now full of police cars. I wonder who was inside of it. I don't think they got out in time he said shaking his head at the spectacle.

Hector then heard a soft knock at the back door that pulled his attention away from the accident. He and Maria looked bewildered at each other surprised by the knock, wondering who that could be. Don't answer that Maria said, it's too much going on right now that could be dangerous. Not with all of these police around here, who would be foolish enough to do anything right now. But I'm going to grab this baseball bat just in case he said as he walked over to the back door.

Looking out of the window Hector could see no one. He glanced quickly back and forth, but still saw no one. He was about to walk away when he heard the knock again. Who is it? Hector shouted through the door but got no answer. Frustrated he swung open the door and lying on the ground covered in blood was his childhood friend, Little-d. What happened man? That was you involved in all of that chaos outside! What happened? He cried.

Little-d laying on the ground groaning and attempting to breathe, but his breathing was short and quick as he struggled to talk. He moaned something but Hector couldn't make out what he was saying, so he moved in closer to Little-d attempting to give him some type of comfort.

It was Mr. Ray he said faintly. You were right to not trust him man. It was Mr. Ray, he told us where to be and what time to be there for the carjacking. When we got there, I saw him standing there with the police smiling, and waiting on us. We tried to surrender, tried to turn ourselves in, but then they just started shooting at us for no reason. Little-d uttered in a hushed tone. They kept shooting and shooting, I tried to get out of there with those two kids' man, but I couldn't. You were right, you were right Little-d uttered taking his last breath before succumbing to his injuries.

Little-d! Little-d! Hector shouted in desperation, breathe man you can make it, breathe! He shouted in futility. By then the police had arrived at his back door. They followed the blood trail left by the mortally wounded Little-d and were standing there watching Hector attempt to help him without offering any assistance.

Freeze! Don't you move! Put your hands behind your back Officer O'Reilly shouted displaying a wicked smile and placing Hector in handcuffs. This guy was part of his carjacking crew I just know it. He said. But Maria came running into the room questioning the officers and why they were handcuffing Hector instead of attempting to render aid or offering any kind of help. We were here sleeping when all of the commotion happened, he's been here with me all night she said.

We still need to bring him in for questioning so we can figure out what happened and how he knew this person laying on the floor. Officer O'Reilly said. He knew that he would have no case against Hector, but "I just want to make him squirm a bit" he said to a colleague there. Turning to Maria he said, if that's the case then there's nothing to worry about, we're the police he said laughing. He took Hector and walked him to a squad car and shoved him into the back seat. Hector, for a moment, believed that his time was up, that this was the end for him.

Chapter 25

Choosing to Live Again

In the midst of all of the chaos and turmoil, Andre Jackson was a man at peace. Two years ago, he was the subject of headlines and drama himself, but now he was living a life of seclusion. Once an up-and-coming young executive in the news and media business, this son of Houston's fifth ward had "made it." Andre overcame the odds and the statistics to ascend to heights that he could not have imagined, obtaining the "American dream." But it all came crashing down for Andre on one fateful evening, turning the dream into a nightmare. An evening that was supposed to be the highlight of his career, a crowning jewel of all the hard work he put in as he was about to be awarded his industry's most prestigious award for the news executive of the year.

However, tragedy struck that very night as his wife Daphne was murdered, and his daughter Renee was gravely injured by an armed burglar in their home. Andre got the news while at the huge awards gala for industry insiders, a banquet where he was being honored, and he fainted upon receiving it, on the night of his life that he had worked so hard for. The news turned the coveted prize into a meaningless trophy, an empty and worthless accolade whose tragic consequences far outweighed its temporary satisfaction. The headlines in the local news shocked the small town of Sun Park, Texas, and were carried on the front page of newspapers in Houston, TX. Andre was the talk of all media outlets in southeast

Texas for months as the story was sensationalized through the press.

Sitting alone in a small room at the offices of Dr. Louis Hernandez, Andre thought about his life choices over the last few years and how they affected those around him. It had been two years since that tragic day and the memories still haunted him at times. The pain would subside over time thanks to the therapy that he'd been going through for the last two years receiving the needed mental health counseling allowed him to deal with the pain more and more each day, but the guilt? That was another matter, it clung to him relentlessly, always there, always attempting to tighten its grip on him, reminding him of his past. Today was the two-year anniversary of that day and the guilt wanted control again.

Andre reluctantly received the mental help he needed from Dr. Hernandez, a noted and esteemed psychiatrist who came highly recommended. Dr. Hernandez helped Andre to climb out of his pit of despair to a place of healing. He helped him to see the need for forgiveness in his life, especially forgiving himself from the destructive self-blame that he was being shackled by.

Andre blamed himself for his wife's murder. It's true that some of his choices played a role in allowing a burglar turned murderer to escape capture the same night the evil deed was done. But ultimately Andre didn't kill her, career criminal Avery Wright was the man who pulled the trigger on that tragic evening. However, he did avoid capture that night because Andre was playing a role outlined to him by Paul, that

WKROC would highlight criminals of color while giving vague descriptions for white assailants such as tall, medium build, medium complexion, wearing a red hat without the mention of their nationality or identifying specifics. This had been a common practice in the news industry for years and one that Andre went along with thinking that he could one day be "on the inside, in a position of change" Paul told him.

His daughter Renee was also shot by the suspect and almost died, but was saved due to the lifesaving surgical skills, and excellent medical care she received at the hands of Dr. Ruth McKenzie. Andre's current wife whom he considered an angel sent from God to rescue both of them. Renee from her physical injuries, and Andre from his mental despair. Dr. McKenzie was a Christian woman who helped to lead Andre to accept Jesus Christ as his personal savior. A strong woman of faith and she transferred some of that faith to Andre, although he didn't realize it at the time.

She also gave Andre his now favorite scripture to help him through his ordeal Psalms 40:2. "He brought me up also out of a horrible pit, out of the miry clay, and set my feet upon a rock, and established my goings." "Thank you, God! You brought me out of my personal horrible pit." Andre said glancing towards the sky.

It was his wife Dr. McKenzie who would finally convince Andre to receive the mental health counseling that he needed to recover from his ordeal. Andre at first balked at the idea of seeing a mental health professional, choosing instead to punish himself by wallowing in his own despair believing that he deserved to be punished, but also, he knew that as the lone surviving parent he would have to take care of Renee, and provide for their household. Andre believed that the stigma of mental health would hurt his career and his chances for career advancement. His dreams for a better life for his family had not ended on that heartbreaking day. Ah, the dream?

Andre's dreams kept pulling at him despite his desperate need for mental health treatment to pull him out of severe depression which resulted from the loss of Daphne but also the loss of "the dream." The depression clung to him, and at times tried to kill him. Several times he contemplated suicide and at one point he even had the gun in his hand all because of "the dream." You see Andre knew he needed help but was apprehensive about getting the treatment because of his career aspirations. He believed that the negative stigma society attached to mental health treatment would prevent him from obtaining another job in the media field and certainly career advancement.

Right or wrong there was some truth to that fear, the negative stigma attached to mental illness and mental health treatment could prevent one from obtaining jobs, career advancement, or success in today's world. Certainly, there are countless people walking around in need of some type of mental health treatment but are reluctant to receive it because of the negative stigma society attaches to it. Andre thought to himself.

Dr. Ruth, he now called her, convinced Andre to accept the help he needed, although she was not his wife at the time. To Andre she was God's angel, a messenger of hope during the darkest period of his life who saved the life of him and Renae. Renae from her physical injuries and Andre from his mental despair. She referred him to Dr. Louis Hernandez, who ironically was the childhood best friend of Alex Alverez who was serving a life sentence for the murder of Dr Ruth McKenzie's brother.

But with his renewed mental health also came back the dreams he once thought possible as a kid growing up in the fifth ward. During this latter stage of his mental recovery Andre kept a book of poetry, a collection of poems from the great black writer and author Langston Hughes. As he sat in seclusion deep in thought inside the small, isolated room he reached for the book and turned to his favorite poem called "Harlem" which for him captured the essence of his current emotions.

"What happens to a dream deferred?" Followed by the first stanza of the poem "Does it dry up like a raisin in the sun? Over and over again the theme of this poem played in his mind. Andre remembered that line from his mother's favorite movie "A Rasin in the Sun" based on the play turned into a movie by another black writer Lorraine Hansberry. The book took him back to a more pleasant time, to a childhood where things were simpler back then. He thought to himself. Reading the poem helped him to get through the hard times he endured lately by bringing up the pleasant memories of his mother Bertha. She would pop some popcorn, make a picture of Cool Aid, and gather the family around the television so they could all watch her favorite movie together. “I think we miss that family bonding in our communities today, now everyone goes off into a separate room and watches things on a device in isolation in their own homes” Andre spoke out loud although he was the only person in the room.

Sitting in that hospital room alone the question posed by the poem “What happens to a dream deferred?” not only made him think about his mother but all of the other mothers in the fifth ward of Houston, in Harlem, the Bronx, and Queens NY. Mothers on the south and west side of Chicago, South Central LA, Jackson, MS, and New Orleans.

I’ll bet there are people in those places that can give me some answers to the question “What happens to a dream deferred? I’m sure they have countless witnesses to gang violence, mass incarceration, lack of economic opportunities, and depression. Andre was having his own personal therapy session, so he grabbed an ink pen from his pocket and started writing down random thoughts to the question.

What happens to a dream deferred?

Maybe the dream gets drowned by alcohol or smothered by drug addiction. Maybe the dream expresses itself in the form of riot or protest. Does the deferred dream haunt you? Chase you down from behind attempting to engulf you with feelings of regret, depression, or anger. Does the dream simply follow you to the grave and is buried with you in your final resting place along with countless other dreams? Or can it be picked up and completed by a loved one who you told it to while the hope of its fulfillment was still alive?

Reflecting on the past, Andre became more aware of the mistakes that he made, concluding that his primary mistake was not holding on to the integrity that his mother taught him. "All my bad choices emanated from that core principle. But God has kept me alive and has given me another chance." Moma was right, God is a God of second chances Andre laughed to himself that's not exactly true, he's a God of another chance because I used up my second chance a long time ago. Andre smiled amusing himself. There was a time not long ago when he couldn't smile.

Andre received a number of offers from media outlets who knew about his work from WKROC and were interested in his services. Time to move on with my life, but there is one person I would like to go see from my time at WKROC. Pricilla Prescott did all she could to help me and prevent me from making the mistakes that I made. I want to go and thank her personally before moving on with my life. Andre said.

Chapter 26

Struggling with the Right Choice

Conrad was up early this morning. As he glanced out of the window, he could see the dawn of a new day appearing as the sun was making its initial ascent over the horizon. The ultimate symbol of new opportunities, he marveled to himself. Conrad was deep in thought about the choices that he was facing and whether this new mission of gun regulation was worth the trouble it was causing his family. He was living out a lifelong dream as the CEO of HEE Inc. The first black CEO in the company's history and the truth was that he was proud of his accomplishments and wasn't in a hurry to give up that life.

I worked hard as hell to get where I am right now. "Why should I give that up now?" I didn't work my way up to this point to become a martyr, even Martin Luther King said, "I don't have a martyr complex." I don't know if I want to give up my accomplishments by committing career suicide. Especially now with what Jordan just had to deal with and the struggle that he'll be facing with all those overdoses of fentanyl down in Florida. Sitting in quiet contemplation, the choice became a heavy burden. Conrad was having second thoughts about his decision.

Walking away from the position of a lifetime for a greater purpose sounded good and noble at the time, but now that the moment of decision was approaching Conrad was struggling with the thought of giving it all up. Wondering if he'll be able to have an effect on the gun industry anyway. This issue is simply too big for one person to challenge it's going to take a lot more than me to go up against the gun industry. And besides, America doesn't like people who go up against the establishment and the culture that we have. We have a history of violence against those who speak out against the laws, accepted norms and customs of this country, even the bad ones Conrad thought, It brings out the worst in us.

Janice walked into the room at that moment, breaking the silence with her cheerful good morning. However, she could see that Conrad was in deep thought about something. What's on your mind this morning? Why the serious look on such a beautiful morning?

I got a text last night from Steven Lawrence, the head of the board at HEE who says they'll be expecting my decision in the next day or so as to whether I'm going to continue with the anti-gun work or give up my position as CEO. Honestly, I think someone is applying pressure on him from the outside, someone above him. I believed I was ready to give it up but now I'm not so sure. I have to consider myself sometimes to you know.

I thought I knew how deep, broad, and far-reaching the branches of the gun industry were, but the truth is I had no idea of the amount of risk involved when I decided to attempt to influence some of the laws affecting guns in America. They have not only come after my job and home but now I'm constantly attacked on social media, and I've been receiving phone threats as well. Politicians, business leaders, and even religious leaders have reached out to me to attempt to get me to stop the "unamerican" anti-gun work we're attempting to do, and we haven't even made any headway. They don't want to give even any inch when it comes to guns a flabbergasted Conrad said.

Yeah, nobody said it would be easy, but is this more about you having to possibly leave your job, or are you really afraid of the threats? Janice asked bluntly. I think you may be having some second thoughts because of this lifestyle as CEO and all that comes with it. I know that is something we don't want to give up so it can't be easy.

Damn right, it's not easy! Conrad responded. We grew up in the projects and now that we have a great life with all of the perks, I'd like to hang on to it for a while if people don't mind. Janice laughed, which forced Conrad to laugh along with her.

I understand, she said. But when you attempt to take on big business in America there are usually a lot of hands in the cookie jar, and they all want a piece. There are people making big money off of guns behind the scenes, not just the gun industry itself. There are banks that finance them, financial companies that invest in gun company stocks, and others who have a financial interest in keeping this industry going Janice continued.

You know it's also not just the money we also have to contend with the gun culture that has been created in America and the messaging from the gun lobby. They have created a culture that for a lot of people is fully vetted into the fabric of America, heroic even. That's why we are the only country in the world that can't get any common-sense gun control laws passed. No matter how many people are killed, even with children being targeted at schools people are not willing to bend.

At some point, you would think that people would be placed at a higher priority than gun ownership, but I guess we haven't reached that point yet. Not even the slaughter of innocent children is enough to move them from their radicalized positions on gun ownership. It's become a culture, a religion with no end in sight Conrad said as he leaned back in his seat mentally tired from the conversation.

For Conrad doing what he believed was the right thing was coming into conflict with his own personal ambition and goals for himself and his family, he also had to take the threats and the protest seriously. "Martyrs don't pay bills," he thought to himself as he pondered his next moves. I hate having to give up what I worked so hard to get and I shouldn't have to he thought.

Chapter 27

Living With the Consequences of Your Choices

Conrad decided to send a text back to Steven Lawrence who unbeknownst to him was a secret member of the Neo-Nazis group led by Rex to inform them that he would come in to give his decision to the board the next morning on whether he would resign or not.

Steven Lawrence just smiled when he saw the message. He was having breakfast with Rex Rutherford at the time giving him updates on the status of the company and asking Rex what direction the company should move in. He showed the text to Rex. It looks like the pressure we've placed on him is working, tomorrow we'll know for sure. In a way it's kind of a shame we've made a lot of money off of this boy.

I don't care! I'm not going to allow a nigger to run my company I don't care how much money we've made. It's not about the money, I play the long game not the short one. He's no longer of use to us so now I'm done with him.

The only reason I gave him the job in the first place was to get Harry on our side. Our movement needs men like Harry, both you and Harry are corporate men, and our movement needs men who see our vision of America and can work within the system to make it happen Rex said.

I'll keep working behind the scenes to keep things moving in the right direction. I think you should offer the job to Harry, it should have been his anyway. But I think he'll be better equipped to run my company now that he's seen the light of our vision and the plight of the Christian white man in America who is always being discriminated against. Me giving that job to a minority over him will help him to better feel the pain of the average white man in this country whose jobs are being handed over to those immigrants, and the evilness of this diversity, equity, and inclusion stuff. Harry will be pleased!

Harry sat alone in his mansion like on most evenings, the "movement" that Rex recruited him into two years ago had isolated him and turned him into a man with almost no social contact with people. He only ventured out of the house when he had business to take care of. His house became his cave, a silo where he could live in seclusion in the middle of a thriving community.

Most of Harry's days were usually spent on the internet working under the pseudonym "Blood & Soil," or watching extreme right-wing news channels. He devoted his time to either creating the next conspiracy theory or helping to spread another. "Blood & Soil" now had a cult-like following and he used it to recruit, and radicalize people into the Nazis, and white supremacist movements. Harry's commitment to the movement was unmatched. After hours alone each day, it became harder and harder for Harry to distinguish himself from the online alter ego he created as the personality frequently dominated him.

However, he did maintain the thirst for revenge that he believed he needed to get over the death of his son Harry Jr.

Using the pseudonym “Blood and Soil”, Harry through his online rhetoric and white supremacist teachings was able to recruit a new generation of members, people from all walks of life. Harry worked tirelessly at teaching them about the dangers of immigration and the plight of the white man in America. Their very way of life was being threatened, “Blood and Soil” taught them that they would need to “fight like hell” it they wanted to have a country.

Harry sacrificed a lot since joining the nazis group two years ago, but lately he sensed something was wrong. He couldn’t get over the feeling that came over him the last time he and Rex met that he was not telling him something. Harry was trying to get some resolution on the death of his son Harry Jr. who had paid the ultimate price for the reckless choices he made over two years ago.

Harry chose the movement over the life of his son that day and his son succumbed to his illness, soon after his wife Judy left him as well, and he has been unable to live in peace since. Harry sensed that Rex was not attempting to help him, so hired someone in the network of their Nazi movement to do some work in secret, someone who could hack into the hospital system and discover who was the mysterious second donor. Maybe then I can get some closure on my son Harry thought.

Harry was sitting at home alone when he received a phone call. Good evening, Brother Harry. Rex said in a polite tone displaying a southern drawl. Rex was always polite, a gentleman, an educated racist, whose southern manners were in contradiction to his racist beliefs.

I have some welcome news that I thought you'd like to hear regarding your friend Conrad James, it looks like the pressure campaign with the media and the threats have worked. He's coming into the office in the morning to give his decision, I think he's going to resign, but even if he doesn't, he'll be fired Rex said, anticipating a response. Harry remained quiet on the other end. Anyway, I thought you'd like to be the first to get the news. I know that you said you wanted to be there when Conrad was relieved of his duties.

What time is the board meeting? Harry finally responded. I definitely want to be there when it happens. I want him to know that I was involved in him being sent back to Chicago where his kind belongs.

Harry could feel a little tension between Rex and himself for the first time, an uneasiness in their relationship. He had quickly become the number two person in the organization and worked closely with Rex over the last two years in the movement, helping to implement the plans that Rex had for the white nationalist movement in the state. Because of Harry his work through recruiting on the internet, their membership had multiplied.

I'll be there in the morning to meet Conrad personally, is that all for now? Yes, Rex replied followed by the click of the phone being turned off. Rex looked concerned; something was wrong he thought to himself.

Harry's next call was to the person whom he hired to hack into the medical records of the hospital where his son died. Any progress? Harry asked after being greeted over the phone. Progress, but not the results you wanted yet I should have the information you need soon though, I've been working on it nonstop replied a female voice. Great, I'll get the final payment to you as soon as you get me that information. Just remember to keep this strictly between you and me. Harry said hanging up the phone.

Chapter 28

Choosing a Future Over the Past (Andre's Redemption)

Andre and his wife Dr. Ruth McKenzie were coming home from the last of Andre's treatment sessions with Dr. Hernandez and were ready to move on to the next phase of their lives. However, Andre wanted to make a stop on the way to the place where all of the recent pain emanated from, he wanted to stop at the news station WKROC hoping to get the closure he needed to bring this painful chapter of his life to an end.

"I don't want to keep living in the past Andre said to Ruth, but I do have one person I'd like to stop and see and that's Pricilla Prescott over at WKROC. I feel I owe her a debt of gratitude and I want to say some things to her in person if it's possible. If it'll help us to finally move forward with our lives then I'm all for it Andre, are you sure you're ready to go back to the place that's been such a part of the hurt that you've experienced in the last two years? Ruth asked. I'm sure Andre replied matter-of-factly.

Pulling into the station parking lot Andre took a deep breath. I think it's best that I do this one alone, I know that you're with me, and without you, I would not have been able to pull myself out of the cave that I was stuck in, but I think it's best that I handle this one myself he said.

Getting out of the car and taking in the familiar site of his old workplace brought back feelings of regret and pain, but he also remembered some of the good times and the accomplishments that he had there. Andre hesitated for a moment but then moved with purpose, he was a man on a mission, he knew who he was there to meet with and where she was located. There was one person left in his past he needed to make peace with, and he walked directly to her office ignoring the stares and the onlookers who were whispering about him and pointing in his direction.

Walking by his old office he could still see the sign that he had installed above the door "News Director." Boy I still remember the pride I took in getting that position, I thought I had made it Andre said to himself. He could see Jamal inside with a phone to his ear looking out into the work area. Reaching Pricilla's office, he knocked softly and could see her with her back turned to the door typing on a computer. Andre knocked harder. Come in, Pricilla said without turning around.

Andre simply stood there quietly, waiting for her to turn around. Well, can I help you? Pricilla finally said revealing a deeply Texas accent, her back still turned. You already have Andre replied. Pricilla turned around to see a smiling Andre inside her office.

Pricilla excitedly walked over to embrace Andre, giving him a warm hug and smile. Wow! How have you been Andre, you're a sight for sore eyes around here to for sure Pricilla said with genuine enthusiasm.

I'm doing well now; I just completed the last phase of my therapy and hope to begin a new chapter soon. Andre said.

I just wanted to come here and thank you Andre said. Thank me? For what? She replied. For all of your help and advice when I was working here, you're the one who helped me to reach the level of News Director, but more importantly, I want to thank you for trying to help me when I was making all of those bad choices, bad decisions helping Paul to cater to the bias and prejudices of people through the news. I know that I became a poor listener, and should have listened better, but I really thought I was going to be in a position to help others in the long run.

In the long run, it's always better to do the right thing, but I know that you're a good person at heart Pricilla said. See like that Andre said, and they both laughed.

When I was allowing Paul to manipulate my ambition for his own self-interest you were always steadfast in your level of integrity, always willing to stand up for what's right, stand up for the news and not give in to sensationalism or the shifting morals of the times. I hope to take some of those qualities that I saw in you into my next position. Andre said.

They hugged each other again as Andre was about to leave, he could see Jamal peering through the glass at them, looking intently. I see Paul is still at it, the same Modus Operandi, standard operating procedure Andre said nodding towards Jamal. He likes to have a black person do his racist bidding for him so that he can remain in the background. Andre said.

Well, at least he has you to lean on Andre said. He doesn't lean on me, in fact, he's replacing me with someone more to their liking. I'm glad you came by when you did Andre because this is my last week here, I'll be leaving the station for personal reasons which I'm sure you'll soon be hearing about but for now, I can't say what they are. Just keep that information between you and me Pricilla whispered in a serious tone.

How did the meeting go Ruth said to Andre as he got back into the car. It was really good to see Pricilla again and to be able to thank her for all of the hard work and advice that she gave me back in my time at WKROC. I felt like I needed to come here and thank her personally Andre said.

Then why do you have that bewildered look on your face? Like something is wrong Ruth said. Something is wrong, but I can't put my finger on it, there was a strange vibe in the air at the station and it wasn't just because I showed up. I could feel it the moment I walked inside, especially when people saw that I was there to see Pricilla.

She told me that this was her last week working there, that she was leaving the station, but the odd thing was there were no signs of that. Nothing was being moved or packed away and her office looked like she would be staying there for a while. Andre said.

Did you run into your former mentor Paul inside? She asked. No, but I see that he's still up to his usual tricks, he's hired another younger black man to take my place. He's from Chicago, Pricilla said. Paul went all the way up there to recruit a News Director who looks like me to do his bidding Andre said shaking his head as they drove along in silence.

Chapter 29

Choosing Truth Over Popularity

A couple of days later Andre was awakened by his wife who was excited about the headlines she was seeing regarding a written story in one of the daily newspapers. “The McMasters Family secret. The bombshell story revealing the perverse secret life of rich and prominent families uncovered” by former WKROC news anchor Pricilla Prescott. The story was being run on news segments across the state and was even making national news due to its sensitive subject matter, and the prominence of the people involved.

A story by Pricilla Prescott, a True Account of My final days at WKROC, a “third person narrative” from your favorite news anchor.

Pricilla Prescott did what she always did in life and while working for WKROC being the obedient soldier. She was always taught by her father who was a Pastor that God wanted her to respect authority. Pricilla served as a mentor for the newest anchor and started pouring all of her knowledge and experience into the younger Laura, whom Jamal thrust upon her at a team meeting. She knew Laura had no experience as an anchor, but Pricilla did the best she could to provide her with the foundation she would need when the time came that she would be in front of the camera. And as the most experienced and seasoned news anchor at the station, she was not threatened by her young and eager pupil. However,

Pricilla was yet unaware of the true motives of her new young protégé.

Laura was talented, career driven, and ambitious, but she was young and lacked patience. She always dreamed of becoming successful on television, however, she didn't want to wait for it, she wanted instant success and allowed her ambition to get the best of her and was making a series of bad choices. Laura was put into the office next to Pricilla and placed under her care to keep an eye on her for Paul with whom she was having an affair, and to report to him if she saw her doing anything he might find suspicious.

Pricilla had been colliding with Jamal from the time he arrived at the station and was more than uncomfortable about the ultra-right-wing direction Jamal was taking the station in. She at first saw him as another Andre. Pricilla remembered Andre fondly but tried to warn him of the path he was taking, and the dangers that it posed to him and the community. I always liked Andre she remembered telling a colleague, he had a good heart but allowed Paul to play on his emotions. I believe that he truly wanted to make a difference. However, with this new Director Jamal I sense nothing good emanating from him.

Jamal and Pricilla went back and forth almost daily, and Jamal seemed to take pleasure in censoring and covering up some of her stories. Whenever Pricilla would excitedly come with a new lead on a new story Jamal would be there to halt it, or at least make her change key parts of it. Telling her "Stay with the format and direction of the station, we only give conservative news around here." Sometimes Jamal would agree to allow Pricilla to run with a story only with the condition that she allowed Laura to break the news on air and be the lead person on it. The replacement plan was moving forward.

Pricilla had become ostracized at the station by Paul and Jamal. Mostly because of her truth-telling and her high standards of journalistic integrity. Those principles were in complete contradiction to the men placed above her. Pricilla started to contemplate her life and career at the station. The only place of employment that she had ever known since college, and a place where she had grown into adulthood.

After a couple of months of going back and forth with Jamal regarding the direction of the station one particular incident was enough to push Pricilla over the line. It was to serve as a point of no return, a journalistic line she would not dare to cross.

Pricilla allowed Laura to sit in and take notes on an interview she was to have with the best friend of the now-deceased daughter of one of the most prominent families in south Texas. The McMasters family. Fearing for her own safety and not wanting to be shunned by other members of their affluent community, the best friend wanted to remain anonymous for the story. She agreed to sit down with Pricilla because she wanted to do something to stop an evil hidden practice and keep what happened to Susan McMasters from ever happening to anyone else.

Pricilla and Laura met up with this "mysterious best friend" who had contacted Pricilla and wanted to share the story with her. Pricilla had become a trusted face to the young lady because her mother would always be watching Pricilla on television. They met at a local coffee shop on the outskirts of Sun Park, Tx. A barebones nondescript location chosen by this "best friend". As Pricilla and Laura sat in the shop waiting for about 15 minutes it appeared they may have been stood up and had wasted a trip.

The upscale Laura didn't like the lack of amenities and plain décor of the place. Laura grew impatient and she remarked to Pricilla this is a waste of our time maybe we should just go back to the office are you sure it's safe here? She said clutching her purse. Journalism 101 stories aren't found inside of an office, the real stories are out here with the people Pricilla said. Just be patient and order some coffee or something. Also, you can stop looking so uncomfortable while you're at it, people can sense when you consider yourself not like them. They can tell when you're an outsider Pricilla retorted annoyed by the highmindedly elite attitude of Laura.

Moments later in walked a tall young 20-something year old white woman wearing shades with a stylish floppy hat covering almost half her face. She was smoking a cigarette although there were clearly marked signs that read no smoking, she sat at their table staring at Pricilla from under the glasses and giving her a nod for a greeting. Pricilla spoke to her while Laura only coughed and waved her hand in a futile attempt to prevent smoke from being in the air.

Who is this, the mysterious young lady asked referring to Laura who attempted to reach out to her and shake her hand, but the request was ignored. This is my protégé Pricilla said. She's here to assist me with any note-taking or help I may need it's ok Pricilla assured her.

The young lady nodded while continuing to ignore Laura, there was something about Laura she didn't like, but she trusted Pricilla and wanted to get her story out. She took one last drag on her cigarette and got right to it.

This is a story about a friend of mine, Susan McMasters was a young honor roll student who was from one of the most wealthy and influential families in South Texas. The McMasters were a proud and influential family who lived in the suburb of Sun Park, Tx. They were prominent members of the evangelical Christian church and held strong to their Southern upbringing and traditions. They owned one of the biggest and most expansive spreads of land in the area that had one big house but also a couple of smaller houses on the land. Also, a ranch with several horses, cows, and other animals.

The McMasters were the epitome of what you would call "old money" living out the American dream. The land was at one time the original sight of one of the largest slave plantations of the old Antebellum South. The McMasters were said to be the largest owners of slaves in south Texas, maybe in America and their land was converted to its current state with its stately mansion, marble floors, and perfectly manicured grounds maintaining the nostalgia of the old south including monuments and tributes to General Robert E. Lee.

The McMasters were one of the families who helped spearhead the rebellion against then President Abraham Lincoln who dared to free the slaves with his "illegal emancipation proclamation" they called it. They lead a defiance of this proclamation by continuing to own and work slaves for up to two years after the signing of the emancipation proclamation. It wasn't that after two years they gained a conscience and decided that they could no longer participate in the immoral, and now illegal practice of slavery, it simply took the northern Union Soldiers two years to make their way down to Texas and enforce the laws that freed the slaves, an event now celebrated by blacks as Juneteenth.

Susan was born into the wealth and extravagance produced by the 200 years of free labor made possible by slavery, and into a family that was one of the biggest contributors to the evangelical church in the south. The McMasters were very active members of the church, especially the pro-life movement.

Like I said before, she was an honor roll student and considered someone with a bright future ahead of her. Her father was a man of great influence in the political and media realms and helped a number of would-be politicians get elected to public office; those who would carry out his ideas and beliefs and help with legislation that helped his many business interests. He dreamed of one day getting Susan elected to the United States Senate and was already laying the groundwork for that goal although she was only a college freshman.

However, Susan was walking around with a secret, one that she knew would cause a scandal because of the prominence of her family. She started dating while in college and became pregnant. Knowing all of the dreams that her father had for her in politics or maybe the family business Susan felt like she was in a situation that would bring ridicule, embarrassment, and harm to her family.

Her mother, with whom she had a strained relationship, was one of the leaders of the anti-abortion pro-life movement and held meetings and functions for planning and financing pro-life events at the McMasters mansion regularly. While her father was a leader on the political side of the movement, he worked behind the scenes to get the laws passed that banned abortion in the state of Texas. However, Susan was also unmarried, and she knew the scandal that becoming a young unmarried woman would cause in her high society and "deeply religious" circles back home. "After all my mother is the leader of the pro-life group back home." Susan told a friend.

Torn after being burdened down by her secret and not knowing what to do Susan finally got up the nerve to talk with her parents on a trip home from college. The conversation didn't go well, and she was taken aback by what she felt was a lack of compassion and selfishness by her parents. They got into a huge shouting match about the pregnancy and what they called her reckless behavior. Her dad who had her life carefully scripted out for her expecting her to graduate college, go to law school, and become the youngest Senator from Texas by the age of 28 was in an uproar.

Her father yelled at her about preserving the sanctity of the McMasters' name. Saying "our family has been a pillar in this community for over two hundred years, we've become known for our standard of moral excellence" he yelled angrily at her. Then her mom chimed in "and what am I supposed to tell my church group when they come over, we meet every Thursday evening now" she cried. Dad, our home is located on the very spot of the biggest slave plantation in Texas, and our family has owned thousands of slaves. And mom I don't care what you tell those sanctimonious old women. Susan responded defiantly to her parents. This resulted in a hard slap to the face from her mom and more yelling from her dad. The "mysterious best" friend paused for a moment and lit another cigarette.

The back and forth apparently went on for about an hour before a semblance of peace was restored and they were able to talk with one another. The family meeting became civil, and they talked about Susan's options and what she wanted to do. The family knew that it was only a matter of time before Susan's secret became public knowledge and her shame would be known throughout their community. The family, known for its upright moral standards and behavior was now in protection mode and looking for more room in their closets to cover up more dark family secrets.

They sat in silence for a while contemplating the situation and what was said in their family meeting.

Finally, Mr. McMasters spoke up. I know someone who can help us and do it in a way that is never found out with no medical records or even appointments to worry about. You would never have to worry about newspaper headlines coming back to haunt you in the future, and our family name would still be intact. Our family and other high-level families in our tight-knit circle have been using their family services for generations now and never had a problem with them, we've always been able to trust them with our secrets. We have always been a part of the best of the best and we must stay above reproach so that the lower classes of people can't use it against us.

You mean an illegal abortion? Asked Mrs. McMasters in shock. That goes against everything that I believe in and the work that I've committed my life to. And you're one of the main forces behind us getting anti-abortion laws passed. She said to her husband. It's my job to protect this family and that's what I'm going to do, he responded. You and Susan may not know this, but this is not a new thing for this family, it would not be the first time that its been done. I already have the connections and can have this problem taken care of quickly and discreetly. Mrs. McMasters looked stunned and in shock by the revelation of the family secret. Oh, don't just sit there in your pious self-righteous indignation Mr. McMasters said to his wife we have to live in the real world. But illegal abortions are illegal, and no one is above the law in the United States Mrs. McMasters said to her husband. You don't actually believe that nonsense, do you? Mr. McMasters arrogantly replied.

Susan sat there silently listening to the back and forth of her parents regarding the illegal abortion and family revelations. She had never heard her mother debate with her father about matters of importance before and it seemed strange to her. Susan never believed she could talk with her mom about things that happened in her life they had a strained relationship. To Susan, her mom appeared to be unapproachable about real-world events, always judgmental, and radical about religion. In the end, both Susan and her mom did what they always did, giving in to the decisions made by Mr. McMasters. Susan was exhausted by the burden she carried around and now just wanted it over with.

Susan and Mr. McMasters soon afterward traveled via train to the state of Louisiana for the purpose of having an illegal abortion. Susan at first felt forced, obligated to cater to her father's wishes like she's always done, but now there was a sense of relief that had her at peace. Although Mr. McMasters was one of the driving forces in getting pro-life legislation passed in the state of Texas, he was illegally headed to another state with his own daughter to circumvent that law. He was armed with a couple of envelopes full of money, it was always a cash-only transaction. "Cash is untraceable and doesn't know or care where it came from or where it goes, and neither does the person who receives it" Mr. McMasters said to Susan.

Don't feel bad about it, this is something that rich plantation owners, wealthy and influential businesspeople, and others in high places have been doing for years, he told Susan. It may not seem right to you, but there has always been a great need for the rich and upper class to protect their names and images. Some of us are part of the evangelical Christian movement, some part of the pro-life movement, some in politics, or unnamed organizations, but all upstanding members of our community he said.

Arriving in New Orleans there was a car waiting for them prearranged by Mr. McMasters and they drove for over an hour outside of the city limits to an area that looked like the middle of the woods. Susan knew they were near the swamp lands because the temperature appeared to go up another 15 degrees due to the extremely high humidity. There they would meet the great, great granddaughter of a former slave who had inherited the illegal abortion practice from her. It was a “family business” that served the affluent community from other states for decades. Inside of a two-room shack that served as a point of death for many unborn children, and a harbor of a long list of family secrets for generations.

This day the temperatures were extreme already over 100 degrees when they arrived in New Orleans. Now in the swamps it felt like 120 degrees, a dangerous temperature to perform normal everyday activities in. This was not a normal activity. During the procedure Susan’s body was unable to overcome the physical pain and trauma that was inflicted on her by the illegal abortion, there were inadequate facilities, no air conditioning, the homemade anesthesia that this amateur “witch doctor” used on Susan to numb the pain only exacerbated it. The extreme heat had corrupted the anesthesia and turned it into a deadly cocktail that burned hot once put into her body. Susan screamed loudly and attempted to flail her arms, but they were strapped to the bed and tightly woven around them. Susan let out one last scream that was so agonizing and ear-piercing that even the sounds of nature stopped for a moment, nearby animals seemed to pause from their natural activities and cry out as they heard the sound of a horrible death echoing in the air.

Days later came the headlines from WKROC that temporarily rocked their quiet affluent neighborhood. Local honor roll student from one of the most prominent families in the area succumbs to covid related illness!

The "mysterious best friend" stood up and lit another cigarette signifying that she was done for now. Susan reeling from her emotions, and Mr. McMasters both made bad choices that cost Susan her life, and Mrs. McMasters was complicit by not standing up and speaking up for what was right.

When you are the one person who is thinking clearly or know right from wrong in these key moments of decision in life, you have the opportunity to be the voice of reason in a tense situation. I believe that God intentionally and strategically places us in the middle of these situations so that we can prevent tragedies like this from happening. Instead, she fell back into the old way of submissive wife thinking., That brainwashed Stepford wives syndrome of allowing her husband to lead their family down the path of destruction. You know how to reach me if you need to talk on this again she said as she strode from the room.

Pricilla and Laura sat there in quiet awe for a moment. Both taking in the tragic tale of a young and promising life needlessly loss. After about two minutes Pricilla said to Laura this is going to be a bomb shell of a story there are some heavy hitters involved here, we had better tread lightly on this one. But it's a story that we have to get out to warn all women of the potential dangers of this type of thing, and the American people need to know that its more common than we are being led to believe. As they got up to leave. Laura was already texting Paul Wilson we need to meet she said to him.

The McMasters Family secret headlines would go on for days and cause a number of prominent people to attempt to disavow any knowledge of the wicked practice of illegal abortions and to attempt to reaffirm their commitment to the pro-life movement. Pricilla had exposed a huge hypocrisy from one of the most prominent families who are one of many who have used the dangerous practice of illegal abortions while working in the "pro-life movement.

Chapter 30

Choosing To Look Away

Karen Rutherford knew and understood her role as the wife of the man leading the white nationalist movement in southeast Texas, Rexnord Rutherford. The role had come to be well defined even if left unspoken by thousands of women in her position throughout history. Remain faithful to her husband no matter what they've done, while staying out of their way. Remain pure, directly outside of the pain and misery their husbands were inflicting on the people who were the target of their racist scorn. Be informed but not directly involved, publicly compassionate but never critical of their actions, while in silent agreement with the actions of their husbands, who throughout history had openly oppressed the "inferior races" of people in their country. This is how we preserve our way of life she was taught.

When Rex and Karen were a young couple living in Mississippi, It was difficult at first for her to adjust to his way of life, but she understood that one day it would pay off big. Rex was a young man on the rise, a son of the South who believed in the "old way" of life. Rex would sometimes come home with blood-stained clothing and a menacing look in his eye. His heart still pumping fast from the adrenalin that flowed through his blood after a late night in the woods of Mississippi. Rex had grown up in a town known as a "sundown town", or "grey town" which referred to a community that set rules intended to keep blacks from living there.

Blacks could come into town and work, doing the manual or demeaning labor that whites did not want to do, but by "sundown" they had to be out of the town or be at risk of harassment, arrest, beatings, or even lynchings. Rex was raised by his grandfather who allowed him to come along with him and his crowd as a little boy, they patrolled the town looking for blacks who dared to miss the proscribed curfew by even a minute. Sometimes as punishment for a perceived insolence from their workers, and sometimes simply to amuse themselves some of the whites who employed the black workers would keep them a little later than normal with the intention of having them fall victim to this vigilante justice. This is the landscape that shaped the beliefs of Rex and lead him down his current path.

His grandfather although a leader in the Ku Klux Klan and involved in multiple lynchings in the back woods and dark roads of Mississippi was also a white southern Evangelical Preacher. He carried a bible around with him wherever he went and was always ready to throw out a scripture when he believed someone needed teaching. He felt empowered by the same teachings that soothed the mind and consciences of his parents and grandparents to justify their slaveholding, segregation, and the brutal treatment of blacks in the state. "The Curse of Ham" is what they were taught in church on Sundays as a way for them to be able to continue with their way of life. Ham, the son of Noah brought about shame on his father and was forever cursed to the "dark races," imposed by Noah on Ham's son Canaan.

Rex's grandfather and great-grandfather were wealthy men, the benefactors of the free labor that slavery provided their family for over 200 years. Their farmland produced large amounts of cotton in Mississippi, and tobacco in North Carolina. Through this wealth, they were able to pay off who they needed to and be able to produce illegal alcohol as well.

Two years after President Lincoln's emancipation proclamation on Jan. 1st, 1863, the Union soldiers finally made their way into the deep South to enforce the law of the land to free the slaves. The Rutherford family, which was one of the wealthy families that still had the uninformed slaves working, decided to move into a new area, a new vision they saw for the future. Prison building and ownership. The Rutherford's saw prisons as the potential new slavery, a new way to confine and profit off of the newly freed slaves.

It was all of this wealth brought about by the vices of the land that Rex inherited and became one of the country's wealthiest men when his father died. Rex choose to run all of the companies that he owned from the background, never taking an official position or title with any of the many businesses.

Karen Rutherford simply wanted to live the "American dream" – a life with her husband that was unaffected by the social ills of American society. She dreamed of a house with a white picket fence, two children and a dog. A way of life that could not be infected or tainted by the life that her husband lived.

She also believed blacks, Jews, and immigrants to be inferior, but didn't possess the internal hostility or propensity for violence towards blacks that her husband possessed. Karen only wanted to live the life that she saw her mother and grandmother live with the same inherent benefits that they enjoyed in the American South of the "good ole days." Karen was from a long line of women who didn't agree with everything their husbands did but believed they were protecting their way of life.

Karen wouldn't be someone who took an active role in the suppression of blacks and other races, that would be "unladylike." But when her husband came home with blood stains on his robe and clothes, she would nonchalantly place them into the laundry with all of the other clothes of the household to be washed. "I don't care what you do, just don't let your actions come back and touch our family" Karen would say to Rex. Able to maintain her dignified place in American society, a woman of God who was active in her local church, she served as his shield to the public, providing a sense of normalcy in the midst of his depravity.

Rex's actions within the Neo nazis white nationalist movement bothered her for a time at first, but over time her outrage grew less and less before setting into contentment. Now she was comfortable with Rex and the movement believing that it was having no effect on her and her family.

On a particularly hot summer evening, Karen sat on the porch of their ranch outside of Houston. A picture of lemonade made with freshly squeezed lemons sat beside her. Karen the "good wife" knew about what time Rex would return home for the evening and she liked to have things in order the way that he liked them. Karen was a great cook in that old southern tradition and had the evening supper already prepared and warming in the oven. The aroma of fine scents rode on the gentle breeze that was flowing, mixing beautifully with the dawn of a Texas evening.

Rex waved at his wife as he pulled into the driveway, home from another day of planning and managing his many business interest, but his main interest was always in maintaining their "way of life." That is what always occupied his mind, even more than all of the money that he was making because of the great wealth he inherited.

Good evening, darling Karen said. I hope everything went well today.

Today was another good day. I just need to keep on top of things and keep them headed in the right direction, our movement is at a key moment Rex said tersely.

You and that movement, I was talking about the businesses and the plans you have for your business interest. You always have that movement at the front of your mind, she laughed.

I have to it's my mission to wake up the masses to the fact that this country is at war, and the war is being fought on our own land not in the jungle. I have to awaken the white man to the truth that he won't have a country if we don't do something about all of these illegals coming over here to steal the jobs of good white men and women. A lot of our people don't see what I see, but God has given me the vision just like he did for my grandfather that we have to claim our natural place as leaders over the inferior races. Only then when the natural order of things are in place will everyone be truly happy, truly free.

Blacks aren't happy in leadership; they don't have the brain capacity for it. The Jews aren't white, they are nothing more than a threat to the white race like Hitler said, and Hispanics don't want to be in leadership they're happiest when working in the fields.

I didn't mean to get you going, I was just saying hello Karen laughed. That's all fine, I know you are going to do what's best for us, I only ask that none of your activities effect our family.

Don't worry, I know how to keep business separate from personal and I won't allow it to touch our home. You promise? By the way, I agree with you about the inferior races just keep that stuff away from our home Karen said with a big smile on her face.

Is there anything else because you seemed to have a different look on your face when you first drove up? Is everything ok? It's Harry. I'm starting to sense a little tension between us that was not there before, he's being a little standoffish, like he's holding something back.

You know that it's around the time of the second anniversary of his son's death, he's probably thinking a lot about him and what happened. You don't think he knows anything about your involvement do you? That you were the second donor but did not come forward Karen asked. I don't believe so, but I don't know Rex said. Maybe you should just tell him the truth and explain to him why you could not come forward.

No! He wouldn't be able to handle that and besides it's bigger than just him and me. It would hurt the whole movement. I told you that I couldn't be identified as being the match for the blood transfusion because James Jordan was the other donor. People will start saying that me and that nigger have the same blood and we can't have that! The white man's blood must always be considered pure and above all others Rex said emphatically. That's fine as long as this doesn't affect our household Karen said.

Chapter 31

Face to Face With Reality

Harry was spending his day the way he had most days in the past two years, alone in his mansion in front of his laptop with a grim look etched across his face. He went by the pseudonym "Blood & Soil" when he was at work doing what he could for the "movement." The white nationalist work required an online presence and Harry was the one who was handpicked by Rex to lead the recruitment and radicalization of young white men into the movement. Although Harry was frequently engulfed in this work, spreading conspiracies, and rumors of the demise of the white man in America, it gave him no joy or fulfillment. His days were spent as a voluntary outcast from society, choosing instead to live in the shadows among fringe groups and like-minded individuals on the internet.

Although a wealthy man and relatively young in his forties, Harry rarely ventured outside to enjoy what life had to offer him. He possessed an abundance of riches from his time with Rex, but rarely enjoyed the perks of it. Instead he spent his days online in a personal cocoon shielded away from the real world. He no longer enjoyed the work he was doing because it had lost its newness. He robotically performed the work that he had committed to do after Rex gave him the assignment.

Harry did take some solace in how he was able to easily control people and manipulate their thoughts with his conspiracy theories, rumors, and the latest disinformation campaign. "These people are like ants, I can make them dance to whatever tune I want," Harry said as he took delight in the latest conspiracy, a sinister smile unconsciously developing across his face.

Harry in fact had the biggest house in the community of Sun Park but since the days of losing his son and wife, he chose to confine himself mostly to one room sitting in front of the fireplace lost in his thoughts. He only ventured outside when in need of the necessities of the house and for meetings with the brothers in the movement. The majority of the house was empty to Harry and had been collecting dust for the past two years. The result of a self-inflicted two-year confinement Harry imposed upon himself.

Blood & Soil's number of followers had multiplied exponentially since Harry took over the assignment and he had become a force in the Nazis movement. But lately, with the second anniversary of Harry Jr.'s death approaching, he was sensing that something was not right inside of the movement and with his relationship with his leader Rex Harry thought as he was lost in his thoughts.

A text came through jarring him back into consciousness. 1488, he saw and replied back the same message to the sender. It was from the obscure person that Harry hired to hack into the medical records and find the information on the second donor, who was he? We need to meet the person said. Meet me at the spot in one hour Harry responded.

Harry grabbed one of his suitcases that were filled with money and started heading towards the meeting. Somehow he believed he was about to receive some unpleasant news.

Arriving at the park in the designated area where they knew no cameras could see them, Harry sat down for a moment lighting a cigarette in anticipation. Harry laughed, “when the hell did I start smoking,” he said to himself knowing the answer was about two years ago. Suddenly his operative emerged from the shadows. A striking female wearing sunglasses, giving him their familiar salutation. 1488 she said. 1488 Harry replied.

You appear kind of nervous is something wrong? Why are you being so secretive? You know that this is our designated area and no one can see us Harry asked. I got your information she said nervously, I just want to give it to you and move on from this. Are you sure that my involvement in this cannot be traced back to me? She asked. I’m sure, but why are you acting so strangely about this?

I just want to fulfill my commitment to you and put this past me and never hear about it again. She said handing Harry an envelope with the information he requested about the second bone marrow donor who never came forward. Harry attempted to hand the woman a suitcase that contained her payment. I don’t want that, this never happened, and I don’t want anything else to do with this. I just wanted to be square with you and leave it in the past said the nervous woman walking away.

Harry stood there for a moment watching her walk away and thinking what could make her act so strange and leave without receiving her payment? Opening the letter Harry then flopped down on a nearby bench in shock at what the contents revealed. The second donor who could have saved his son's life, Rexnord Rutherford!

Chapter 32

Facing Your Choices

Conrad woke up in a troubled state of mind and it made him both angry and disappointed in himself at the same time. Man, I thought giving up this position for the calling I felt God was calling me for would be easier. But to be honest, I've been having second thoughts Conrad said to himself. How were those twelve disciples able to drop everything and follow Jesus? I guess I'm more selfish than I am noble, believing that I would be glad to give up this CEO position to concentrate on the anti-gun violence Initiative. The reality is that I've been having second thoughts about it and it's easier said than done.

Just then Janice walked into the room. Good morning baby she said joyfully, hiding a sheepish grin. Good morning Conrad replied. Why are you so cheerful this morning? You know I have to go before the board with my decision this morning, don't you?

Of course I know that. I just believe in the vision that God has given you and I'm confident that He'll see us through. Change is not always easy, but it's sometimes necessary Janice said.

I wish I had more faith like you and was as selfless as you are. The truth is I know that these positions don't come around every day, especially for us. I've been having second and third thoughts about the decision even though I know it was the right one Conrad said. I'm not worried about your position, and neither should you I know that we'll be all right because we're following what God intended for us to do. And besides, this may be an opportunity for us to start our own engineering company instead of working for a large international one. When God closes one door, He opens another one Janice said.

You're not rethinking the gun reform work we're trying to get accomplished are you? Because the problem is getting worse and worse every day Janice asked.

No, I know something needs to be done about that. I just don't know if what we can do will be enough. We're fighting against not only big business, but also a gun culture that has been established in America Conrad said. Not by ourselves.

But we're not by ourselves. Most people in America believe that we have a serious problem with guns. It's the big business and that gun culture that needs to be called out. I think we ought to have a moment of prayer before you leave.

About ten minutes later, strengthened by the prayer, Conrad was out the door to meet with the board of directors at HEE.

Conrad sat alone in his office for a few moments attempting to prepare and compose himself for the meeting. "It's been a journey of a lifetime to reach this level, but I have better things to do with my life than make money. Money is good but not everything" he said to encourage himself. He sat alone soaking it all in thinking about his ascension to the top of his profession, coming from the west side of Chicago to the top of a fortune 500 company doesn't usually happen. The odds are better that you can be a professional basketball or football player than to obtain the professional status that he had. But he displayed a level of discipline growing up that few people could match. The guidance of his mother, and God's grace had brought him further than he could have imagined. Conrad sat in silent contemplation thinking of his mother who died ten years ago.

Wow! I'm still amazed by the level of integrity my mother showed while we lived in those projects in Chicago. She never once compromised herself or did anything that she believed would bring dishonor to her family. "My mother was very much into the preciousness of a name, the meaning attached to it. She'd always quote Proverbs 22:1 whenever we were faced with hardships. "A good name is better than great riches, to be esteemed is better than silver or gold" She'd always say. Her faith was her shield, and she wore a belt of truth and a breastplate of righteousness. Conrad sat silently contemplating his mother at this moment of truth.

A loud and sudden knock on his door startled him back into real-time. Conrad looked at his watch thinking maybe he was late for the meeting, but he wasn't. Who could that be he wondered. Conrad strode to the door and opened it without asking and was shocked by who it was. There standing in front of him was his former co-worker and neighbor turned adversary Harry Jacobs.

Harry stood there for a moment with a look of satisfaction on his face before speaking. Mr. CEO, I just wanted to be here today to show you that I haven't forgotten how you swooped into town and stole my position out from under me and that I knew this day would be coming soon. The time for quotas, affirmative action, and discrimination against the white man in America is coming to an end and a new day is dawning.

Well, Harry, it's a surprise to see you that's for sure. However, I see that you're still operating under the same delusional thoughts about how I got this job as well as the condition of this country.

I'm not under any delusions! I know how you got the job and about the direction of this country and I'm here to reclaim it for the rightful heirs to this country as well as reclaim my job. The menace of diversity, equity, and inclusion is over Harry said.

Yeah, I know about some of your exploits on social media. You're still spreading that Neo-Nazi, white nationalist propaganda. "Blood & Soil" right? That's the pseudonym you go by online. I've followed some of your movement just to keep tabs on dangerous people like you from time to time as you spread your lies about the plight of the "poor white man in America." The absurdity of that would be funny if it wasn't so dangerous. So why are you here this morning? To take pleasure in my leaving the company, right?

You think that you can take guns away from law-abiding citizens with your anti-American beliefs about unarming true patriots? This is America! Gun ownership is a God-ordained sacred right here Harry said with a smirk on his face.

Gun ownership is not God-ordained, nor is it sacred. It's simply a right given to people under the constitution that needs to be amended and loopholes closed to stop dangerous people from killing innocent people including kids.

Still trying to save the world huh Conrad? Guns are a way of life in America and we're not going to stand by and watch people like you attempt to lie about our great nation. People need guns for their own safety and protection. Guns keep us safe from the criminal element that needs to be disposed of and sent back to their own countries. People like you hate the second amendment and want to take away people's rights.

I don't hate the second amendment; I just love my children and people more and you can stop the grandstanding and talking points. There are no television cameras around. If guns made people safer, America would be the safest place in the world. There is no place in the history of the world that has more guns than America. And by the way, who is it that is making it easier for criminals to have guns? It's the same people who are making huge profits from guns, violence, and prisons. America is the only place in the world where people can simply walk into a store and purchase guns as if it's candy or a carton of milk. Hell, if it were up to you, they'd have guns in vending machines.

Don't you think responsible gun owners are tired of irresponsible people creating a narrative of them not caring about what is happening in America with guns? Portraying them as a part of some radical cult.

Guns have become the number killer in America, not cancer or any other illness. Guns are the number one problem solver for Americans whenever we get upset, angry, or offended we quickly grab that convenient solution sitting right beside us. Without any regard for the consequences until it's too late.

I see you've decided to continue down this path of destruction. You know it's ok to choose to turn your life around, to head in another direction away from the dark side. God has given you the power of choice. With life there is hope and you have the power to choose life over death, it's all in the power of your tongue Conrad said. That's what your son Harry Jr. did, he and my son Jordan became best friends and I'm sure that's what he'd want you to do.

Yeah, I heard your speech a couple of years ago about choosing life Harry laughed. I've chosen my path. I'm a Christian just like you. I'm just a far-right Christian Harry replied.

What does that mean? I guess you're going to wait until you get to heaven and then change huh? Is heaven segregated in your far-right Christianity or just here in America? Conrad asked.

You have no idea the power I have over you right now. I've decided to allow you to live for now, but your life is in my hands. If I wanted to end it right now I could Harry continued.

You have no power over me, my life is in God's hands, not yours. This movement of yours has made you delusional. I can see how much it has changed you since you started down this self-destructive path.

Harry laughed. By the way, he said as he turned to walk away, I'll be replacing you as the new CEO of HEE. A position that should have been mine in the first place. I'll see you at the board meeting in an hour.

I'm not surprised that you'll be there. I know that groups like yours and the KKK have come out of the closet, you've become shameless in your evil. You have exchanged your masks for suits now. You're running for public office and passing laws.

Conrad walked into the meeting with the board of directors at HEE confident in his decision and without any remorse for the actions that he felt he needed to take. Surveying the room there was one face that he did not recognize, who didn't sit at the table with the others but stayed in the background. It was Rex, the true majority owner of the corporation who Conrad quickly deduced was the man pulling the strings.

He only had a clipboard with the number of mass shootings in America. Holding up the sign 215 and counting, Conrad said. There have been more mass shootings in America than there are days passed in 2023, and with no signs of anything changing soon. That's the culture that the gun industry and its lobbying arm the NRA have created. Along with the media outlets that continue to cater to the profits and political power that they crave as they exploit people for profit and turn guns into a religion in America.

Unfortunately, it's not a religion that looks to save lives but is only a merchant of death. So, with that, I choose to continue the work that we started with the Sabrina James Nonviolent Initiative and respectfully resign as CEO of HEE Inc.

I know better than to attempt to reason with the unreasonable or to attempt to negotiate with people who are not well-intentioned. You have my resignation and with that, I bid you goodbye. Conrad said turning to leave as members of the board attempted to give him their prearranged arguments for why he should resign. Conrad was already gone.

Chapter 33

Dealing with Life's Cruel Moments

Hector Rodriguez sat alone in his jail cell that night. Time stood still for him in a moment of torturous emptiness. It was as if he was reliving a nightmare.

I can't believe that I'm back in the one place that I dreaded coming back to. This is the last place I wanted to see again, I've attempted to run from this life, but like a relentless predator, it keeps pursuing me. I've been in and out of jail since I was 16 and this time, I did the best I could to not come back again and yet here I am. Hector thought to himself. It looks like I'm destined for this life. No matter how hard I try not to, I keep ending up back here he said aloud.

I can see now that all I have is myself. I tried to live a Christian lifestyle and look what that got me, back in the same place. I believed in God and the promises that He made in the bible. I listened to Alex and those other preachers in jail, and nothing is happening for me. In the end, I'm here in this cold dark cell alone and abandoned by God and everyone else. Little-d was right, at the end of the day, all we have is ourselves. Now I have to figure out how I'm going to get out of this mess.

God, I thought that you would open doors for me but they are still closed. I couldn't even get a job when I got out because everyone looked at me like I was a criminal. I guess I can't blame them for that though, I'm the one who decided to put these tattoos in my face and on my neck, but that shouldn't keep me from making a living. I still have to eat and pay bills like everyone else. No matter what I do people keep judging me by my past and slamming doors in my face. Enough!

The cell was cold, dark, and eerily quiet as Hector stared up at the ceiling while lying on a bunk. The perfect environment for his thoughts to haunt him and haunt him they did. He couldn't help but replay over and over in his mind the last moments that he had with his childhood friend Little-d and the final words that he said to him while dying on his back porch.

"It was Mr. Ray. You were right to not trust him man. It was Mr. Ray, he told us where to be and what time to be there for the carjacking. When we got there, I saw him standing there with the police smiling and waiting on us." "We tried to surrender, tried to turn ourselves in, but then they just started shooting at us for no reason. They kept shooting and shooting, I tried to get out of there with those two kids' man, but I couldn't. You were right, you were right Little-d uttered in a hushed tone, taking his last breath before succumbing to his injuries." Hector shook his head in an attempt to clear it.

Damn! That racist and corrupt Parole officer, he's the criminal, he's the one responsible for me being here. The death of Little-d and those kids. There's no telling how many people Mr. Ray has sent back to prison who have been trying to turn their lives around only to have to deal with him and this corrupt parole system that keeps people under the hand of the law well after they've served their time. This corrupt

Parole and probation system is worse than being in prison, it's like walking around with a weight around your neck. That's how they're able to keep the revolving doors open to prison by using this system that is stacked against us. No wonder when you hear people talking about prison reform you never hear them attempting to address the probation system. They know that's how people are kept in the system years after their initial incarceration.

Damn! I can't sleep, every time I close my eyes I can still hear the screams of those two teenage boys, screaming in agony from the fiery crash attempting to get away from the onslaught of bullets being hurled at them. I've been tossing and turning for so long that I don't even know how long I've been here, or what day it is.

Hours later Hector, who had been finally overtaken by exhaustion woke up in a cold sweat. The moisture ran down his head and into his eyes before ultimately covering his shirt. He had managed to get some tortured sleep before the screams woke him up again, jarring him back into reality. Looking quickly from right to left he realized he was still in jail.

The more time alone in the jail cell the more his thoughts haunted him. But now there was a drastic shift in his emotions as they turned from fear and disappointment into anger. Hector's anger grew and grew by the second and he was becoming enraged at the prison system, and particularly his Parole Officer Mr. Ray. How much money is Mr. Ray being paid to keep the prison doors open for people who look like me I wonder, and who's really funding it?

Mr. Ray doesn't have that kind of money, he's just a pawn for someone much more powerful. How many people have Mr. Ray wrongly sent back to prison, and for whom? Mr. Ray has lied to me, mistreated me from the day I was released from prison, and then attempted to set me up like he did Little-d and those kids.

Two days passed but Hector had no idea how long it had been. The police had 48 hours to charge Hector with a crime before letting him go, but they had no intention of charging him. Officer O'Reilly was just keeping Hector for the full 48 hours to let him "sweat it out." He and Mr. Ray talked and agreed to release him after the time required to charge him expired. This charge may not stick, I'll find a stronger charge to get him on soon Mr. Ray promised Officer O'Reilly. You can let that immigrant go in two days They both laughed hysterically.

Time passed slowly for Hector as he sat alone. The prison that surrounded him became secondary to the prison of his mind as his thoughts wandered uncontrollably. Sleeping intermittently, Hector was able to manage a comprehensive thought. "My future seems to be in dire jeopardy" he said managing a laugh. Little-d there was a time when thoughts about the future were for other people, not for people from where we grew up. Nobody believes in us, so we have to make our own future, you always used to say to me Hector said laughing as he attempted to hold a conversation with his now-deceased friend.

Realizing what he was doing Hector wondered "Am I going crazy?" Who am I talking to? I don't know if they are ever going to let me out of here, but if they do one thing is for certain, I'm going to kill Mr. Ray! Hector determined.

Moments later he was startled to hear his name being yelled from a distant hallway, "Hector Rodriguez pack it up you're free to go." His last thought echoed in his ears "I'm going to kill Mr. Ray."

How about a ride home, a couple of officers mocked Hector as he left the police station that afternoon. I'm good, I know the way and I've had enough of your hospitality I'd rather walk he answered.

Hector thought to himself, It's only about an hour from here and I need time to clear my mind and think, I can't get those screams out of my head from those kids in the car . I told them to go back home that they had no idea what they were getting involved in, but I didn't know it was this deep. Mr. Ray is a wicked man who deserves to pay for all he's done.

Hector stumbled towards his Fifth ward home feeling disappointed and disillusioned. I must have been a fool to think this time would be different. I allowed myself to believe that God would be there to help me through my troubles and that He would care about someone like me. I had better stop believing in things I can't see and concentrate on what's in front of me. Now I have no idea what I'm going to do. I still have no job prospects, I'm out of money, and not even God is on my side. This is just getting to be too much. I feel like I'm close to the edge.

Just then Hector received a text from Mr. Ray. "Congratulations number 120-111-141-1847-2051 on your release from prison, you know tomorrow is our scheduled monthly meeting day and I expect to see you there in the morning." This thing is never going to end, they're never going to allow me to move on with my life. To them I'll always be a part of the system, always a criminal, always a number.

I'll be there in the morning all right, but I've had enough of all of the dancing for these people I refuse to live life this way, I'm not going to spend the rest of my life bowing to this corrupt man. Hell, I was better off in prison, that's the one place that I can get the truth from it seems, I'd rather go out on my own terms not catering to some racist PO. I tried to walk the straight and narrow, tried to live a different way as a Christian, but I guess not even God is on my side. Hector said shaking his head as he took the long walk home.

Hector finally arrived home that night, but when he walked inside, he found the house empty. Maria had gone along with their young son. Hector called for her and ran from room to room in a desperate yet futile search for Maria, but he discovered that all of her belongings were no longer there. She moved out of the house while he was in lockup for the past 48 hours.

Hector slumped down on the floor feeling exhausted, desolate, and inconsolable. Maria finally had enough and was gone. I can't blame her I guess; I would probably leave me as well he blurted out managing a fictitious laugh. I guess my moma was right all along when she kept telling me as a child that I would never amount to anything. He glanced at the text from Mr. Ray again, I just have one last score to settle before they take me.

Hector woke up the next morning still struggling with the way his life was turning out, depression was setting in and he struggled to get out of bed. Forsaking his usual morning prayers Hector instead walked around the house once again as if he was hoping it was all a dream. That he would find Maria and their son in their usual areas of the house with Maria starting breakfast and their son nearby in his playpen.

Hector Rodriguez left home that morning with his mind in a state of confusion, swinging back and forth from disappointment to disillusionment. He felt betrayed by everyone he knew and everything that he believed in. Naive about his faith, Hector believed with all his heart that this time would be different. That with God "on my side" nothing is impossible. That's what Alex told me, that's what the preacher said, and showed me that in the bible. Hector thought to himself as he prepared to leave for his monthly parole hearing. I wonder what the hell he wants to talk to me about. Whatever it is won't matter because it'll be the last time he gets to talk down to me. Time to get ready to go.

An hour later Hector was out the door on his way downtown, walking with more of a purpose this time he seemed a man on a mission. The voices and screams were back inside his head as he made his way. Only this time the screams appeared to be more intense than the last, and the faces of the two kids were stuck in his mind. The kids had been recruited by Mr. Ray after he was assigned to them as a parole officer, and he presented them to Little-d as easy help for him to continue the carjacking ring. Walking further he could hear Little-d telling him with his last breath "It was Mr. Ray, he set us up." With each step he took Hector grew more and more angry. I'm fed up with people lying to me and treating our people like dirt, acting as if we're criminals when the people we are supposed to report to for help are the bigger criminals. They don't really want people to turn their lives around, they're making money off of this criminal justice system.

Hector pausing for a moment of reflection thought about his childhood friend Little-d and felt a single tear rolling down his face. My mind is being attacked in all kinds of ways and I don't know what to do about it or where to turn to for help. My prayers are not being answered. It's too late to turn back now I've made my decision; I can't live like this anymore. I won't be a footstool for these people, I'd rather go back to jail. It's time to put an end to it once and for all.

This guy has been allowed to run over people after they've been released from prison for years and he's more than comfortable doing it. It can't just be him, there must be someone else with a lot more power that is behind it. Little-d said that someone was paying a lot more money to keep the carjacking ring going, and Mr. Ray doesn't have that type of money or power.

Hector intentionally arrived early at the downtown office of Mr. Ray knowing what time he was scheduled to come in. I want to be there when he walks in and see the surprise on his face, I'm tired of him threatening me with his comments about sending me back to jail and his hypocrisy about me getting a job. He knows damn well he don't want me to have a job, he wants me to be a crook and work for him. Well, I have other plans.

As Mr. Ray walked into his office, he could see that the door was already open and the silhouette of a man inside, sitting in his seat behind his desk. This disturbed him and he began to move a little quicker to see who would dare to enter his office uninvited.

Seeing Hector, a look of contempt quickly came across his face. What the hell are you doing boy? You have the nerve to let yourself into my office and sit in my chair, behind my desk? Don't you know I have the power to put you back behind those prison walls with the rest of your kind right where you belong? How dare you! Barked Mr. Ray going into his usual insolent, and rude behavior.

Sit down and shut up! A defiant Hector shot back. It's not going to be that kind of meeting today. Seeing Mr. Ray's eyes look towards a desk drawer where he kept his firearm, Hector pulled out the weapon from his waist. Looking for this? A dangerous grin came across his face. That's why I'm here early. I knew where you kept this gun and wanted to make sure that I got it first. I know how cowards like you need to use a gun for everything.

Chapter 34

A Time to Kill?

Your text said that you wanted to meet with me, so here I am, only today I'll be the one running the meeting and you'll be the one doing the listening. All of this time you've been talking down to me, calling me names and threatening me with going back to prison if I don't get a job soon. You call me a criminal when you are the biggest criminal in Houston? What kind of scam racket are you running here and with who?

You don't know what you are talking about or who it is that you are messing with boy Mr. Ray shot back. Our organization is bigger than you can understand, and more powerful than anything you know. If it wasn't for us none of you immigrants would be allowed to be here. You kill me and you won't live to see another day that's for sure, now give me that gun and maybe we can work something out. You can take Little-d's place, I'll put some real money in your pockets and get rid of this parole thing for you. How does that sound? Mr. Ray teased.

It sounds corrupt, like it's coming from someone who has used his position to his advantage for years all the while stepping on the necks of men who come out of prison looking for to change, a new life, but instead they get you. And you find a way to keep them in the system while satisfying your racist, and depraved feelings. I'm not here to work for you I'm here to kill you! Hector said as the temperature of the room started to rise.

Wait a minute! We can work something out. I was only doing my job, only doing what I was ordered to do. The people I work for have a plan and I'm just a pawn in all of this just like you. Mr. Ray pleaded.

The people you work for. Who are they, and what do they have to do with this prison and parole system? Hector demanded, pointing the gun directly to the head of Mr. Ray.

They own it! They're the ones making the money off all of it. You think that this prison system is the way it is by accident? They set it up to keep all of the niggers and immigrants in check, it's like the new slavery for modern times we're still making money of the backs of blacks and immigrants. Don't you see? It's set up that way Mr. Ray said in desperation.

So why did you kill Little-d and those two boys that were with him and wanted to have me to go down with them? He was loyal to you, why'd you have him killed? Because his time was up, and I was ordered to have him removed.

Hector thought about all of the obstacles that he faced since his initial incarceration at 16 years old, all of the setbacks, and roadblocks that came from that. He thought about his dad who was currently locked up, Alex, and the others that he'd met while in prison. The results of intentional "mass incarceration" of neighborhoods like his all over the country and he started to get emotional.

He thought about his conversion to Christ while in prison and the fellowship that he enjoyed with the other men who had turned their lives around while in prison, the stories that they told about their children. How the time away from their kids was hurting them more than themselves. All of the prison related jobs and businesses that these small towns used to flourish off of the bused in blacks, Hispanics, and others who came from other parts of the state.

Tears welled up in Hector's eyes as he allowed his mind to think about the promises that he made to God while in prison. "If you would give me just one more chance, I'm going to devote my life to you no matter how hard it gets." His emotions were getting the best of him while Mr. Ray kneeled before him shaken by the fear of losing his life not looking up but continuing to beg for his own life. With his head bowed to the floor in fear, he never saw that he could have easily disarmed the equally shaken Hector.

He thought about all of the hopes and dreams he had, the optimism that welled up inside of him when he left the penitentiary. Armed with a new faith and trust in God, Hector saw nothing but straight roads as his future. He remembered excitedly sharing the faith that he possessed with Maria, and his old gang from the neighborhood and the hope that it would help to change their lives as well. But now Hector saw no other way out.

I Guess now your time is up as well, I know that I'm going back to prison anyway and that people like you will never allow me to live a regular life, so it doesn't really matter what happens to me anymore. I know that this prison system is stacked against me. But at least I can get a small amount of payback by taking out a low life like you. It may be too late for me, but at least I can keep you from doing this to someone else. Hector said as he cocked the pistol that he gripped tightly in his hand.

Suddenly, in burst police Officer Eric Kemp with a few of his fellow officers from another precinct. Halt! Stop right their Hector, don't do it. Don't throw your life away for a person like this. I beg you to put the gun down. You don't want to do this he's not worth the price that you'll have to pay if you pull that trigger. Hector stood still for a moment with a puzzled look on his face.

Officer Kemp then continued. We've been monitoring this parole officer for the past couple of weeks along with the racist cop Officer O'Reilly and we have them on tape plotting and planning a number of crimes, you don't have to kill him. How is that possible Hector asked. You guys don't take the side of someone like me over your own.

I went to internal affairs with some of the things I witnessed inside of my precinct with Officer O'Reilly and his crew and Mr. Ray's name kept coming up, so we decided to monitor him as well. We know that he's a criminal and that he's been using some of his own recently released parolees to commit crimes, threatening them with incarceration. Paying them for performing carjackings, we were just waiting to see if we could find out who was financing this operation, but I couldn't let you go through with this.

Hector stood there as if frozen in time, not knowing what to do or even think for a moment. But why would you care what's in it for you he mumbled. Nothing. I'm about to become an outcast with my own precinct and maybe even the entire police department, but I couldn't stand there and do nothing about all of the corruption and blatant racism that I was seeing. I made a choice; I crossed what's become known as the "thin blue line" and did what was right. What God would have wanted me to do. So now it's your turn. Will you choose to live and not die, choose God over evil, will you choose life? Officer Kemp said stretching out his hand for the gun. Hector handed it to him and broke down weeping uncontrollably.

Chapter 35

Controlled By Bad Choices

Jamal Reynolds sat alone in his office contemplating his next career move, the room was quiet enough for him to hear the sound of the old-fashioned wall clock that he hadn't noticed before as it ticked away in the night. It was nightfall and the offices at WKROC had been closed for a while, but Jamal sat in a silent moment of reflection as he thought about the pending consequences that were just starting to come down from the release of the whirlwind story that Pricilla Prescott uncovered on the McMasters family. It felt like a calm before the storm for Jamal and his mind was meandering back and forth about his uncertain future and his next career move

The story that Pricilla released was a bombshell, no wonder Paul was being pressured to stop it from getting released, he said as he glanced at the headlines on his computer. "Daughter of prominent Evangelical Christian and anti-abortion pro-life family dies in an illegal abortion attempt." I didn't know that Pricilla had that inside her, that she was that good of an investigative reporter, but I have to hand it to her, she blew the cover off with this one. People are shocked by the news and the family that's involved, but in the words of Gil Scott-Herron, "America leads the world in shocks."

Jamal laughed to himself. I was just reading about the McMasters family, and I can see how prominent their family has been down here for the past 200 years. I see they are one of the biggest agricultural producers and employers in the south. Hell, that just means that they were probably one of the biggest slave owners in the state before that, Pricilla's article mentioned that their estate was once one of the biggest slave plantations in Texas, so why should I care about their family secrets getting out?

But now I know that I might as well start packing my bags because I'm sure that Paul will be getting someone else to replace me. That's fine with me, I'm ready to go back to Chicago anyway. I don't care about what these southern white people are doing I've got my own stuff to worry about.

I just wish I was leaving here with Janice like I'm supposed to be doing. That's my only regret that I have to leave her here with that damn Conrad. Every time I think about how he stole her from under my nose it makes me cringe in anger. One day I'll pay him back for how he stole Janice away from me, the life that we had planned. One day he'll get what's coming to him, I'm never going to let go of that anger. I do feel like something is in the air though, I'm getting an eerie feeling like something is about to happen, we'll see.

At the same time, Paul Wilson was nervously on his way to a meeting with Rex his boss, and the leader of his white supremacist group. Paul didn't know if his life was in danger or not, but he knew it could be, he respected Rex because of the enormous growth in white Nationalism and the Neo-Nazis movement that he's been able to direct since moving to southeast Texas. Paul knew that Rex wanted to talk about the story that was released by Pricilla Prescot and what the next steps could be.

1488 Paul said to Rex after arriving at the meeting, 1488 Rex replied. But this is an unpleasant time to greet each other with our mantra. One of our brothers, Mr. McMasters, is hurting, and he wants answers as to why we could not stop this from happening, we're supposed to be covering each other at all costs. He's extremely angry and wants some heads to roll. This has become a national story; they're calling it the "McMasters illegal abortion scandal." It's being covered by all of the networks and puts his family along with other prominent members in an unfavorable light. They have an image to uphold as one of the most upright families in the South. Plus, they are big contributors to the pro-life movement, and his wife hosts several anti-abortion events at their home to raise money for pro-life groups every year.

What would you like me to do now because Priscilla's story has already broken, I figured you were calling for this meeting to let me go, to fire me. I thought Jamal had it handled, and we would be able to give Pricilla back her old job, but she's a product of a world gone by, still living in the past, she still believes in things like honesty, integrity and we couldn't buy her off.

Mr. McMasters wanted you fired but I was able to convince him that you are still needed at the station and are a valuable member of our movement so for now you're safe. He does want retribution though and someone has to pay a high price, so I was able to convince him that offering up Jamal would show people that there is a stiff price to be paid for messing with one of our members Rex said.

And he was willing to accept that? Not at first, I had to lay out a plan and some assurances for him. His initial response when I suggested that Jamal be used as a temporary substitute, a sacrificial scapegoat for all of this was "What the hell does that nigger have to do with this story getting out." But I assured him that in the long term, this will go away and that you and your news anchors would do what you've always done, distract people from the truth and give them something else to be outraged about.

He's a convenient fall guy for now, someone we can paint as a "dark villain" in all of this. I need to keep Paul in charge of media for now until we can get a handle on things I told him, and that's where you come in. I need you to convince Jamal to travel to Mississippi. There's a big media conference that will be held there soon. Tell him it's for up-and-coming young media executives like him and that you'd like him to attend. Offer him whatever monetary incentive you need to entice him to go Rex said.

He's not going to go to Mississippi not even for money I know this boy he says he hates rednecks and that he would never go to Mississippi, not for any amount of money. Then tempt him with something else, whatever it takes to get him there, and I'll have my people take care of the rest.

I think I know of something I can use to get him to go that is a stronger incentive than money. Hatred, envy, and revenge. Paul smiled as he thought about the look he saw on Jamal's face as he talked about Conrad. It won't come back to us, will it? Paul asked.

There are hundreds of unmarked, forgotten graves scattered about the woods, dark roads, and highways of Mississippi. From the time of slavery to the days of lynchings, he'll be just another "ghost of Mississippi." If we can do it to those three civil rights workers, Emmitt Till, and Medgar Evers we can certainly do it to him. The next day Paul came into the office of Jamal who was unaware of the plans that Rex had for him. Good morning, Jamal, I wanted to talk to you about what happened with Pricilla and to let you know that I don't blame you for what is going on with this McMaster's story. That's good that you don't blame me for that because I had nothing to do with it. I made the offers to Pricilla that you and I discussed, offered her more money and even her old job back, but she turned it all down. I guess she still believes in the news Jamal replied.

Paul took a deep sigh, well regardless, the story will blow over soon enough and people will find a new scandal to be outraged about. That's why I pay you to help us push the new stories out there, to distract our viewership from harmful stories like this one. It hurts our viewers, this station and our bottom line when pillars of our communities like the McMasters are caught up in disrepute or gossip. "Pillars of our community?" Ok if you say so, so what did you want to meet with me about? I nominated you to be our representative at the big media conference in Mississippi, it's for up-and-coming young media executives like you and I wanted to give you the good news face to face. HAHAHA! Good news, man you know that I'm not going to no Mississippi. I told you that before when you came to Chicago to recruit me, I'll pass on the conference. "Mississippi Goddam" in my Nina Simone voice. But I didn't tell you about the stipend that was attached. See our station needs representation like you at the conference. Representation like me? Jamal jumped in, you mean that you need a feather in your cap, and increase your DEI numbers to look better as a company, right? DEI? What's that Paul replied. Diversity Equity and Inclusion you know what that is. I thought we weren't going to play games with each other, just tell me how much is the stipend? Paul wrote down a large figure and Jamal smiled.

That's a really big number and very tempting, but you know I've made quite a bit of money here already and I'm thinking about my next career move, I'm not sure how much longer I want to live down here. I'm not interested in traveling to Mississippi, not even for that type of money. Jamal stood up signaling the end of the meeting.

Ok, that's fine, but I wanted to save this for last. I'm privy to some information on a friend of yours that you may find interesting, someone in your past. Who is that? Jamal asked. Conrad James. Hearing that name compelled Jamal to sit back down and his mind went to a different place. For a moment it was like no one else was in the room with him, like he had been transported to a different time and dimension.

The "root of bitterness" that he held on to against Conrad grabbed hold of him grabbing his attention. Allowed to go unaddressed those old unresolved feelings of hatred, betrayal, and anger came back to him. Jamal hated Conrad for years, but he was able to bury it when needed, allowing them to have a semblance of a friendship for the past 25 years, and for him to stay close to Janice. The secret envy and Jealousy he carried around held a place in his heart becoming a stronghold for him.

At times they would paralyze him and leave him in a state of depression. Other times it was the anger and pure hatred that was produced by these emotions that seized control of him. But regardless of what shape the emotions took they always hampered his decision making. Jamal! Jamal! He heard a voice saying, "You all right? Snapping out of his temporary trance yeah, I'm fine he said. Tell me more about Conrad.

The station really needs you to go to this conference and if you do I promise I'll give you something on this Conrad that is just as big as the McMasters family and will tear his family apart, Paul promised. There's some information about what happened with the big fentanyl overdose in Florida last week that resulted in nine deaths that we may be able to tie to his son if we play it right.

The thought of tearing his family apart was just too tempting for Jamal to pass up. Finally, Janice and I can live the life that we were meant to live, I can finally have my soul mate back, the woman he stole from me. I can finally have my revenge.

Two days later Jamal boarded a plane that would take him to Mississippi for the media conference although he had no interest in the conference at all. He was being pulled by a force that was more powerful than his need for money or material wealth, stronger than his personal ambition or career goals. It was revenge that compelled Jamal to board the plane and travel to his destiny. He would never be seen or heard from again, Jamal became another "ghost of Mississippi."

Chapter 36

Presented With a Choice

Andre sat in disbelief as he read the article from Pricilla Prescott on the "McMasters family scandal," a secret illegal abortion from the pro-life, anti-abortion rights leaders that cost their only daughter Susan her life in a Louisiana swap area. The story dominated the headlines and was the talk of southeast Texas. He and his wife were waiting for Dr. Hernandez who wanted to talk to them about his childhood friend Alex Alvarez who was about to go before the parole board based on his recommendation.

They were intrigued by what Dr. Hernandez had to say about his childhood friend. Dr. Hernandez is the current co-worker of Dr. McKenzie and was the primary mental health counselor for Andre when he was going through a tragic time in his life over two years ago. It was due to the help and professionalism of Dr. Hernandez that Andre was able to recover and reclaim his life when he was in a deep state of depression. Because of their relationship and the respect they held for Dr. Hernandez, they agreed to discuss Alex with him, although they had no idea what he wanted to talk about.

Dr. Hernandez arrived on time for the meeting as he usually did, walking in with a nervous smile. Good morning, and thanks to both of you for agreeing to meet with me. I know that the two of you are probably wondering why I wanted to talk to you about Alex Alverez. I know that his name will bring back some bad memories from the past, but I wanted to talk to you about him and the person that he really is, then I will give you the reason that I'm bringing him up now.

Alex and I were best friends growing up and he was the smartest person I ever knew. A straight-A student who was about to become class valedictorian. He wanted to be a doctor himself and no one who knew him ever doubted it would happen. He was also voted most likely to succeed.

But all of that changed on that tragic day when Alex shot and killed two people, including your brother Dr. McKenzie. He brought the gun on a whim one day when we were coming home from school, not intending to ever use it. One bad choice that will live forever. In fact, on the day of the shooting, he left the gun in the house but forgot his hat, and when he went back inside to retrieve the hat, he saw the gun and thoughtlessly decided to put it inside his gym bag. A fight broke out in the park that day and as we were leaving a group of people started charging towards us, that's when he took out the gun and fired the shots, one of which killed your brother.

Since he's been incarcerated, he's been the picture of rehabilitation. He graduated from college and has become an ordained Minister while in prison. Alex has become famous in the prison system for the number of young men that he has mentored, helped to obtain a high school diploma, and given their lives to Christ in jail. The number is staggering, and God has done some amazing things through the life of Alex despite his past mistakes. Alex has become a model not only for rehabilitation, but more importantly redemption.

So, you want us to feel sorry for Alex and forgive him is what you are getting at? Andre interjected. No, I want to go deeper than that. I want to recommend him to the parole board for a clemency hearing and I was hoping that you two could find a way to forgive him to the level of testifying on his behalf at the hearing.

A clemency hearing? That means to have him released from prison, is that right? Do you want me to testify on behalf of the person who killed my brother so that he can be released? Dr. McKenzie asked in amazement.

Yes, that is correct. But I'm not going to recommend him for the hearing without your blessings, without your approval Dr. McKenzie. I know the tremendous amount of pain that he caused you and your family by his actions on that day twenty years ago. The other part of this Dr. McKenzie is that you can finally release the weight of the past, the hurt and pain that it brings whenever you think of it. I believe this can be freeing for you as well, a catharsis of the spirit that can purge you of the bitterness that it brings.

Andre chimed in. You're asking a lot Dr. Hernandez I know that you've done a lot to help me get past my own family tragedy, but to ask my wife to testify on behalf of her brother's killer and get him released.

I realize that Andre, and I know that it won't be easy. Also, there's no guarantee that it would even work, it's a long shot at best, and clemency for someone is not something that happens very often. First, you have to go before the Texas Board of

Pardons and Paroles and convince them. Afterward, if they agree to it, they write a recommendation on behalf of the inmate to the Governor to grant the clemency. But it's only a recommendation the Governor doesn't have to accept it, so this entire process is a longshot at best, but impossible without your help.

I know that this is a lot and I'm not expecting an answer, at least not a yes today, but if it's flat-out no I do understand. In the meantime, I have a number of letters here on behalf of Alex written by other inmates and the impact that he has made on their lives. I believe they will give you a better idea of the true person that Alex has become. I'd like to leave them here with you to read if you don't mind.

Chapter 37

Choosing Redemption and closing the Past

The next morning Andre woke up to bright sunshine coming through his bedroom window, he turned to see that Ruth had already quietly gotten out of bed. Walking into her office to check on his wife Andre could hear a faint sound that he couldn't figure out, so he continued towards her office. He stood in the doorway and watched his wife who was reading something that had her mind completely focused upon it and she didn't even notice him at the door. She sobbed while reading.

You ok honey? What are you reading that has gotten you so upset, so emotional this morning? Those letters that Dr. Hernandez left from the inmates at the Huntsville State Penitentiary. There are some miraculous redemption stories of how one person can have such a great impact on the lives of others. However, I can't help but think about the impact that this same person has left on me and my family. He killed my brother 20 years ago and I've been carrying around the hurt and pain of that with me for years. I've been hiding it, and busying myself with my career pursuits, but that day changed me forever. I realize now that I have never been able to forgive this person and it's been hurting me more than it's been hurting him.

Don't beat yourself up too bad for that. The man did kill your brother so it's only natural to harbor ill will towards him. No one can deny that you are human. Yeah, I know but that's how I was able to help you get past your hurt by showing you the need to forgive yourself while I've been holding on to my own past. Dr. McKenzie said holding back more tears.

So, what do you want to do then? How can we both let go of the past? Andre asked. This can be the bridge to the healing that this family needs, I'm so thankful to Dr. Hernandez for presenting this opportunity to me. This is a chance to bring healing to this family and I'm going to take it. Call Dr. Hernandez and tell him that I'm going to testify before the parole board for Alex to receive clemency. She broke down crying. What's the matter honey? That's the first time I've been able to even speak that name since my brother died.

That's a start to the healing process, Andre said. I learned from Dr. Hernandez that the process of forgiveness doesn't start until the acknowledgement of the hurt. Now the mending can start, and there is no set timetable for how long the process towards forgiveness will take, but we have to take back the power that holding on to unforgiveness has over us.

Dr Louis Hernandez was on his way to the Huntsville, Tx penitentiary to visit with his childhood best friend Alex Alverez when he received the call from Andre that his wife Dr. McKenzie would indeed testify on behalf of Alex. "She wants to start the process of reconciliation so that we can both become whole again," and she wanted me to thank you for giving her the opportunity to do so. Dr. Hernandez smiled in gratitude and assured him that he was the one who should be thanking her.

Now I have some extra hope that I believe Alex will need when I share with him the news about submitting him to the parole board for a clemency hearing. Why am I nervous? He said to himself as he entered through the visitor's doors, submitted to the process of being searched, and walked through metal detectors all part of the process of visiting with a prison inmate even for employees of the system like he was.

He sat alone waiting for them to bring out his best friend, attempting to busy himself by reading a magazine that held little interest to him. After a while, they brought in Alex, with shackles around his ankles, and wrists. The sight of the former valedictorian, and the one voted most likely to succeed coming out as a convicted felon, was still shocking to Dr. Hernandez although this wasn't his first time visiting. He shook his head in amazement. Choices! He said under his breath.

Well, if it isn't the doctor coming down from his perch to visit us small folks Alex laughed as they exchanged a quick hug, not to get too much attention from the prison guards. It's good to see you man and I'm glad you're doing well.

I'm doing fine, at least that's what they tell me. Don't take this wrong, but you seem to have adjusted to prison life and your situation.

I'm making the best of it. I don't have much of a choice at this point. But it's still prison. It's not like I'm pretending that I'm at home or doing what I wanted to be doing with my life, I'm just trying to make the best out of the new life God has given me here in prison, the ministry that he has provided me.

I've heard. You know that I'm a prison psychologist and a part of the Texas prison system, so I get to hear some things. You've become somewhat of a celebrity in here a lot of people talk about you. I knew that you were destined for great things growing up, but I could have never guessed this as the way God would use you Dr. Hernandez said in a serious tone. That makes two of us! They laughed.

I do have something I wanted to share with you. I wanted to get your permission to submit your name before the Texas Parole Board of Pardons and Paroles as a potential candidate for clemency.

Clemency! Me? That has never occurred to me to be a possibility considering what I've done. The crime that I committed to get me here in the first place, I'm here for murder.

Yeah, I know I was there, remember? I also know that you didn't go to the park that day intent on killing someone, that the circumstances lined up perfectly, and that we were about to be attacked as well. Plus, I know the work that you've put in since being incarcerated here - graduating from college, becoming an ordained Minister, and all of the people you've helped to graduate from high school while here. Plus, mentoring hundreds of youths since then, I believe that all of these things make you an ideal candidate.

I've gotten used to being able to help youths who come inside cope with their new reality, to deal with the fact that the life that you once dreamed of, or that your parents dreamed of for you will never happen. For most of us by the time we do get out of here, our parents will have died, relatives and friends will have moved, and your old neighborhood will be changed while you're in prison. Hell, the whole world will be different.

I don't want to give you false hope or anything, it's going to be a long shot at best, but I think it's worth taking a shot. There's a two-step process and we must first convince the Parole Board, and if a majority of them are willing then they'll submit a letter to the Governor recommending clemency, but he can say no as well. Lastly, I met with Dr. McKenzie who was the brother of the bystander that you shot and she's willing to testify on your behalf as well, she knows about some of the work you've been doing and wants to find her own forgiveness in this tragedy. She's willing to help.

Alex just sat there in stunned silence, tears flowing down his face uncontrollably. This went on for a couple of minutes before he finally was able to speak. "I'm at a loss for words, I never thought I'd ever even have a chance at life on the outside again. I'm also amazed by the depths of our friendship, that you have been with me throughout this entire journey. Even if it doesn't work out, I'm eternally grateful, and thankful to you my friend, God can do anything but fail so I'll be ok with the results.

Returning back to the jail cell that he's called home for the past twenty years, Alex Alvarez flopped down on the floor half sobbing with tears of hope and joy.

Unable to speak as he was overcome with emotions. It was his intention to pray but he could not find the words, neither could he fully wrap his mind around the possibility that he might one day have another opportunity at life. "I know that I'm not deserving and that I committed a horrible offense that caused someone their life I wish I could redo that day, I've relived it in my mind for the past twenty years Alex sobbed.

He lay prostrate on the floor in worship for hours, not speaking or attempting to move but in silent communion with God. Out of the darkness of the night God spoke to him and gave Alex the confirmation that he needed to move forward, and instructions on what he would be doing when he gets out of prison.

"I have spoken My word on your behalf, and I will surely bless you in your current circumstances. I will bless you with freedom and a new life, you will have a new ministry outside of these prison walls. Because of the extraordinary faith that you have shown in me under these circumstances, I will bless you with a new ministry. When you are released, you are to minister to others who are coming from these same circumstances. I will bless you with clothing, food, and housing to provide for former inmates and help them to re-enter society. When you get out start by reaching out to your brother Hector, who's in trouble and is struggling with his faith. Your story will be one of redemption and show how far, how wide, how high, and how low my grace can reach."

After this Alex went to sleep and continued to conduct himself with the same faith that he has had since his conversion. He never once questioned God or became anxious about how long the process of the clemency would take, or whether it would be approved. Alex rested in the confidence he had in God's word, and he knew that it would work out.

During the clemency hearing, Alex was able to speak directly to Dr. McKenzie. "I want to say to Dr. McKenzie how sorry I am for her loss, a loss that I caused by my foolish and reckless actions on that day. I realize that no number of words or contrition can bring back your brother, but I want you to know that his loss and my role in it haunts me to this day. Not a day has gone by since then that I don't think about and regret taking a life that was not mine to take. I hope that you can one day find it in your heart to forgive me."

Dr. McKenzie then gave a great testimony that God used to spearhead Alex's approval and eventual release on clemency. The parole board agreed by unanimous decision to send a letter recommending clemency to the Governor's office immediately afterward. Not long after this, after being lobbied by several church Pastors and Dr. McKenzie herself, the Governor signed the order for clemency for Alex.

Chapter 38

Consumed By Bad Choices

Harry Jacobs arrived at a new crossroads, one of several that life challenged him to navigate through over the past two years. It seemed to him that one life-changing decision after the next was coming his way and now he was not sure about the direction that he had chosen for his life. He sat in stunned silence as he contemplated his next move, still trying to process the new information that he received regarding Rex.

Harry waited with eagerness to hear from his operative about the information she found about who the second donor was for his son Harry Jr's bone marrow transplant and how he would plot his revenge against him. However, he was astonished by the results he received. Rex the one who recruited him to the white nationalist movement, and the leader of the Neo-Nazis sect in southeast Texas was the second donor that Harry had been searching for, the person who could have saved the life of his son but refused to come forward. Harry sat motionless in his quiet room while staring blankly at the information before him, not knowing how long he sat there as time ticked along.

Finally, freeing his mind from the daze, Why? What could this possibly mean? Harry said out loud to himself. Why would Rex allow my son to die when he could have saved him, and I could still have the life that I wanted before all of this happened? "My life has spiraled downhill since my son's death and not long after my wife's departure." She blamed Harry for not wanting to allow Jordan James who Dr. McKenzie said was a perfect match to be the bone marrow donor.

Harry's mind reflected back to that day when he informed his brothers about the two matches for the blood transfusion and the excitement that he had when he told his "white nationalist brothers." The renewed hope that the news created for life for his son Harry Jr. However, Rex and the rest of his white nationalist members said to Harry that God would find a better way than to have a nigger give a blood transfusion to the "pure white Christian man." "God would never contaminant the blood of the pure Aryan white race with the blood of a nigger! God will find a better way, a better solution." Rex was adamant about that Harry remembered.

That was only one of many sacrifices Harry has made for the good of the "movement" and the "taking back of America" from all of the illegal immigrants, and sinful talk about diversity he was taught. Now, staring blankly at the hypocrisy of Rex and all he'd done to help push his agenda Harry was faced with another pivotal decision on his uncertain future.

Boy Conrad is one lucky monkey. I was going to kill him before I found out about this information on Rex, but I don't have the time and energy to waste on him right now I have bigger fish to fry. I'll just let him go back to Chicago with all of that anti-gun garbage he's talking about, he's going to need it up there, that's one of our main targets for gun distribution and violence, plus we have several operatives up there who keep the mayhem and violence going. One day soon though his time is coming.

Harry's mind wandered off again as he thought about all that he lost because of his decisions over the past two years. The fog was back, controlling his mind and taking over his thoughts. He found himself unconsciously walking to his car and started driving, not knowing where he was going or what he was about to do, he just knew he had to get out of the house for a while. The demons were there, and they haunted his thoughts.

Suddenly, a familiar voice came through his mind, this time instead of haunting him it was the familiar voice of his mother who died over 20 years ago. How far are you planning to go on this ruinous path that you've chosen in your life? This path to destruction, I taught you a long time ago that hate leads to the path of destruction, it is a road to perdition said the voice.

I didn't choose this path it chose me; I didn't ask for this. I only wanted to live a quiet life with my family, but life started coming at me.

But now you listen to all of this white supremacist, and Nazi rhetoric that's not the way you were raised, that's not the Christian upbringing you were given.

I'm still a Christian I just found a better way, a new calling that God placed on my life to help our race.

God is not concerned with race, He created all men, and He only looks at the heart. The voice replied.

God has forgotten about me at times, He allowed my son to die, and then my wife left me. She blames me for his death. I miss my son. I wish I could talk with him and take away his pain.

Harry Jr. is not in pain, I see him every day, he's with me. Harry heard his mother say. Harry shook his head to regain consciousness. Damn, I must be losing it. Realizing where he had driven and that he had been driving for 45 minutes.

Chapter 39

Choices that Affect Those Close To You

Rexnord Rutherford and his wife Karen sat down for the evening to discuss some of the day's activities. Rex rarely had this type of quiet evening available to him, usually his many business ventures, and leading the movement kept him out until later in the evening. However, tonight he was home earlier than normal attempting to have some time to unwind before he got back to "his work."

You seem a little preoccupied, nervous about something Karen said to the normally calm and confident Rex. It was that confidence and his family pedigree that had gotten him to his current status as the leader of the white nationalist movement, and he was in the process of making some major moves for the movement. He believed that the time was ripe for a more outward appearance from its membership, a coming-out party for all to see.

Gone are the days when we needed to move about in secret in our own country, the days of masks, white sheets, and fake names to cover us from the judgment of this country are over. The events of the past few years have shown us that we don't have to move around in the dark or lurk in the dark anymore. The time is right for our members to come out of hiding and show themselves to the world, no matter what their job title, position, or status is. We have people from all walks of life now, teachers, policemen, the US Congress, and Senate, and even the supreme court. It's time for the white man to take back what's his and take back this country Rex said.

How did it go at HEE Inc this morning? Did you have the board to replace Conrad as CEO of your company? Yes. And I'm going to have them install Harry as his replacement, the job should have been his a long time ago, he's the rightful CEO. I just needed to install Conrad in his place over Harry so that he can feel what most of our brothers out there are feeling in everyday life. That this diversity thing is a scam, diversity, equity, and inclusion initiatives are a threat to this country and especially to the white man. These people are not qualified to be in leadership and Harry needed to experience how it feels to be passed over for a job that is given to a minority to give him a little boost to join our movement, a little extra incentive.

I've been with you for over twenty years now and I've always told you that I won't attempt to interfere with all of your extra-curricular activities as long as our family is not affected by it, keep them away from our household and some of those things to yourself. We have an eight-year-old son Rex Jr. to think about as well. Extra-curricular activities? Like what? Rex attempted to feign ignorance of what those might be.

Those nights in the woods of Mississippi when you'd come home with blood on your clothes, on your hands, and that bloodthirsty look in your eye, who do you think washed the blood out of your clothes? The meetings that you lead with all of your white supremacist friends, and colleagues, and all of your prison building and mass incarceration plans, you don't think I know about all of this stuff? We've been married for over 20 years, but I've been the one who has needed to shield you, and our family reputation. I've been the President of the women's auxiliary club here for three years, I'm the one who goes to church every Sunday, and because of me, we are seen as pillars in the community, a strong and traditional American family.

Haven't I always kept those things away from the family? You don't have to worry about that. You can continue to have your church functions, tea fundraisers, and committees while being a pillar in the community he laughed.

You can laugh all you want but without me by your side, and my help you wouldn't be able to do all of those things. I'm not a racist like you, but if it wasn't for me, you wouldn't be able to do all that you do in the business world or other areas of society. I believe you when you say that you're just protecting our way of life, that it's best for all people when white men are in charge. My only request is that it won't come back to hurt our family, as I've been saying for twenty years.

The couple sat in silent contemplation for a moment thinking about their life together for the past twenty years, and the ups and downs that they have experienced. Rex went to his liquor cabinet and pulled out an old bottle of scotch that he'd been saving for a few years, waiting for the right moment.

I want to celebrate you and provide a toast to our family and heritage. You have been a big part of this family and have been the rock for me in times when I needed you most. And I want us to continue to move forward and work for the uplifting of our people. Let's toast the mantra for our movement 1488 and say it together. "We must secure the existence of our people, and a future for white children."

Just then a loud knock broke through the joyful mood of the room, interrupting the celebratory toast, Rex looked puzzled by the lateness of the visit. Who the hell could that be? Peering out of the window he could see Harry standing there, believing there was a problem Rex went to let him inside.

Sorry to interrupt your evening, I can see that you guys are celebrating something, that's the old bottle of scotch that you've been saving for a joyous occasion I remember you told me. Yes, and you're just in time to celebrate with us I'll pour you a glass so that we can toast our brotherhood.

Brother huh? Harry said, reaching out to accept the drink and finishing it in one gulp. I've been thinking a lot about our brotherhood lately, all that we've gone through and accomplished over the past two and a half years since you brought me into the "brotherhood." Somehow my mind keeps bringing me back to the death of my son, there has always been something that would not allow me to let him go. It's like I've been missing something, and that has gnawed at me.

Grief is a strange thing my brother, sometimes it simply takes time. Rex jumped in. No it's not just that, I've always had the feeling that something wasn't right about the circumstances of his death. That second donor who signed up to help people never showed up when needed, don't you think that's strange? Well, I do.

So, I did some digging, and you know what I found out Harry said as he reached into his waist to pull out a 9mm handgun, that it was you all along, that you betrayed me, and my son, and have been lying to me ever since! Harry said with a bizarre look in his eyes and a shiver in his voice.

Wait a minute brother Harry, be careful what you are saying and what you might be thinking about doing. I don't think you know exactly who I am or what I can do, just give me a second and I can explain his voice rising with fear. I'm listening Harry replied, so now would be a good time to explain yourself.

We all have to make sacrifices for the good of the movement, for the lifting up of the white race, we're under attack in our own country and we have to take it back. I had to think about the long-term consequences of coming forth as the blood match Rex said in panic. Explain?

After the black boy next door Jordan James came forth as a potential donor, as a perfect match. As the leader of the white Neo-Nazi movement, I could not be seen as having the same blood as that of a nigger. You heard what all of the brothers there were saying about that blood, that you couldn't mix it with the "pure white Christian man." Word would have got out that he and I have basically the same blood and it would have hurt the movement.

Harry moved closer. So, you decided that you'd rather keep your position in the movement than to save the life of my son is what I'm hearing. You don't care about no movement, all you care about is having a position, a title.

Harry you'd better think before you do something foolish, you can't do anything to me and get away with it my reach goes well beyond what you can even imagine. My family is from the old confederate south, one of the riches in the country. We owned plantations that have helped to build the wealth of this country Rex said proudly, regaining some confidence.

Pausing for a moment Harry thought to himself. "Rex is right, he's probably too important, too ingrained into the system, and from too important of a family for me to shoot and kill. His reach is too far.

Drink up. Harry said pointing the gun at Rex and his wife Karen, signifying that he wanted her to drink as well. Drink up! He demanded again. Drink up. Again, and again, and again. Harry wanted to make sure they both got good and drunk. He wanted them to consume the entire 5th of the scotch if possible.

Meanwhile, Karen started to plead for her life, and the life of their eight-year-old son, Rex Jr. "We had nothing to do with this, please don't kill us. My son and I are both innocent bystanders, we had nothing to do with this. Don't kill us please." Turning to Rex, you said that you would not allow your outside activities to come back to touch our family. Karen cried to Rex in despair pleading for her life.

A sinister look came over Harry's face. You're no innocent bystander, you've been right there with him in the middle of all the things that he's done, the people he's killed. You've been posing for pictures in the community newspapers, hosting women's groups, and playing the "good wife" in the midst of all of the misery he's produced. You've been his buffer allowing him to live a double life. You looked the other way because his lifestyle has kept you in a position of privilege all these years. Now Drink up! Harry demanded.

Harry turned to Rex with disdain on his face. So, you're one of those "passing negros" we hear about huh. Pretending to be white, you do have the same blood as Jordan James, that's what you were trying to hide when you let my boy die.

This went on for over an hour because Harry wanted the entire bottle consumed. He wanted to have them both completely incapacitated before he made his next move. Still unsure of how far his revenge would take him.

Walking over to Rex, he smacked him across the head with the 9mm rendering him unconscious, Karen was already unconscious. Then he went upstairs to the bedroom of Rex Jr., their eight-year-old son. He paused for a moment, thinking about the conversation he had with his long-deceased mother while on his way over here to the Rutherford home. "Are you going to follow God, or people?" his mother would ask him. Harry picked up the sleeping child and carried him down the stairs and into the family car where he placed him in the back seat.

Coming back twice more to the house Harry placed Rex and Karen in the vehicle as well. It's a good thing you guys live out here on all of this land by yourself, no one can see me he laughed.

Placing them inside the car Harry stared at them for a moment. "Everybody gets to live out their dreams but me. When is it my turn? Why do I always have to finish second?

The next day another tragic heading was plastered across the news headlines that sent shock waves throughout the Sun Park community. Prominent local couple was killed in a drunk driving accident on I45 known as the most dangerous highway in the United States.

Harry became a shadowy figure in the "white nationalist movement," operating mostly online by his adopted pseudonym "Blood & Soil." He was suspected by some of his fellow brothers in the movement for the death of Rex and they wondered about his commitment to the movement. However, others revered and feared him for his boldness. Unable to prove whether or not Harry had any involvement with the death of their former leader only added to the legend and mystic of Harry with their underground network of followers.

Chapter 40

Living With The Realities of Our Choices

It had been an eventful and consequential week in the Houston suburb of Sun Park, one that the residents won't soon forget. The week started with a carjacking ring being discovered that was led by Mr. Ray, a corrupt Parole Officer and officer of the court. Two kids he recruited died in a fiery car crash attempting to escape the scene of a carjacking. The carjacking ring was exposed as a result of the investigation into a rouge police wing that Police Officer O'Reilly was in charge of. The two men are suspected of having Neo-Nazi ties.

Then the CEO of the town's largest employer, HEE Inc. Conrad James, resigned under pressure from the gun lobby, residents, and WKROC news rather than cease from continuing his anti-violence initiatives. WKROC news is also reporting from Florida that his son Jordan James may have been involved in a party where nine people died of fentanyl overdoses.

Afterwards came the release of an explosive article by Pricilla Prescott on the McMasters family that would reverberate throughout the prolife movement. The couple were high prolife and active members of the prolife movement and the evangelical church, whose daughter Susan, we now know died in a secret illegal abortion done in the wooded swamplands of Louisiana, a practice that had become a custom of those in the wealthy McMasters circle for decades. Hidden by their wealth and influence the McMasters were members of the “old south” who believed that the law applied to everyone else. Finally, as a culminating catastrophe to the week came news of the drunk driving deaths of two of the area’s most prominent citizens Rexnord Rutherford, his wife Susan, and their eight-year-old son in a drunk driving accident. Rex’s death sent shock waves throughout the Neo-Nazi movement leading to a void that Harry triumphantly filled as the new leader.

By this time Conrad and Janice James were back in their hometown of Chicago, there was no reason for them to remain in the Sun Park community other than the job that Conrad decided to resign from so they headed back to their roots. After all of the drama and chaos of the past two years, they wanted to get back to familiar surroundings and stand on the foundation that raised them.

I never heard back from Jamal, Janice said. I’ve reached out to him several times since our last conversation and he’s not responding, I hope he’s doing all right. I know that he’s no longer at the news station he was working for because they’ve hired a different news director. No one has seen or heard from him in a while, it’s like he’s a ghost or something.

Jamal’s like that sometimes, he’ll simply disappear and then reappear at strange times. He’s always been something of a mystery man, a hard guy to figure out. Conrad replied as he looked at the local headlines in the newspapers. Wow. It’s going to be hard work, this gun problem is out of control, look at this, 30 people were shot over the weekend. There’s an evil presence at work here, someone is working behind the scenes to keep this gun violence going, profiting from the violence. I believe that it's coming from the outside, someone not from here manipulating this.

This is not gang violence; you rarely hear about one gang firing at another these days. Now it's about firing on innocent bystanders, people out going to the grocery store, at a high school graduation party, or coming from school. What does that have to do with gangs? No. That's the presence of evil in the world around us, and people become willing participants in it.

The mass shootings keep coming, this is an uniquely American phenomenon of people firing indiscriminately into crowds of ordinary people whom they have never met, without any thoughts or cares about who gets hurt and it happens almost daily in this country Conrad continued.

I know that it was tough for you to give up that CEO job, but you've always done what was right when it counted, even when it's a struggle for you to do so you find a way and I'm proud of you for that.

Tomorrow, we kick off the Sabrina James Initiative for Nonviolent Change right here in Union Park. Janice said as they drove through the old neighborhood. In our hometown of Chicago, this is the place where it's most needed. Talk about coming full circle that's the park where we played as kids. I know your mom would be proud to see that.

It was tough for me to give up that job, and the security that it provided for us, but God will make another way for us. When He closes one door, it's because He has another one waiting for us to walk through. God speaks through doors both opened and closed ones.

I believe that He has shown me my purpose, and that's much greater than having a certain job. We live in a world where people crave more. They want more money, more power and influence, more popularity, and more ratings. But God has given us something greater than any job He's led me to "find, follow, and finish" my purpose for Him, and there is no greater purpose in life.

As they continued to drive down Washington Blvd. and cross Wood Street in their old neighborhood he couldn't help thinking of his mother, Sabrina James. I still remember my mom's favorite scripture whenever she was facing a tough decision. Proverbs 22:1 "A good name is more desirable than great riches; to be esteemed is better than silver and gold."

It's a shame how many people today are throwing their lives away on a whim like their life is worthless. People are reactionary today and don't want to think, they have no process for decision-making, so you have people dying or spending their lives in jail cells because of stupid reactions. Forfeiting their reputations and careers for political figures who care nothing about them, or killing people over trivial things that don't matter.

I used to watch how my mom would deal with decisions in hard times or in harsh circumstances. My mom didn't graduate from college or anything, but I later came to understand she developed a process for her decision-making. She never called it that, but I would later define it by the acronym PCEE. She would **P**ause, **C**ontemplate, **E**valuate, and **E**levate above her circumstances. It helped her to overcome what life threw at her.

During this "tour" of their old neighborhood they couldn't help but be struck by how different it now was. They saw the people playing tennis and walking their dogs, all of the current investments that had occurred in this community since all of the old residents were uprooted. None of the people looked like them or knew anything about them.

Janice sighed in a moment of reflection. "The Henry Horner projects that we grew up in are now gone, they once served as an unwanted backdrop to the old Chicago Stadium, inevitably to be torn down. A regretful campus too close in proximity to Chicago's now famous west loop and downtown areas.

A short-term mistake in city planning is now erased for the long-term good of the city. A wrong, now made right in the name of city progress, I'm sure. No more ghettos or projects stationed too close to the vibrant downtown communities someone must have sighed in relief. Now the area is populated with brownstones, condos, and two flats used for Airbnb which provide easy access to downtown for tourists." Janice shook her head in amazement.

Getting out of the car near the United Center on Madison where the Chicago Bulls play and walking around made Conrad reminisce about how they'd always hang around the old Chicago Stadium, the original “The Madhouse on Madison” as they called it back then, hoping to get a ticket somehow. The stadium was just outside his window so he had a clear view of it and had to walk by it every day to go to school but couldn’t afford to attend the games. An ironic cruelty for those who lived nearby.

Boy! They have invested a lot of money in this area since we’ve been gone. Malcolm X College has a whole campus over there now. Janice commented, pointing in the school’s direction. This seems intentional. Yeah, but it’s not new, it’s done in cities all across America. Janice replied.

Yeah, I know, It’s hard to put into words the emotions you feel walking through the neighborhood that you grew up in that was devoid of any type of investment, opportunity, and even hope. Now an eclectic community with people who don’t look like you are enjoying the fruits of the current investment in the community. Most probably don’t know about the people who once lived around here, most don’t care, but I wonder how they’d react if I could talk to some of them about it. Conrad said.

“The truth is I don’t even know how to express how it feels because I’m not sure how I feel about it, but I know it doesn’t sit right with me. And I know that it is an intentional and common practice in America’s cities. The creation, and then the dismantling of “ghettos” in America. Damn, gentrification!”

Epilogue

I want to take this time to express my heartfelt thanks to you the reader for joining me on this journey. I encourage those of you who have not read my first novel "Choose Life" to do so. I believe that it will provide in-depth insight into how some of the characters in Surviving Life were shaped and formed by their past decisions into the people they became.

This novel has been the experience of a lifetime for me, a journey that I started when I believed that God was leading me down a path of using the art of storytelling for His glory, revealing to me things He wanted me to see, and leaving the action I would take up to me. Choose Life, and Surviving Life are the culmination of some of my own thoughts, notes, and experiences lived in the past and inspired by God.

The accompanying workbook is titled "Surviving Life! The workbook. Inside you will find an interactive way to help you in your individual life choices. It has been designed to help people think about developing a process for their own decision-making and hopefully making better life choices. I believe that it would be especially beneficial to youths, young adults, book club discussions, or anti-violence groups.

The thesis of this novel is to demonstrate how our choices in life can take us down roads and paths that we would not have thought possible. Both wanted and unwanted, pleasant, and unpleasant. Whether the choices are good ones or bad ones they build upon one another, gaining momentum like a train when it first exits its station, soon it will develop the power to overrun most things in its path. Becoming almost unstoppable. Likewise, an undisciplined mind, untrained to set barriers or stop itself from poor and reckless thinking will have thoughts like a runaway train. Ultimately leading to a pattern of poor decision-making and self-destructive behavior.

My hope is to give the reader the needed motivation to make choices that will bring them into a relationship with God, and choices that will honor their families. To not be defined by our mistakes, but to realize that it's never too late to change directions in life.

Some of the scenes in Choose Life and Surviving Life are drawn from my own real-life experiences and interactions with the police, racism, and other people. The characters were developed based on the stories that needed to be told through their lives and my own experiences.

Explosively radicalized opinions on topics like the 2nd amendment, racism and white nationalism, the prison system, biased media reporting, abortion, and now politics place a large segment of Americans against one another.

Not only do I not expect everyone to agree with some of the topics addressed in this novel, I would be disappointed if they did. For some are opinions and opinions are shaped by a number of factors including life experiences, upbringing, age, and education. This is how diverse thought is formed.

Issues addressed in the book like gun control and the gun industry I realize are deeply divisive among Americans. And I know that they stir up emotions entirely different for a number of people. However, we should be able to agree that mass shootings and other gun violence have become commonplace and are a huge problem in the country. But so has the response to these problems from the people on both sides of the issue. Leading to a paralyzed society, and politicians forcing political gridlock that is more interested in gaining the needed talking points than on problem-solving.

The primary characters in the book Conrad James and Harry Jacobs I have intentionally left in a state of limbo, irresolution, or without finality. Purposely done to match the two main issues the two characters were pursuing in America. The problem of gun violence and the ever illusive "race problem" in America.

Some have simply decided on an "ostrich solution" believing that burying our head into the ground is an escape. This will only allow the problem to fester and grow. Telling people who have been the object of racism for about three hundred years that it simply doesn't exist may be soothing to the mind and consciousness of a nation but is certainly unrealistic.

I would be more than happy to respond to anyone who would like to leave me a comment on any of the characters, issues, or stories written about in any of my writing. The primary way to do that would be through my website listed below. I will respond to some requests on my social media which I will also list below but will not be engaging in any type of debate on social media. Questions of dissent, objections, or opposition would probably be better left on my website.

Finally, my hope is that in some small way, this book was able to bring some type of enlightenment to those who may be in need of it during times of trouble or need.

Author contact information

Website

Authorbriannelson.com

IG @authorbriannelson

FB authorbriannelson